M000086631

CJ West

The End of Marking Time

John,

Good luck to you too.
Please call if he needs help.

CJWest

22 West Books, Sheldonville, MA
www.22wb.com

© Copyright 2010, CJ West

All rights reserved.
No part of this book may be reproduced, stored in a retrieval system, or transmitted by any means, electronic, mechanical, photocopying, recording, or otherwise, without written permission from the publisher.

Requests for permission to make copies of any part of the work should be mailed to the following address: Permissions, 22 West Books, P.O. Box 155, Sheldonville, MA 02070-0155.

The following is a work of fiction. The characters and events are of the author's creation and used fictitiously. This book in no way represents real people living or dead.

Cover design by Sarah M. Carroll

ISBN 10: 0-9767788-4-X
ISBN 13: 978-0-9767788-4-4

Acknowledgements

Special thanks to Julie Rosenthal for helping me understand the current state of the corrections system in Massachusetts. Julie was incredibly generous with her time and expertise. Her insight into our judicial and penal systems was invaluable for me to understand not only how our system operates, but where it falls short.

Thank you to Abbe Nelligan for a firsthand look behind the walls at MCI Cedar Junction. I've also spoken with numerous court and police officers about their hopes and frustrations over the years and I am indebted to them for their candor.

Thank you to my beta readers Jady Babin, Kerilynn Newman and my wife, Gloria. Thanks also to L.J. Sellers for her patience and witty comments as we prepared this work for print.

Other Books by CJ West

Randy Black Series
Sin & Vengeance
A Demon Awaits
Gretchen Greene

Standalone
Taking Stock

To my many champions for their support and encouragement.

Frank Cinnella
Marla Cukor
Sherry Davis

Dale Arnold
Jady Babin
Keith Boggs
Vicky Buonasaro
Courtney Clift
Patty Flood
Terri Streetman Krause
Joey Mitchell
Patrick Moore
Kerilynn Newman
Toni Osborne
Alynn Parr
Brenda Rodrigues
Cindy-Lee Samuel
Adrian Smith
Sue Violette
Stephen Welch
Patti Whitney

Punishment brings wisdom; it is the healing art of wickedness.

Plato

He that is taken and put into prison or chains is not conquered, though overcome; for he is still an enemy.

Thomas Hobbes

CHAPTER ONE

I wasn't surprised when the Plexiglas partitions shot up out of the floor and locked me in front of this window. I had seen the breaks in the tile floor and I knew what was underneath because Wendell has done this to me before. I know this time is different. I'm not going to pretend I'm not scared to face your decision. If you were on this side of the glass, you would be scared, too. You can tell yourself you're too good to end up where I am. That you're not like me. But how different are we really? I wish I could see you, to see the difference for myself, but I understand why Wendell is hiding you. You probably have a steady job, a house, and credits in the bank. You could never imagine doing the things I've done. All you want is to get this over and go back to your life. You might even be ready to push the red button and get on with it, but put yourself in my place. For the next few hours I'm going to tell you my story. I hope you'll give me a chance.

It was my destiny to be trapped in this tiled hallway with you watching me through the one-way window. Maybe not from birth, but certainly from the time I opened the can of peaches I stole on Longmeadow Drive. I had been on my own five years by then and I was at the top of my game. I was cocky, but I had good reason. I chose my targets well and I moved like a ghost when I worked. I hadn't been arrested in three years, not even a close call. Maybe that's why I watched Leno from behind the couch while the middle-aged fat guy drifted in and out of consciousness right in front of me. He snored one minute and laughed at some politician's latest gaffe the next. I watched the show, ate my peaches, and wondered how this buffoon afforded such a huge place all by himself. It wasn't just him. The whole street was full of little kings and I couldn't imagine there were so many kingdoms in America. Don't get me wrong. I was glad to have them around because I worked my way through the royal suburbs week after week. I should have been paying attention instead of wondering why someone with so much money lived by himself. Unlikely he had a mother like mine. Or maybe he was just like my father.

Usually I cleaned up after myself so well that my marks weren't even sure they'd been hit. Plenty of them blamed the shifty-eyed kid next door or raged against a child they suspected of buying drugs. Normally I would have cleaned the fork and put it back, then rinsed the can and left it with the recycling, but that night I left the can on the end table, the fork leaning down into two inches of syrup. I knew I could never come back. I had been through half the houses on this street, pinched a wad of cash here, a diamond necklace there. After I slipped out with the Mercedes that night, the neighbors would take a closer look around their houses and the emails would start flying. There would be meetings with the police, talk of a neighborhood watch, a few of them would even buy guns. Sometimes when I was done with a place like this, I'd tip off a real bungler, a smash-and-grab type hyped up on drugs, and send him stumbling into a hornet's nest of nervous housewives and angry husbands. Sometimes the druggie barged in and out so fast he got away the first time, but eventually he would end up cuffed in the back of a cruiser. That satisfied the neighbors and covered my trail nicely. Everyone was happy except the guy forced to detox in a six-by-nine.

I should have sent one of them in my place, but I wanted the Mercedes. It took me five minutes to creep out of the living room and up the stairs to the master bedroom. The keys to the Mercedes were right on the bureau in plain sight, as was his wallet with five credit cards and six hundred forty in cash. Who carries that much cash anymore? I left him twenty for breakfast and took all the plastic. If he had more cash lying around, I couldn't find it. I checked the sock drawer, then felt under the bureau and along the back edge with no luck. He might have had a safe behind one of the oil paintings, but I couldn't risk taking them down with him in the house. I was sitting at the desk in the corner with his checkbook in my hand when he decided he'd had enough of Leno and lumbered upstairs. The room was massive, but there was only one way in and one way out. I gambled. I could have headed for the door and whacked him when he came in with his eyes half open, but that wasn't my style. I slipped to the floor, crawled into the opening under the desktop, and pulled the chair in behind me. He topped the stairs, trudged past me, and flopped face first on the bed without even looking in my direction.

It took him ten minutes to start snoring regularly. I got back up onto the chair, reassured by the irregular nasal bursts. My gamble paid off. There in the top drawer I found a two-sided sheet of paper that listed every credit card, bank account, and Internet site logon the guy had, complete with passwords. I had his debit card and his PIN, but I wasn't stupid enough to walk into an ATM and use it. I could find some kid I'd never seen before and split the max withdrawal with him, but that was risky. The magic was the plastic. Since I had his list of customer service numbers, it'd take him a day to contact the banks. All I needed was a few hours and he'd be asleep longer than that.

I stopped at the bedroom door to look back and wonder if I'd ever own a place like this. With an eighth-grade education, probably not, especially where I went to school. But for the next thirty minutes, I'd be driving a top-of-the-line Mercedes with a pocket full of cash and plastic.

The garage door opened smoothly. I drove out and hit the remote like I lived there. I was pretty full of myself when I made the corner out of the neighborhood without a soul to see me. I couldn't stop thinking about what the fat guy would do when he woke up. He might not notice his wallet was lighter, but he'd definitely be pissed when he couldn't find his keys. He'd have a fit when he went down to the garage looking for them and realized the Mercedes was gone.

The whole thing would sink in then. He'd call the cops and he'd stomp around the house looking to see what else I'd taken until they got there. It would really hit him when he found the empty peach can on the end table.

Eventually he'd remember hearing the fork tap the bottom of the can. He'd turned around once but hadn't really been looking. He felt safe in his home until that night. All people did. They had to. Otherwise they'd go nuts jumping at every noise and shadow. They knew there were criminals out there, but not in their houses, not while they were home. The poor guy wouldn't sleep for weeks.

He'd turn the night over and over in his mind until he realized he'd picked up the clicker just a few feet from where I was hiding in the shadows against the wall. He'd be terrified then. He expected criminals to be violent and unpredictable. He never expected someone like me. I never panic. I know the cops take twenty minutes to get most places and that's more than enough time to disappear if you're not in a rush. I always plan two exits, a hot one and a cool one. I always keep my head and most of the time, like that night, I glide along the cool road home, careful not to get stopped.

Unfortunately, I had no idea who I'd just hit or the shit storm I was about to set off when I sold those credit cards.

CHAPTER TWO

I dialed the numbers from memory when I was twenty minutes from the drop site. "Hey," I said into the phone. "I could really use a ride." I didn't boost many cars anymore, but my familiar voice was enough to get me a meet. Cars were my living when I hit the street at fifteen years old. It was the easiest and safest way for a kid to survive. Double taught me to open doors and start cars without doing any damage. I crashed a few learning to drive, but in three years I'd never led the cops to the drop point, never got busted, and never led anyone back to the factory. They kidded me about moving up the ranks when I started breaking into houses, but they respected my skills and were glad to snap up what I had whenever I dropped by.

"Ok," was all that came from the other end.

It was one A.M. by then, prime time for a drop-off. Some people might be sleeping at this time of night, but I knew my old friend had been waiting for someone like me to call and he'd be ready to go in minutes.

Later, I turned the corner onto a quiet street with a balance of apartment buildings with protected parking lots and single family houses that jostled for on-street parking. No one lived here long enough to get protective about the neighborhood. There were enough boyfriends visiting so that an extra vehicle hanging around for a few days or even a week went unnoticed. Crusher made sure no one in the know boosted rides from this street, and since cars weren't disappearing, the cops never had a clue how many cars traded hands here or how long we'd been doing it.

When I parked halfway down, Double came up alongside in a BMW 530i. He waddled out big as ever. He got the name Double back in school because like most of us he got free meals, but he always took double lunch. He was eight years ahead of me, one of those guys we looked up to as heroes. Back then he was the biggest kid for seven blocks, so he was recruited by every gang around. When he made his choice, the balance of power in the neighborhood shifted. He was big enough to avoid the gangs altogether. He told me so a year before my mother chased me out. He was twenty-two and had been busted four times for selling drugs. I could tell he regretted what he'd done, but by then he was trapped. He'd dropped out of school in ninth grade. He was committed to the gang and even if he could get out, who would hire a guy with an arrest record three pages long? Even now, six years later, he was still working for the guy who convinced him to join his gang all those years ago. They'd moved out of drugs and into cars, but I had little doubt Double was going to spend serious time in prison. Crusher had a good system, but so many cars disappearing couldn't go unpunished forever.

After my talk with Double, I started acting like I was Swiss. I knew who was jumped in to which gang, who the leaders were, and what they were after. I couldn't bring them together and work out a treaty or anything, but I didn't care about that. I just wanted to stay neutral and make enough friends inside to get myself out of trouble if I offended someone. Trust me, these guys got offended real easy. I only worked in the suburbs, far from their turf and that's how I stayed in one piece. Double was the best mentor I ever had. What he told me kept me safe for a long time, but he couldn't protect me from what was about to happen.

I flashed the keys as Double finished his walk around the Mercedes.

"Couldn't make the payments?" he joked.

He bounced back into the street and nodded toward the kid getting out of the BMW. I tossed him the keys and took his seat as Double squeezed behind the wheel against the desperate pleas from the shock absorbers.

Double fanned four hundreds in my direction.

"I don't think so," I said.

"You know the rate."

"Not for this car. It's worth eighty grand."

"That's not up to me. You know that."

"Let's go see the man."

Double gave me a second to reconsider. When I shut my door, he took off with the kid in the Mercedes right behind us. Most guys were afraid of Crusher, but I knew he got his nickname crushing beer cans and not gang members. The name was even more apt now. He bought totaled cars from insurance companies and swapped the VIN to an identical stolen car, then he crushed the evidence and sold it for scrap. Ironic, the insurance guys saw him as a good business partner because he paid top dollar for the cars he wanted, while he made a fortune off their losses.

Crusher told me you've got to be patient to get rich. A lot of what I do is modeled after him. He takes cars off the street and hides them in an underground garage for two years. That gives him time to dig out the anti-theft devices and gives the hot cars time to drop to the bottom of the insurance company lists. Even the victims have stopped looking for their cars by the time Crusher sells them. It took me a long time, but I learned to do the same with a safe deposit box and stolen jewelry. The cops only worry so long about stuff taken in a house break then they give up. I'm careful not to take anything too unique or possibly sentimental, and by the time I bring my stuff into the pawnshops it has long cooled. The way things were going for me, I could have taken a year off and it wouldn't have crimped my style a bit.

Double parked out front and I followed him through the dark office and downstairs. The basement was one huge room glowing with neon light from every corner. I walked around the couch and stood halfway between Crusher and the car chase playing on a sixty-inch plasma. He loved car chase movies, watched them over and over. He ignored me, intent on the action. I couldn't help but smile. He had this narrow little beard under his chin that hung straight down like an extra finger. One day I imagined that it continued up, joining the short mustache and matching eyebrows, like a dragonfly had landed on his face. Since then I couldn't look at him without connecting his eyebrows, his nose, and that goofy beard into an insect. To top it off, he framed his face with narrow blond braids. The guys around him were too frightened to tell him he looked ridiculous. I could probably get away with it, but I wasn't into taking unnecessary risks. I kept my smile to myself.

When he finally looked up, he smacked my hand. "What's up, hero?" He flashed a look at Double and said, "You're not getting greedy on me?"

"I brought you a Mercedes SL six hundred."

He leaned forward on the couch. "And four hundred doesn't quite cover it?" His eyes lit up knowing how much he was going to make. "If you had the balls, you could sell it for ten grand. It's worth a hundred."

Ten grand would save me a lot of night work, but I didn't want to look too interested. I didn't even want to think about a hundred grand on one score. Infringing on Crusher's business wasn't a good idea, even for me.

"You don't want to do that, do you?" he asked softly. Then he raised his voice with a decisiveness that required a response. "What's it look like, Double?"

"Mint. He brought the keys."

"Sweet. You know those keys cost me four hundred bucks?"

"Glad I got 'em then."

Crusher fanned a handful of hundreds and I took them without counting. Later I'd find he'd doubled the regular deal. I would have been happy with six hundred. With fourteen hundred in my pocket and the credit cards, I was due for some downtime.

"Wanna beer?" Crusher asked. "You earned it."

"No thanks. I've got one more stop."

Double perked up and jingled his keys. I gave him a thumbs-up, thanked Crusher, and headed for the BMW. I told Double I was headed for the hospital and he knew just where I meant.

"Nice ride you boosted tonight," he said.

"You're not doing so bad," I said, meaning the Beemer.

He quieted down and focused on driving. I knew the Beemer belonged to Crusher, but I never knew it bothered Double until then. He lived with Crusher underneath the junkyard and had everything he really needed.

A mile later he said, "You think Cortez has it right?"

Cortez was the first Latino in the South Side Slashers. He worked nights in the hospital. He bought my plastic and resold it for extra cash. "Buying plastic? You ain't into that?"

"No. I mean working for the man."

I couldn't imagine what he was thinking. Double wasn't a bad guy, wasn't born to be a killer or anything, but he made his living by making two or three ten-minute drives a day. That and he ran errands for Crusher. I'd thought about nine-to-fiving a few times so I could buy a house and file taxes like a regular guy, but what could I do? Who would pay me enough to live on? If I couldn't do it, Double had no chance.

"Why you want to do that?" I asked.

"Didn't say I did."

"Why you asking?"

"Just thinkin'."

"Don't you have everything you need living with Crusher? Why would you want to screw that up?"

He didn't answer, but just hearing my own question I knew. "Who is she?"

He turned and drove for a few blocks before he said, "What about you? You ever think about going straight and settling down?"

He was twenty-eight. Girls were starting to ask him about settling down and having kids. Big as he was, it must have been hard finding girls. If they knew he'd probably never have a legitimate job it'd be even harder. He couldn't have them sleeping in the basement at the junkyard.

I wondered if he'd been saving money like I had. My safe deposit box held enough cash for a down payment on a house, but I couldn't tell a loan officer that I made sixty grand a year robbing houses. I could save enough to buy a house in cash, but the cops would be all over me then. I'd made my decision when I was fifteen. I'd spent the last five years becoming a world class housebreaker and that's what I'll always be.

"I wouldn't know where to start," I said.

Double was going to have to work out his woman problems on his own.

9

CHAPTER THREE

Double dropped me a block from the hospital. I wished him luck and called Cortez from the sidewalk. He gave me the usual about being busy and that he'd meet me at the regular place when he got his break. I didn't care. My timing was good. The bars had closed an hour earlier and only a few stragglers wandered the streets. I adopted a far-away look and a casual walk on my way to the diner. Anyone who looked too awake at two-thirty A.M. was up to something. I wanted to look like I'd had a few, but not so many a cop would hassle me while I still had the plastic and the list of account numbers and passwords in my pocket. Once I dumped this stuff on Cortez, there was nothing to link me to the fat guy's house.

The place was hopping when I walked in. The late night crowd was hungry for greasy burgers and breakfast food to sober up for the drive home. There were a few seats at the counter. The only open table, a booth right next to the door, was a little more private, but not much. I sat down and watched a guy sitting with three women in the next booth. He desperately needed a wing man to create a diversion. The blonde he was talking to was smoking hot and sloppy drunk. She kept bobbing forward and cupping his face in her hands. He kissed her a few times, but the friends kept reaching across the table and breaking them up.

The waitress interrupted. I ordered scrambled eggs, OJ, and French toast and went back to the scene in the next booth. Why did gorgeous women always have friends who couldn't get a date on a bet? It had to be a safety thing. One of the women laughed like a mule. When the other turned, she might as well have been one. Wow. No sober guy would throw himself into the mix, not even for all the cash in my pocket. Nothing could keep those two girls from putting an early end to that guy's night.

Cortez walked in. I shifted my eyes to him, but I was still thinking about the poor guy paying for four breakfasts in the next booth. We'd both had an exciting time and we were both going home lonely. Unfortunately for him, he was emptying his pockets while I was stuffing mine.

"Not bad," Cortez said with a nod to the booth behind him. "Want some of that?"

"Don't think I can deal with the complications."

He tugged his uniform and said, "Too much for you?"

I meant the rabid guard chicks, but I didn't like the challenge in his eyes. Like I couldn't hold a real job. I was good at what I did. The best. I was invisible moving in and out of houses. Why couldn't I do some weenie job in a white uniform?

"What's so hard about what you do?" I asked.

"Nothing. Most of it's just showing up and getting bossed around. I wheel sick people from place to place, deliver supplies once in a while. It's cake. Especially at night."

"And you think I can't do that?"

"You'll let someone tell you what to do day after day for eight bucks an hour?" My face must have gone slack. "That's what I thought."

"Why do you do it?"

He reached in his shirt pocket and pulled out a picture. I knew he had a kid, but never thought much about it. In the picture, the kid was on the floor surrounded by stuffed animals. She looked too small to ask many questions.

"What am I supposed to tell her?" Cortez asked.

"You think you're some hero because you wheel toilet paper around the hospital?"

"To her, yes. She thinks I help sick people."

Women, families, they screwed everything up. Would Double end up doing the same thing in a few years? Serving the man so he could go legit and pay the way for his family? Would it happen to me some day? No chance. No kids for me. This wasn't some stage I would grow out of. I wouldn't go straight for some skirt. Cortez and Double weren't either. They were pretending, covering so the girls could hold their heads high. But they couldn't make it working for the man. Never would. That's why they had to meet me after midnight.

"What you got for me?" The question brought me back.

I took the cards from my pocket and slid them across the table.

Cortez took them one by one until he got to the bank card. "This is no good without the PIN."

I pulled the sheet from my pocket. "Got a pen?"

He forgot about the cards and focused on the paper in my hands. I slid it to him and watched. His eyes got big when he saw the account numbers. This was going to be a great payday.

"Let's have that back," I said.

"Wait a second. What do you want for it?"

"Slide it back," I said a little louder and he did.

"When'd you get that?"

"Two hours ago."

"Anyone see you?"

"Nope."

"I'll give you five hundred."

I couldn't imagine it was worth that much. It might have been worth more, but I had no way to get rid of it and I wasn't going to a bunch of ATMs and getting my face on camera.

"Deal." The instant I said it, he walked out with the cards and the password list. I knew where he was going so I didn't chase him. My food came a minute later. I started on my eggs, picturing him running down the street to his favorite ATM. He paid some kids to keep the camera lens blacked out with spray paint. He was out there making the cards pay for themselves. We both knew it. The thing about free money was you can't have it all. You have to share, but there was plenty to go around if you knew where to look. Cortez was getting the cards and the numbers for free. He'd have a profit after ten minutes work, and then he'd go online and start selling the credit cards over and over again. The accounts would be maxed in a matter of hours and a bunch of banks would take it on the chin, but bankers were worse crooks than either of us.

Cortez came back long enough to drop me six hundred twenty-five bucks and give me a line about his break being over. Neither of us said anything about the fresh bills and neither of us mentioned that he'd made more in his fifteen-minute break than the rest of his day. He'd be online soon making a bundle that was tax free and safe from his wife spending it on toys the kid would break and clothes she didn't need.

The guy, the hot blonde, and her two ugly friends got up and walked out. I was twenty years old. What was ahead of me? Was I going to keep chasing chicks like the guy in the booth or was I going to slow down and start acting like Double and Cortez? Those two were lying to themselves, pretending to be something they weren't to impress women. I knew who I was and that wasn't going to change.

As I stood up and headed for the cash register, the overhead television was crammed with police cars in front of a big house all lit up with spotlights. I pulled a twenty from my front pocket. At once I realized that the fat guy was buying me breakfast and that the front of his house was on the screen. His name was Jeremy Whitehouse and he was the Suffolk County district attorney. All those years ago in the projects, Double taught me to keep out of trouble by keeping a low profile. Tonight I'd broken that rule in the most spectacular way. Lots of crimes went unsolved, including most of mine, but this one would be different. There were half a dozen state police cruisers there helping the Sherborn cops.

I was shaking as I took my change. The car was good. Crusher wouldn't sell it for a long time and it wouldn't see sunshine until then.

The cards were the problem. Cortez had already nailed the DA for six hundred at least. In an hour there'd be dozens of people using Whitehouse's credit to buy all sorts of things. I tried to remember if his social security number was on the paper I sold Cortez, but it didn't matter. They'd crucify me for the trouble I'd caused him. I left the diner looking for a deep hole to disappear into.

13

CHAPTER FOUR

I counted four sirens rushing by that morning while I tried to sleep. I hadn't been arrested in three years and I didn't expect they'd be coming for me that morning, but the piercing sounds forced me to sit up and listen. They wouldn't come for me with sirens wailing. And they couldn't trace my work so fast. I knew it, but I also knew they'd pull out every weapon they had to get justice for the DA. It was lunchtime when I pulled the covers off. The DA's credit cards were all maxed by then. If they hadn't shut off ATM withdrawals, his bank accounts would be emptied by now, too.

Most of my crimes went unpunished, but the cops weren't going to give up this time. If I didn't feed them someone to bust, they'd arrive on my doorstep sooner or later. If I had a job it'd be easier to convince them I'd gone straight. They'd rather think that than realize I'd been hitting three houses a week for years and they just couldn't catch me.

The sirens went away and left me in the room over the garage.

It was just a room. Not a palace like those places I hit out in the suburbs. The family that lived downstairs threw up a partition and added a bathroom, stuck a stove and an oven in the corner, and called it an apartment. They turned a little extra space into some extra cash each month. That's what I lived on, the extra that people had lying around. From my place to my livelihood, I took what people didn't really need. Mostly the world didn't notice. I was just one guy. I didn't need much to live.

You might think I'd have great stuff since I'm in and out of really fancy places three times a week, but the truth was, I didn't allow myself any connection to the places I hit. When people were out of town, I could get away with couches and beds, silverware and glasses, but I didn't use stuff every day that linked me to being dirty. Most of my furniture the Berniers put in here for me, the rest Double and I picked up on the side of the road. I kept some jewelry until it cooled off, but it was always hidden where no one could ever find it. I always keep myself looking clean. I had problems for a few hours in the middle of the night when I worked, but beyond that, I looked like a solid citizen with a lot of free time on his hands.

I cleaned myself up, put on some jeans, and went around the corner to Dunkin's for breakfast—a large coffee and a Boston Kreme donut. I could never cook something this good. My mother never cooked so I never saw why it was important to try.

I headed down the block when I was finished. The guys were playing three on three in the park. There was a guy on the side who wanted to jump in, but hoop wasn't my thing and I wasn't into getting sweated up. The Red Sox were playing at seven and I thought I'd go to one of the bars around Fenway, have some fun, and chase a little action. Until then I planned to hang, people watch, and see who showed up in the park. I waved the guy off and sat down.

The game went back and forth. Several of the guys dumped in long shots, shots I knew were way outside my range. Some of these guys were here day after day. I wondered if they considered this work, like they'd go pro someday. I couldn't help feeling bad for 'em, knowing how unlikely it was some kid from West Roxbury would be bumped from obscurity to the pros. They had to know they were just killing time, but if they didn't, I wasn't going to be the one to tell them.

Every so often someone came off the street to watch the game for a few minutes. After the third short visit in twenty minutes, I realized the guy watching from half court was selling drugs out of his bag. The customers eyed me suspiciously as they headed for the sidewalk, but no one from the game hassled me. At least one player must have recognized me from the neighborhood. Not many white guys my age shaved their heads. It made me easy to spot, but that's not why I did it. I learned about forensics watching cop shows on TV. If I didn't have hair, I couldn't leave it behind.

I was alone until a car pulled up and Melanie Michaud wiggled across the sidewalk to me. We'd had a fling a few months earlier when I was lying low. She liked the way I threw money around when I was flush from a big hit and I liked how friendly she got once she had a few drinks in her. Her timing couldn't have been better. I hadn't planned anything for the next week and I would have been happy to spend the whole time with her. My plans changed when I saw the nasty look in her eyes.

"Where you been?" she said, like I'd been hiding from her.

It was months since I'd seen her. I'd been busy working and she knew I wasn't looking for anything permanent. I didn't promise her anything but a week of fun. That was long over. I didn't get why she was standing there with her hands on her hips until I saw the bulge at her waist. She shoved it out so I couldn't miss it, but I knew it wasn't my fault. Kids on the court kept score of how many girls they knocked up. Not me. I had lived that life and I wouldn't put my kids through it. I'd been swiping condoms for seven years, even though I knew it was better without them. A lot better.

"What are you trying to do?" I asked.

"Don't give me that. You better own up, boy."

I stood up and stepped closer. "You looking for a husband?" I whispered. "Cause I ain't playing that game." If she'd talked to Double, she'd have known. "I was careful, very careful. I didn't do that to you."

"My father's thinking different."

The one girl in the neighborhood with a live-in father had to come and make trouble for me. "Listen," I said. "You're a hottie, Melanie. If I was going to get married, it'd be a girl like you. But that ain't my kid in there. You know I'm careful. You tell your father, when he brings me the DNA test to show it's mine, I'll be there at the altar. You, me, and the baby."

Melanie looked like she'd pass out.

I kissed her cheek and she hustled back to the car.

CHAPTER FIVE

I did go to Fenway that night after Melanie cornered me in the park, but every time I thought about chasing a skirt, I started thinking about what Double and Cortez were doing. That life didn't fit for me and just thinking about it set me off. I left the bar alone and I spent the whole week walking around the neighborhood, watching the tube, and wondering if I was missing something by not settling down. I drank four or five beers the whole week and didn't get laid once. Some vacation.

When Cortez called to say things were slow and ask if I could throw some plastic his way, I was more than ready to get back to it. I called a guy who toted bags in a fancy San Francisco hotel. He spent his whole day getting sneered at by rich people on vacation and he was only too glad to sell me the names of his nastiest, worst-tipping clients.

For fifty bucks he gave me three names and addresses in Massachusetts. The one that stuck out was in a great neighborhood in Westwood. When I got there I couldn't believe how huge the place was or how thick the trees grew around it. None of the neighbors could see the house and once around back, I was invisible from the road. I had to cut through a glass door to get in without setting off the alarm, but then I had the run of the place without worrying about anyone coming home. I stayed two hours looking for, finding, and eventually cracking a basic wall safe hidden in the master bedroom. Inside the safe was the deed to the house, the titles to three cars, and some other crap that was useless to me, but I did find fifteen grand in cash and a serious diamond necklace.

There were two cars in the garage. Crusher would have given me five hundred for either of them, but with all the heat I brought down when I hit the district attorney, I decided to steer clear of Crusher until I cooled off. He was not a guy I wanted to disappoint. I didn't find anything for Cortez either, but not because I was worried about him. He didn't have guys like Double hanging over his shoulder ready to break my leg. Unfortunately for Cortez, the only plastic I scored was a single card sitting in the safe with the activation sticker still across the front. The card was mint. Never used. They must have taken all their regular cards with them. Not something I'd advise a family bring on vacation.

Cortez called while I was driving home. I told him the card was no good, but he wouldn't take my word for it. He practically begged me to meet him at the usual place. He said he needed a few bucks to get through the week. I'd just scored enough cash to hold me for months, so I didn't see any harm in loaning Cortez a few hundred. I wish I'd thrown that card out, but I didn't see the harm in giving it to him.

The diner was quiet, but I was earlier than usual. I knew Cortez was desperate when I saw him in the first booth waiting for me. His breaks were short and he never beat me to the diner. He looked nervous, like a guy in deep with a bookie who was threatening to start breaking things. Looking back I should have known what was coming, but Cortez and I had done this hundreds of times.

"Anything for me?" Cortez asked as soon as I sat down.

"Nothing good. Why so nervous?"

He sat stiffly like he was afraid to move. I checked the time and scanned the empty tables. This time of night, the diner was usually jumping, but tonight almost every table was empty. There were three guys at the counter to my left, but other than that, the place was deserted.

"Couple things came up at home," he said. "I'm a little short and if I don't get something going, checks will start bouncing."

"This is all I got." I slid the card across the table. It was still as shiny as when they printed it. I hadn't peeled off the sticker. I wasn't trying to sucker him. He should have agreed it was worthless. He should have asked to borrow some cash. But he didn't. He picked it up and headed for the door.

"Be right back with your cut."

"Forget it," I said, getting up.

I hadn't ordered food. That almost saved me. Without breakfast holding me there and with so much cash in my pocket, I was glad to give him the card and be on my way. I told him so.

His eyes pleaded with me to sit down and that's when I knew I was in trouble. The three guys on the stools behind me swiveled their heads around and I saw their faces reflected in the glass door.

"A few minutes won't hurt," I said real loud and started for the booth.

When the three men turned their backs, I bolted past Cortez out the door. My Chevy Z24 was sitting at the curb ready to make a run, but there was no time to get in and get it started. A uniformed cop dodged around either bumper toward me on the sidewalk. I cut hard to my right and sprinted down the open concrete. There was too much light on the main drag. I needed to get into a neighborhood. That's where I knew how to disappear. Fortunately, I'd been to this diner with Cortez so many times I'd thought plenty about where I'd go if things went bad.

Another uniformed patrolman popped out at the corner with his gun drawn. Idiot. Like he'd shoot me for running. He held his ground until I almost reached him, then he threw out an arm to grab me. I swatted it away without breaking stride and kept on going, my sneakers slapping pavement, the gap between me and the cops widening.

Things were looking a little better then. I was twenty and still dressed all in black from the hit I'd just pulled. I don't work out, but most of the guys chasing me were in their thirties and forties. I had a lot more to lose than they did and my running showed it.

I've been chased before, but usually it's just two cops, and if I can't outrun them it's easy enough to hide and sneak away when they give me a little too much space. I'd already counted six guys and that wasn't the end of it. Sirens wailed. Lights flashed. As I ran for the shadowy neighborhood another block away, three cruisers raced past. One went ahead to the next intersection and swerved sideways. The other two blocked off the side streets.

Two guys stepped out of each car. Nightsticks came out immediately and I was surrounded by a dozen cops. There were a couple of cars for me to dodge around if I wanted to run, but not a crack between buildings for me to slip into.

I thought about starting one of the cars on the sidewalk. I was fast, but not that fast. My record had been clean for years and I didn't want to screw it up by adding grand theft. Resisting arrest was bad enough. I was going down. Had I known how hard, I might have smashed a window and taken my chances in a car chase.

The ring closed in and I started thinking about what they really had on me. Cortez had sold me out, for sure. Why? For one damn card? Not likely. They'd gotten him on the DA hit. He was the weak link. Somehow they'd traced the cards back to him and he'd pointed the finger at me to save his sorry ass. I should have stuck to what I knew, jewelry and cash, but the cards had been easy money until then.

Probation was about the best I could hope for. Maybe if I was lucky I'd get a lawyer who knew something about entrapment, because this whole night felt like a setup.

They made me put my hands on my head. They cuffed me. They frisked me. They cheered when they found the fifteen thousand and the necklace in my pockets. Otherwise I'd have walked. It was a supremely unlucky day in an otherwise charmed five years.

CHAPTER SIX

They fingerprinted me, photographed me, took everything valuable or dangerous I had on me, and they stuck me in a cell for two hours. A few years earlier I'd had an idea to disappear out of their systems. I considered tearing up my license and social security card, so if they ever caught me, they'd have no way to prosecute because they wouldn't know who I was. In the end I thought better of it. I needed the license to drive, but I had a bigger problem. Nothing was safe in a neighborhood like mine unless it was inside a vault. I couldn't have a regular bank account because they'd report my deposits. I used a safe deposit box and I needed identification to get into the deposit vault. I didn't earn interest on the cash I had in there, but I didn't need to be greedy. I was doing fine. The cops had me and my license. I might do a little time, but it wouldn't be long. Not with a case like they had.

When they finally got organized, the first guy came into my cell. I knew my rights and I also knew how not to help their case. They wanted to connect me to the DA and the only way to do that was for me to slip up. Otherwise it was my word against Cortez's. He had a lot to gain by cooperating. If my public defender had a clue, he'd expose their case for what it was. I wasn't in denial. I knew I was guilty. I just didn't believe they could prove it.

He walked me down to a room with a single table and no windows. I figured him for forty-four, not too overweight for a desk jockey. He introduced himself as Detective Rosenthal. He asked me what I knew about District Attorney Jeremy Whitehouse. I almost started to tell him what I'd heard on the news but stopped myself. I was being recorded and I knew if I added even the smallest detail that wasn't in the newscast, they'd crucify me with it. I smiled to acknowledge how smooth he'd been, then I stared deeply into the second button on his blue shirt and didn't move.

That really pissed him off.

He tried to keep cool by asking me questions about where I was and how I'd gotten inside. He needed to place me at the scene. I knew the only thing I'd left behind was the can of peaches. If they could have gotten any DNA off the fork, they would have done it by now and Detective Rosenthal wouldn't be wasting his time asking me how I'd gotten inside. Didn't the district attorney tell them he left his garage door open until he went to bed? All I did was walk in, hide in the garage, and wait for the house to get quiet. They would never prove I'd been there.

The detective kept on with questions and I tried to count the number of threads that went from buttonhole to buttonhole. I figured it was six or seven, but it was hard to tell because they twisted and overlapped.

The detective banged my cell phone in front of me.

"If you break that, you're going to have to buy me a new one," I said evenly without a hint of anger. The money would come from Rosenthal's pay and that made him even angrier than before.

"Why don't you have your friends' numbers programmed?"

I dialed all my numbers from memory, but I didn't tell him that. I wasn't a techie guy. I wasn't big on the Internet and gadgets. Truth was, I could barely read. I probably could have programmed the numbers in, but it was just as easy to remember them.

"I can get the records from your carrier," he said as if the phone company was scared of him. We both knew he was just a bureaucrat.

I just kept staring. The numbers would lead to Double and the Mercedes underneath the junkyard. The place had been searched before and they'd never found the underground garage. No reason to expect they'd find it this time. The numbers would also lead to my friend in San Francisco and if Detective Rosenthal really did his investigating, that would connect me to the couple I just hit. I tried not to show it, but the detective had the leverage he needed right in his hands. I hoped he'd miss it or maybe a jury wouldn't believe the bellman had sold me the numbers.

He slapped down the cash next and asked me what I was doing carrying that much around. I had every right to carry as much cash as I wanted, but unlike Cortez, I didn't have a legitimate means to earn it. In the detective's eyes I had no right having that money. He knew I'd stolen it. He was right, but my expression never changed. I moved over to his pocket, admired the stitching, and wondered what caused it to bulge the way it did.

I smiled when he reached into that pocket and pulled out a plastic bag with the diamond necklace. He asked about my love life. Like I'd stolen the necklace for some girl. Did he know about Melanie? He couldn't yet. If he did, he'd know a girl like her couldn't pull off a twenty-thousand-dollar necklace. As I stared back blankly, I knew Detective Rosenthal was going after this one all the way. He wouldn't disappoint the district attorney even if this case was outside the DA's jurisdiction.

The card came on the table next. The worthless card was my undoing. I didn't need it for anything. Normally I would have left it in the safe, but I felt bad for Cortez. I was trying to help him out by sliding it his way. I didn't even want anything for it. The name on that card linked me back to the house with a hole in the glass door and a recently emptied safe in the master bedroom. Those people might not have been back for weeks. They might not have reported anything missing. Who knew, maybe they'd stolen the money in the first place. But when the cops called and told them they'd found it, they had no choice but to claim it.

Being a good guy got me busted for the first time in five years.

23

CHAPTER SEVEN

In the old days, courtroom trials had lots of things, but common sense wasn't one of them. The rules were designed to protect the guy the police were trying to put away. I guess this kept the cops from ganging up on people they didn't like and sticking them in jail, but what most citizens didn't realize is that a savvy judge could read my record, discuss the evidence with both attorneys, and figure out a case like mine in about thirty minutes. What most people also didn't realize is that it takes some real effort to get into the defendant's chair. This wasn't my first breaking and entering offense. I had robbed two or three houses a week for five years. Conservatively, I'd hit five hundred houses by the time they caught me. Sure, I'd been caught plenty when I was a kid, and yes, I was something of a perfectionist so I'm not typical. But whatever time they gave me, it wasn't bad for five hundred house breaks and whatever cars I'd taken in that time. If it wasn't the DA's house I'd hit, we would have pled out for probation and I would have been home planning my next job.

A mountain of paperwork wouldn't discourage the lawyers lined up behind the prosecution table from pursuing my case. The court had even gotten me a pretty good public defender so I couldn't appeal for ineffective counsel. They made it harder on themselves, but in their own perverted logic it twisted around and made sense.

We exercised my right to a jury trial. Judges in Massachusetts were notoriously liberal. They gave light sentences most of the time, but given who I was up against, my lawyer thought it best to play the entrapment card for all it was worth. That would sway a jury a lot more than a judge.

I'd let my hair grow out to a normal length while I was locked up and my lawyer got me a nice-looking suit. My job was to sit at the defense table, smile for the jury members, and act innocent. I tried not to bristle the hair on my head, but there was a lot of time to kill in my cell and the habit transferred to the courtroom. I wasn't required to say anything in my defense. Our strategy was to give them nothing and hope their pitiful evidence withered in front of a jury.

The first charge they tried to get me on was the DA's housebreak. They brought Cortez out onto the witness stand and he told them he bought the district attorney's credit and debit cards from me. He also told them about the credit card I took from the couple vacationing in San Francisco.

My lawyer destroyed him during cross examination. Cortez admitted he'd sold the district attorney's credit cards sixty-five times. He'd also personally taken a thousand dollars from the debit card. I watched the jury when Cortez said he'd called me and asked me to get him some more cards. I thought we had beat it then. Cortez was their only real witness, and the jury was a lot madder at him than they were at me. They whispered to each other when they heard Cortez was getting probation for cooperating. That was the high point of my trial.

They didn't have any physical evidence that tied me to the district attorney's house. It was just my word against Cortez's. The jury liked me and it was easy to believe Cortez was pointing the finger at me to get himself off. I thought we'd done it, but it was pretty clear that I'd hit the Westwood house while the owners were in San Francisco. People liked things to make sense. My jury was no exception. When the prosecutors put the two charges together like they did, they made it harder for them to let me go. If I'd hit the couple in Westwood, it made sense that I'd hit the DA's house, too.

The prosecutor had all the cops from my arrest there in the courtroom. He filed them up on the stand and each said they saw me with the money and the jewelry. If we'd been thinking faster, we could have put Cortez back up there and said I was buying the necklace from him. It could have worked, but having both items from the safe in my pockets torpedoed me. We didn't even try blaming Cortez.

What happened next surprised me and my lawyer.

They trotted in my landlord and made him testify to how much I paid in rent. Later I'd learn that they threatened him with tax evasion because he wasn't reporting what I was paying him. He told them everything about me. Where I liked to eat. When I came and went. He told the jury everything he knew. When he was done, they brought out some accountant to add up what I was spending. They spent two hours creating a little budget for me right there in court. When it hit me, the surprise must have shown on my face. I wasn't collecting welfare or unemployment. I hadn't filed taxes in my life. I didn't hold a job. So, they asked, where was the money coming from?

That was the moment the jury turned.

They scowled. They gawked.

They were angry that they were going to work every day and I was making an easy living breaking into people's houses and taking stuff. They probably knew someone who had been robbed and they knew how awful they felt afterward. What I did wasn't easy, but I couldn't tell them that. They wouldn't understand how hard I worked to be good at what I did.

The prosecutors celebrated behind their long wooden table. They knew they'd won retribution. They wanted the car back and they wanted the money. Fortunately, everything I owned was tucked in that safe deposit box and no one was going to find it. They could fine me all they wanted, but I'd never have to pay. Their smugness convinced me to start collecting welfare when I got out, so they couldn't use that trick on me again.

Their anger went beyond what I'd done to the DA or those people visiting San Francisco. To them I was evil. Career criminals were a cancer to those men in suits. The cops would be all over me when I got out, ready to throw me back inside the moment I crossed the line. I was an easy target now, a convicted felon. They couldn't know it, but something extraordinary was about to happen. Something that would foul their plans forever.

CHAPTER EIGHT

Have you ever been to prison? Did you know that if you get arrested for a felony you go from a lock-up at the local police station to the house of correction? I was there for months while my trial dragged on.

After my trial was over, my lawyer filled me in on another interesting piece of information. In Massachusetts if you enter someone's house at night and try to rob them, you can be sentenced to up to twenty years. They figured people are home at night and if you break in you're likely to run into them and then things could turn violent. That made sense most of the time, but I knew that couple was in San Francisco. That's why I was in their house so long. And the DA, I was only six feet from him. I could have stuck my fork in his throat while he was sleeping, but I'm not that kind of guy. I was just trying to make a living like everyone else.

I knew a dozen guys who had been arrested for breaking and entering and gotten off with probation. I must have gotten the one conservative judge in the whole state, because he wasn't so accommodating. He even gave me a lecture before he sentenced me. He was really upset that I'd never had a job and that I hadn't graduated high school. Heck, I'd never made it to high school, but I didn't tell him that. He said I was unable to contribute to society without making major changes in my life. The first change he made sure of—a change of address. He sentenced me to five years.

That may not sound like much. It worked out to about four days in jail for every house I robbed. I was fortunate considering the judge could have sentenced me to forty years, twenty for the DA and twenty for the couple from Westwood. Five years might not sound like much next to forty, but it's significant because anything over two and a half is the difference between hanging out in the house of correction and doing hard time in state prison. I should have known I'd end up there. The judge had intense pressure to hand down a heavy sentence. Getting five years wasn't bad.

I wasn't excited to bunk in the house of correction. Most people wouldn't be, but living there wasn't much different from living back in the projects with my mom. It was dangerous, but all you did was hang around and watch TV until someone fed you. I didn't have anyone on the outside waiting for me. I didn't have a job I could lose by going away. The food was free, so it wasn't that terrible being locked up while my trial was going on. There were some rough characters inside, but a lot of them were in for DUI or drug possession and just wanted to serve their time. The hard core criminals, the murderers, rapists, and gang leaders who would shiv you for looking at them the wrong way, they got sent to state prison. Now that my trial was over, that's where I was headed.

The whole night before my transfer I kept going over the stories I'd heard. Guys got raped in the showers and beaten if they didn't go along. Lifers spent all day making weapons out of pens, toothbrushes, and anything they could steal from the kitchen. Gangs governed life inside. I'd spent my entire life avoiding gangs in my neighborhood and now that I was old enough to be free of them on the outside, I was getting sent to a place where they were unavoidable.

At five-nine and one seventy-five, I was a lightweight inside. Feminine to some of those brutes behind the wall. Every time I closed my eyes that night I dreamed of a three-hundred-pound, hairy monster who'd be sharing my cell for the next five years. By the time morning came my eyes were bloodshot, my head buzzed, and my cheap prison shoes felt like they weighed ten pounds each.

Breakfast went on as usual, but when I was finished, they led me through the maze of locked corridors and made me dress in an orange jumpsuit. A chain around my waist threaded through the loops in my suit and kept my cuffed hands from leaving my sides. My feet were shackled so

I could only shuffle my way into line with the others bound for MCI Cedar Junction. The officers took our court clothes from storage and stowed them underneath the bus. Like the wealthiest of travelers, we weren't allowed to touch our bags, though the reasoning in our case was quite different.

The correction officers scrutinized checklists.

They processed paperwork for each prisoner at a painfully slow pace while we stood in a line of orange. I watched the guards as I waited and soon understood that they were leery of the men in line with me. They controlled men that society could not and yet they gave a wide berth to the nine inmates chained in a line against the concrete wall. The discovery made my stomach turn. There would be hundreds of men like these at Walpole. If the guards were afraid of them while their hands and feet were locked, how would I survive among them for five years? I was smart, but I didn't have anything to bargain with. Nothing that I wanted to share anyway.

The man in front of me had shoulders that blocked out the six men ahead of us. Standing there, I tried to think of anything I might have in common with the other guys in line, some way to strike up a conversation and make a friend who might help me later. I checked his neck and his arms for tattoos. Looked at his dark hair and wondered about his heritage. A big guy like him would be a good friend to have. I could promise him cash when he got out. Everything in my safe deposit box would be cool enough to sell in five years. I had some fine jewelry stashed in there. Maybe he had a lady.

I didn't say anything in line. Just waited, hoping for an opportunity to make a connection with the big guy on the bus and save myself a lot of trouble later. Pretty soon they moved us ahead single file.

The first two prisoners loaded one at a time, up the steps, through the grated door and back to a seat. They were locked to chairs rather than seat-belted. The officers pulled aside a nasty-looking guy with a thick chain tattooed on his neck. Three officers surrounded him, while another led the remaining prisoners onto the bus one by one. I didn't know what was so special about the guy they pulled out of line, but I didn't even consider striking up a conversation with him. When I got to the head of the line, I

29

kept my eyes focused straight ahead on the dirty steps until they led me all the way to the back and chained me down.

I was glad to be on the opposite end of the bus when the guards coaxed the last prisoner to the front seat and locked him in behind the grate. The three guards locked the door and took up positions behind the driver, two facing us, the other facing forward. Sitting in my own row at the back I felt secure even if I'd lost the opportunity to make a friend during the ride.

Two sheriff's cruisers escorted us out onto the roadway. I couldn't see the cars through the windows, so I watched the guards sneer at the prisoner in the first seat. I was sure he'd be leading a huge gang by the time we reached the prison. He would order men killed and control the guards with bribes. I thought I was enjoying my last twenty minutes of safety, but it didn't turn out that way at all.

The bus driver slammed the brakes and we all flew forward, our chains clinking as we reached their limit, our shoulders and heads hitting the seats ahead of us.

"What the hell?" the bus driver hollered.

The crack of gunfire sounded outside, muffled by the closed windows.

The bus started up again, turned hard to the right, and leaned over as it climbed the curb and lumbered away. Behind us a Chevy pickup slammed into the sheriff's cruiser, wedging it against a parked sedan. Men jumped out of the pickup and opened fire with automatics. The driver frantically worked his radio, but he was dead in seconds.

The bus picked up speed, but it didn't take long for the pickup to catch us. The guards had guns drawn and pointed at the inmate in the front seat. We all knew they couldn't shoot him. We also knew that once his friends freed him, he wouldn't show the same kindness to the guards. I never imagined this was a chance to escape. I'm not sure why, but once I heard the gunfire, my only focus was staying alive. I kept my head down, expecting the shooting to be directed at the front of the bus and hoping that my position in the rear might save my life.

I was half right.

The pickup truck raced by on the opposite side of the bus and opened fire at the driver. I should have had my head down, but I couldn't resist peeking over the seatback. The bulletproof glass repelled the attack.

We'd only driven about a mile, so it was too soon for the police to respond to the guards' calls for help. Gunfire clattered outside. The tires on the driver's side blew out. The crippled bus lurched that way and rammed into the cars parked along the opposite curb.

We jolted out of our seats. I jammed my shoulder so hard I thought I dislocated it. I sat low, in agony, unable to steady my shoulder with my other hand because it was chained down.

I heard gunfire and screaming, but I couldn't tell how they got the door open. It was clear when they did. Gunshots blared and the bus driver's blood splattered all over the inside of his window. The guards refused to open the gate until the intruders shot two of them point blank.

I should have ducked. It was stupid to watch and see these men's faces, but I couldn't help myself. My eyes hovered just above the seatback as the guard offered up the key to unlock the inmate in the front seat. When the chains were off, they chained the guard down and the inmate fired a single shot from the steps.

The bullet should have blown his head apart, but there was no blood.

A horrid crack traveled through me, not in through my ears as if I'd heard it next to me, but through my bones as if the pain was being transmitted by gut-wrenching vibrations.

All I could see was white. The brightest white I've ever seen in my life. It was accompanied by intense pain and absolute silence. I felt myself falling back to my seat, but I never touched down.

CHAPTER NINE

Obviously I recovered because I'm standing here telling you my story, but while I was sleeping the American criminal justice system was completely revamped around me. Everything I knew about getting along was outdated. Every new rule, every new procedure was foreign to me. It was almost impossible for me to adjust. The changes would have been easier to take if I had lived through them like everyone else. I'm not making excuses for what I did later, I just want you to understand how completely my world changed in what, for me, was a single moment.

Ironically, the next thing I remember seeing after the blinding light on the bus was another sort of light. It was muted and fuzzy. When I blinked a few times, I could see I was in a small room under dim fluorescents. The pain in my head was completely gone. I was comfortable, but my arms and legs were pinned to the bed and I couldn't lift them. The last thing I remembered was being on the bus and getting hit in the head. I assumed I'd been brought to the hospital and was strapped down so I couldn't escape.

I tilted my head a few inches and saw an old man asleep in a bed next to mine. He wasn't moving either, and other than him I was alone. A plastic oxygen mask covered my nose. As soon as I saw it, my skin itched underneath. I tried to raise my hand and lift it off, but my hand wouldn't budge. I tried to yell for a nurse, but I could barely hear the hum that escaped the mask. I desperately wanted a drink. I wanted to sit up and pull off the oxygen mask, but most of all, I wanted to know where I was and how soon I could get out of bed. I hoped someone would come soon.

I listened. I moved my eyes back and forth, straining at the limits of my vision. I tried to call but couldn't even hear myself. I lay there for hours like that—watching and waiting for someone to come. Disturbing thoughts wandered into my head. The longer I lay there alone the more terrified I became. A bullet had struck me in the head. Was I paralyzed?

I tried to wiggle my toes for several minutes, but I couldn't see them moving under the blankets. I tried the same with my fingers with no success. I could see the fingertips on my right hand because I was angled that way, but couldn't see if I was handcuffed or even strapped down. I knew better. Nothing was holding my fingers and yet I couldn't move them at all.

I tried to calm myself, but I could hear my heart beating faster with worry. Would I be stuck in bed forever? Would I be one of those people who uses their eyes to move a wheelchair? I thought about how unjust that would be. I'd never hurt anyone. I did what was necessary to survive, but I'd been kind to my fellow man. I'd avoided gangs, guns, and violence my entire life. I didn't deserve this.

I couldn't move and there was no one to talk to, but eventually I started thinking this bed might be an easier place to serve out my sentence than locked behind bars with violent criminals who were ready to tear my arms off. I considered playing dead when the nurse came to check on me, but I had to know why I couldn't move and if it was permanent or not. When she finally came I did everything I could to get her attention.

"Good morning, Michael. How is everything with you today?" she asked in a faraway voice, not expecting a response.

I hadn't seen her until she spoke. She breezed around the bed, working on something I couldn't see. Then she stepped over to me and asked, "Ready to go to the gym?" She must have been thinking about something else or she would have seen my eyes shifting left and right, signaling her that I was awake. She followed her routine with no reason to expect me to wake up on that particular day. That's why she wasn't really looking at me.

She picked up my arm and stretched it up high. I wasn't cuffed to the bed. I just couldn't move. She was exercising my muscles to keep them in shape. Was there hope I could move them again?

I hummed loudly under my mask. The nurse jumped back off the bed with her hands shielding her face. My arm dropped with a thump. I couldn't stop it. I couldn't even slow it down, but I felt my palm hit the blanket.

"Doctor Pearson!"

The doctor didn't come.

She leaned closer again. This time she was intently focused on my face. I shifted my eyes back and forth until it made me dizzy. I turned my head just a little bit toward her and I saw her smile in amazement.

"I'll be right back," she said and then she ran off.

It took a long time for Dr. Pearson to get to my bedside. When he arrived, everyone was a floating head to me because I couldn't see anything unless it was right in front of my face. He had thin gray hair and he looked heavy by the folds of skin hanging down from his neck and jaw line. By the way he grumbled, I could tell he was skeptical about my awakening.

He flashed a light in my eyes and it felt like he stabbed me deep inside my head. I blinked them shut.

"That's a good sign," he said, with more energy in his movements.

He didn't say anything, but I felt him tapping the fingertips on my left hand. He saw me trying to look that way to see what he was doing.

"Can you feel that?"

I blinked.

He moved to my toes and pretty soon he learned that I had feeling in all my extremities. I just couldn't move them. He read my chart for a few minutes and then said, "You really hit the jackpot, didn't you?"

I had no idea what he meant. I grunted.

He shifted my arm and sat on the edge of the bed. "This is going to be hard for you to understand," he said. "You were hit by a stray bullet four years ago on your way to MCI Cedar Junction. The trauma caused your brain to swell and you've been in this bed ever since."

Four years? That's why I couldn't move. I hadn't used my arms and legs in four years.

"The medical community gives up on most people after two years. You were lucky enough to be in the Massachusetts prison system. They get sued so much they didn't dare pull the plug."

I had no idea what he meant, but I tried to follow along.

"There are only two people left in the whole system. You," he pointed to the man in the bed next to mine, "and your friend over there."

What? I blinked. He couldn't really know how confused I was, but he seemed to understand how odd his last statement sounded.

"The whole system was shut down just after you came to us. The Supreme Court decided that long-term incarceration was cruel and unusual punishment and that rehabilitation efforts by the states and even the federal prison system were entirely ineffective.

"So, in a way you didn't hit the lottery. If you hadn't been shot, you would have been released with everyone else three years ago. It was madness when it happened. I don't know what the heck they were thinking, but we seem to be getting a handle on it now."

I'd spent four years in bed when I could have been back in my apartment. I'd escaped countless torments inside prison, but I'd lost four years of my life in the process.

"We're going to start you on therapy, Michael. It's going to take some time and a lot of hard work on your part, but we'll have you walking again. When you leave this bed will be up to you."

If I knew how hard recovery was going to be, I might have just given up, but I was excited. I'd be released as soon as I was able to go home on my own. Unfortunately, I was still in that bed months later.

They asked me if there was anyone I could call, but I couldn't dial a phone. I couldn't talk. I couldn't even give them a name and number.

CHAPTER TEN

When you can't make a muscle, it's impossible to exercise on your own.

Every morning for the next two weeks, Debbie, my nurse, wheeled in a machine with a bunch of wires sticking out of it. She attached the wires to my skin, and when she turned it on I started to twitch all over. The machine shocked my muscles into working. I have no idea how many hours I sat with my muscles jiggling. It seemed like forever, but then one morning when she was done I could make a fist. Pretty soon I was lifting my hands, then my arms, and eventually my legs.

I spent two more months exercising before I felt a little coordination coming back. That was the day Double strolled into my room. When I saw him coming I realized how helpless I was. I couldn't run away. I couldn't even get out of bed on my own. Had the cops busted him and Crusher with the Mercedes? As Double came closer I realized Crusher wasn't with him. Double looked chill as ever. He wasn't there to hit me. He looked thinner than before, like he'd lost thirty or forty pounds.

"What's up?" I said, proud to have most of my voice back.

"Hey, Tin Man, I thought you were toast."

I raised my hands, a feat for me, but it didn't impress Double.

"You getting out soon?" he asked.

"A few weeks they tell me."

Double got all serious and came right up to the edge of the bed. "Things is different."

"Yeah, my doctor said some crap about no more prison. Is he for real?"

"Legit man. Things are whacked. You won't believe it."

"Tell me."

"Cops and robbers, man, it's over."

"What?"

"Some judge decided we can't go to prison no more."

"We?"

"Nobody."

"So what happens when you get busted?"

Double pulled up his pant leg and showed me the tracking device on his ankle. It was loose enough so he could slip it off.

I shrugged and he could tell I wasn't getting it.

"It's all high tech now. If there's a heist and you're anywhere near it, cops'll know." I asked him why he couldn't just take it off. "Guys have tried. They've got it connected to your heartbeat or something. You take it off and they know. You've got to keep it on."

"What happens if you get caught?"

Double struggled for an explanation. I knew I wasn't asking the right guy, but he'd been through the new system and come out ok.

"You go to court, but it's no BS like it used to be. You go in and thirty minutes later your trial is over and you get your sentence."

"How can they do that?"

"Mostly because there's no more juries."

"They can't do that."

"You don't want a jury, man."

"Why not?"

Double thought some more. A lot had happened in four years and he couldn't possibly sum it up in a two-sentence explanation, but he tried.

"They let everybody out three years ago, right?"

I nodded.

"The people went freaking nuts."

"People?"

"Imagine going to rob some guy's house. You get inside, but you don't know you've tripped some fancy alarm. You're going along, looking for some cash or whatever, and bang, you get a bullet in the back of the head."

I looked at him sideways. I was more careful than that.

"Dude, brothers are getting shot every day. People aren't afraid of going to jail anymore. You break into some guy's house, he's not scared of you and he's not calling the cops. He's not afraid of some ankle bracelet any more than you are, so he lights you up."

"Don't they get arrested?"

"Sometimes. But the cops side with whoever owns the property. And even if they do get busted, they get the same as us—reeducation."

"Reeducation?"

"It's probation on steroids. They're serious. You've got meeting after meeting with these guys who teach you how to live right."

Double almost convinced me to go legit, but I didn't know the first thing about getting a job. I couldn't flip burgers all day or stand guard over some warehouse all night. Double was convinced there was no other choice, but I was smarter than him. At least I thought I was. There was no real punishment for crime anymore. Why couldn't he see that? As long as I avoided angry homeowners, I could go right back to work. I didn't know it yet, but I had a lot to learn about the changes Double hadn't mentioned.

Before he left, he showed me pictures of his wife and kid. They had a place not far from my old apartment in West Roxbury. He told me I should move back into the neighborhood and we could play some ball on weekends. He told me I was going to like the way things were.

"Couldn't miss," he said.

I had my doubts.

CHAPTER ELEVEN

Wendell Cummings was the next person through my door that day. He's leaning against the glass behind me now, waiting for me to finish my story. I know you recognize him because he brought you here. He seems patient now. He started off that way when we first met, but his patience didn't last.

The first thing he did that day in the infirmary was fasten a tracking anklet and tell me never to take it off. If it ever came off, even for a minute, I couldn't go more than five feet from it. It could withstand intense heat. It could be submerged underwater to any depth. "Never, never, never take it off," he said.

The nerd was completely serious. He had straight gray hair that hung down in his face. The dress shirt and worn boat shoes made him look like a guy who chose to work in a library where he could keep learning even if they couldn't pay him much. He was book smart for sure, but there was a major problem with his plan to track my movements— the anklet was so big I could almost kick it off. I wondered if he was that much of an idiot? He must have known what I was thinking because he said, "This is serious, Michael. I've taken charge of you. You keep that anklet on and you keep out of trouble. Your trouble is my trouble and I'm not having any of it, understand?"

I tried not to laugh, but I couldn't help thinking how idiotic government people were. I'm no imposing figure, especially after lying in bed for four years, but Wendell was barely my size and he was fifty years old. On top of that he looked goofy and uncoordinated. I had been threatened by some scary dudes and let me tell you, Wendell Cummings wasn't one. He threatened to track me with an ankle bracelet I could slip off anytime I wanted and if I got in trouble, there was absolutely no chance of me going to prison. At that point I couldn't believe anyone chose to go straight. It made no sense whatsoever, but I had a lot to learn.

I don't think Wendell trusted me. I shouldn't have trusted him when he opened the box he brought with him and gave me a can of peaches and a Coke. I hadn't had either since I'd been locked up and it looked like a feast. Canned peaches and a Coke weren't expensive, but when you really want something for a long time, it's fantastic when you finally get a hold of it. I'd wanted peaches in a can since I was six years old. To me it was a big deal.

The peaches were still in the open can with heavy syrup and a fork the way I liked them. The Coke was poured into a glass, something I didn't normally waste time on. As I speared the first peach slice, the snack warned me. It whispered that Wendell Cummings knew me too well, but I didn't listen.

He said again, "I put together your program, Michael."

He acted like some kind of god for creating this program. I had no idea what he was talking about, or why he thought it was so important, but to Wendell it was a very big deal.

"Your trouble is my trouble. Remember that, Michael. We're going to do everything we can to help you. Whatever happens, you cannot be arrested again. Do you understand?"

I nodded, eating my peaches.

He pulled out a black cloth case that held stacks of DVDs. "Each of these runs about six hours, Michael. When you get home, you will find a box attached to your television. You'll insert one of these DVDs and play it each day. You must be in front of the television with your anklet on the entire time the DVD is playing. If you need to leave the room for any reason, you must stop the DVD and restart when you return to the room."

He must have seen my smirk. Everyone he told this to must have had the same reaction.

"Michael, if you don't watch the entire DVD, you get no credit, understand?"

"Credit for what?" I asked before slurping some syrup.

"The program, Michael. The program. You cannot move ahead until you complete each DVD successfully."

"What if I want to watch something else?"

"You can't."

"What do you mean I can't? I can't watch television in my own home? You're out of your mind."

"Things are different, Michael," he said coolly. "We take rehabilitation very seriously. You must complete the program before you can go to work, before you can restart your relationships with your friends, and yes, before you can watch television."

I didn't bother arguing. Wendell Cummings was out of his mind.

He showed me the numbering system on the DVDs. There were fifty-two of them. Once I had watched each one all the way through, I'd receive directions that told me what to do next. I could only watch one each day, and if I didn't complete the DVD in one day I needed to start again from the beginning the next day. There was an instructional video, blah, blah, blah. At this point I was really losing focus. He stressed how important the videos were and that somehow they would help me to make big changes in my life, but my eyelids drooped and I couldn't stop them.

The last thing I heard while Wendell Cummings was in the room was that I should expect my counselors to start arriving the next day. I wanted to ask why I needed to talk to counselors, but my eyelids were so heavy I couldn't hold them open. My head lolled to the left and I fell asleep with Wendell Cummings watching me.

CHAPTER TWELVE

When I woke up, the lights were dimmed to simulate night inside my hospital room. Debbie sat by the door and watched me intently. How could it be nighttime? I hadn't even had lunch. The last thing I remembered was Wendell blabbing on about his program. Did I nod off and sleep through the entire day? Debbie wouldn't tell me what time it was and when I found the tender spot at the base of my skull, she warned me not to touch it. She said I had a sore from lying on the pillow too long and that I needed to leave the bandage alone.

Now I know that was a lie. What they did to me was illegal. How could they plant something inside my head and get away with it? I don't know what kind of justice this is, but you should consider what they did to me as much as anything I've done wrong.

Debbie gave me two pills to help me sleep, and the next morning I met my education counselor, Dr. Blake. He was a big guy, not tall but well-rounded in the physical sense and he had a thick beard and dark curly hair. He was young, probably a newly graduated Ph.D.

Dr. Blake shook my hand vigorously and pulled the single chair close to my bedside. He explained that this was the start of my program more enthusiastically than any bureaucrat had ever spoken to me. Blake was excited to help me go straight and be a productive member of society, yada, yada. So I listened to him babble and tried not to interrupt.

"What was the last grade you completed in school?"

"Seventh."

I guess I should have been embarrassed that I never finished eighth grade. Blake was the first in a stream of people tasked to mold me into shape. Every one of them had been to college. They weren't geniuses or anything, but they'd made the investment I wouldn't make in myself, not that I really had a chance where I came from.

"Did you have difficulties in school?"

"Besides paying attention?" I asked. He wanted to know if I was a moron, without sounding politically incorrect.

"Can you multiply twenty-three by three?"

"In my head?"

"Can you?"

I asked for a piece of paper and he refused. When I couldn't answer, he gave me a few really easy problems I could do in my head. I wondered what multiplying had to do with life but didn't ask. This was serious to Dr. Blake and to his credit, he didn't make fun of me. I was embarrassed by how simple he had to make the problems for me to answer them right. He made a few notes and then handed me a typed page and asked me to read the text.

I struggled with the third word and Dr. Blake make a tick mark on his notepad. In my school if you learned to read and write you were a prodigy. I wasn't a retard, but I spent more time worrying about how to keep my skin intact than reading books someone made up. There might have been a few kids I went to school with who could have read that entire page without fumbling, but not me. I stumbled over lots of words. After a while I stopped trying to sound them out and said pass when I got to a word I didn't know.

When I handed back the page he asked me to name the seven continents. I got North and South America, Asia and Africa. I had no idea what the other three could be.

He asked me who the president of the United States was. You'd have to be dead not to know Barack Obama was president when I went to prison. Hey, I watched TV, but I couldn't have known he'd lost reelection while I was sleeping. Blake asked me to name the two halves of congress in the federal government. I had no idea what he was talking about.

He asked me about the court system and I knew everything about it down to the difference between district, superior, and federal court. He was impressed with my knowledge of appeals and other procedures. The problem, he explained, was that this system had been entirely revamped in the last three years. The only part of American government I was familiar with had been erased. My ignorance earned me a civics class. If I had known he was assessing my weaknesses, I would have worked a lot harder to come up with correct answers.

He asked me about Tom Sawyer, Captain Ahab, Mr. Darcy, Moses, Gandhi, and Muhammad. I knew these people were all famous. Some of them were fictional. I told Dr. Blake that Tom Sawyer was a young kid in a book by Charles Dickens. When he grimaced I knew I was wrong and I didn't try guessing who the other people were. Blake was surprised for a minute but made some notes.

I wasn't worried about all his notes and questions until he showed me the stack of DVDs I'd find when I got home. There were five or six books he expected me to read, and I told him he was out of his mind.

"You don't understand," he said.

"I guess I don't."

He pointed to the red light on the ankle bracelet. "No one will hire you until that light goes green."

"Are you kidding me?"

"That light doesn't go green until you get your GED. And to do that, you've got to prove to me that you're ready."

I didn't know what to say. I didn't need a job. I certainly wasn't reading all those books, but Dr. Blake's intensity made me nervous. There I was a convicted felon and they were paying this guy to teach me things I should have learned for free in high school. I didn't understand what was happening, but I was in no position to argue with Blake.

CHAPTER THIRTEEN

If my conversation with Dr. Blake was a shock, my meeting with Dr. Charlotte Finch was intriguing. I was delighted to see her walk into my room. Her long red hair shimmered under the fluorescents and her taut body waved and curled as she stalked up to my bedside and offered her hand. She saw me check her left hand for a ring and find none. She smiled a knowing smile that was neither an invitation nor a rebuke.

"I'm the family counselor," she said.

She stiffened at my horrified expression.

"Don't worry, this will be the easiest session you'll have this week. We should be done today." Boy was that a lie.

"Don't tell me I need your approval to get that light off?" I looked down at my ankle and the glowing red light.

"Don't think of it that way, Michael. I'm here to help."

"Do you do this for everyone who leaves prison? I mean, how can you afford all this? How many prisoners have been let out in the last few years?"

"That's a lot of questions. Just relax. This isn't going to hurt. Yes, we do this for everyone. We think it's important for you to be comfortable in all aspects of your life. If you are at ease, you can work yourself back into society in a positive way. We've had a lot of practice. We've released two million prisoners in the last three years."

Two million? How could two million felons rejoin society in a positive way? Charlotte, Dr. Blake, and Wendell Cummings were kidding themselves.

"How many years do you have to go to school to be a doctor?"

"Eight years of college usually, depending on the specialty."

I couldn't believe all these people spent eight extra years in school. I hadn't even finished the first twelve, not even close, but it was clear to me you couldn't empty the prisons and expect it to go well. They might have spent a lot of money on fancy educations, but they had a lot to learn.

"Let's get started," she said, opening a folder. "Would you like to talk about your parents or your siblings first?"

"Parents?"

"I only have record of your mother here in the file."

"Does it say 'fat menace' under her picture?"

"Come on now, Michael. You need to be honest with me and yourself. Your mother wasn't a menace, was she? She brought you into this world and cared for you, didn't she?"

"She stuck a gun in my face and said she was going to kill me."

"When was that?"

"The first time, I was thirteen."

She looked surprised, but I could tell she'd heard stories like mine before. All she said was, "Why?"

"I was her original ticket out of the house. She got pregnant with me when she was fifteen or sixteen. It wasn't an accident. She knew the government would give her an apartment in the projects and enough to feed the two of us. It was ok at first, but she never stopped getting her ticket punched, if you know what I mean. By the time I was thirteen, there were six other kids. Money was tight. She never got a job, just kept getting pregnant and angry when there wasn't enough to go around."

"So you started getting into trouble?"

"I was hungry. I clipped a can of peaches from the grocery store and I got caught. DSS and the cops brought me home."

"Your mother had good reason to be angry then."

"She wasn't worried about me. She was worried about DSS taking her kids away. Without us, she'd have to get a job. When she stuck that gun to my head she said, 'You bring DSS here again and I'll shoot you dead, boy.'"

Charlotte had to stop and think about that a minute. "But you stayed until you were eighteen."

"Is that what your file says?"

She turned it toward me knowing I couldn't read the small print.

"One of the kids found some fancy jewelry in my bedroom two years later. My mom went crazy looking for the gun and I split. I was fifteen and I never went back."

Charlotte wrote something in her file. I wondered if she'd bust my mom for collecting when I wasn't even there. It would serve mom right. Charlotte asked about my brothers and sisters and I told her I saw them sometimes on the street. Nothing regular.

"What about your father?"

"Never met him."

"Would you like to?"

"What are you talking about? My mother doesn't even know who he is."

"We have a new program," she said. "When a baby is born without a father, we put the DNA into our computer systems. Every man who gets a DNA sample taken by the government is compared against the list of fatherless children."

"You can tell me who my father is?"

"About eighty percent of the time. Do you want to know?"

I'd never really had a family. My mother didn't count. She was too young to know what she was doing. Finding my father was likely to be a huge disappointment. He certainly wouldn't want any part of my mother and he'd have no real obligation to me. I was twenty-five. What did Charlotte think I was looking for? A handshake? A ballgame?

Charlotte nodded up and down, like I had to find my father to stop the little red light from glowing, but she couldn't force me to do it. I said sure. What could it hurt?

She gave me a clipboard with a paper, pointed to the X, and I signed it.

"That brings me to one last thing," she said. "Children."

"I don't have any."

She looked at me funny and took a picture out of her folder.

47

Melanie Michaud, that bitch. She'd talked to the cops while I was in a coma. How could she? Just like my mother—in it for the money.

The picture Charlotte handed me wasn't Melanie Michaud.

I recognized her curly red hair instantly. I'd spent a week with Kathleen Fitzgerald before I'd hit the district attorney. Seeing her picture I felt like I should have gone back.

Charlotte handed me a second picture. He was three years old, sliding down a red plastic slide in someone's back yard. As I took the photo, I felt foolish for the glances I'd shot at her earlier. She'd known what she was about to reveal, maybe that's why she kept her cool. Maybe she was just playing me and had no real attraction at all. Certainly, being a felon didn't put me at the top of her list.

"Jonathan," Charlotte said. "Jonathan Fitzgerald. The DNA match was conclusive." I'd been careful, but even without the DNA test, there was no doubting he had my square chin and stubby nose. I could almost see his mother's green eyes, but the picture was too far away.

The financial thing didn't hit me right away. Sure, Charlotte was showing me the picture because she wanted me to help pay for little Jon's care. I got that. After growing up with barely enough to eat, I had to help the little guy. It wasn't a mix up. DNA tests don't pick some random girl and it just happens she's the last girl I slept with before I went up. No. It was my mistake not the computer's.

I thought about Kathleen. Was she different now that she was a mother? What would she expect from me?

Charlotte passed me a card with Kathleen's address and phone number in blue ink on the back. I had to see her and work things out. Once Kathleen and I agreed on how to take care of Jonathan, Charlotte, would approve my release from the dreaded red light.

How absurd? How hard did they think I'd work to turn off the little red light on that anklet? The folly was blocked by thoughts of Kathleen and Jon, what I'd find at their new address, and what they'd say when I came to see them.

CHAPTER FOURTEEN

I was overwhelmed. The physical therapy alone was a major strain. While I was learning to walk and talk and move, counselors streamed in, one after another, and told me things that completely upset my understanding of the world. I might have been able to digest the changes if they were spread out over a year, but they came so fast I could barely listen to everything the bureaucrats spouted off. I told them what they wanted to hear, even though I expected to be robbing houses as soon as I was out. I knew the government was going to great lengths to help me. It's not like I didn't appreciate it, but I couldn't picture myself at a mindless job day after day. Sure, I would have been proud to have a legitimate job. Maybe I didn't believe in myself. Maybe I didn't believe anyone would hire me. Whatever my reasons, I dismissed the BS my counselors slung at me.

The next guy to walk up to my bedside really didn't fit with the rest. He wore a dark suit, white shirt, and shoes that shined from any angle. There wasn't a single wrinkle in his outfit. He introduced himself as Morris Farnsworth, my financial counselor.

I stopped him before he could say another word. "What are you doing here?"

"I'm your financial counselor."

"But you? Look at you in that fancy suit. You belong on Wall Street or something. Why are you here talking to a convict?"

"Relearner," he corrected.

A frown crossed his lips. He straightened them quickly and I knew counseling convicts wasn't his first career choice.

"I worked for an investment bank before things changed."

I didn't understand.

He tapped my file. "Of course you don't know about that, do you?" he asked. "A few years ago, when the supreme court mandated changes in the prison system, the government had a major budget problem. Not to mention a major labor problem."

"I can't believe how many people have been parading in here."

"Right. Now multiply that by two million." My mouth hung open while he continued. "It's a big job to help the institutionalized recover what they've lost. The costs are astronomical and the labor effort is immense. The government solved both problems with a couple of wide swings. Unfortunately, one of them eliminated my job."

"And here you are. What were the swings?"

"The first was a tax code overhaul. There are no loopholes anymore, no complications. You make money, you multiply it by the tax rate and you send it in. It's incredibly simple."

"So lots of tax accountants were out of work?"

"Not to mention ninety percent of the IRS."

"What did they do?"

"Financial counseling for inmates. What else?"

"So you were an accountant at the investment bank?"

"No. I was downsized when the banking system was streamlined."

"Streamlined?"

"Instead of backing the banks, the government took them over. There used to be thousands of banks, now there's only one."

I sat there a minute thinking about all the banks that used to fight each other for customers. All the commercials I'd seen on television. All the ATMs along the sidewalk. All the free toasters they gave away. It made sense that one single bank would be much more efficient, but who could we trust to safeguard the money of every American family?

"Frightening, isn't it?"

I wasn't smart enough to know why I felt queasy, but when Morris told me he was there to help me create a budget, I knew he was much too bright for the task. He seemed as embarrassed about being there to help as I was for needing him. I didn't ask him any more questions about what he did before he got this job.

He cleared his throat, a signal it was time to get to work. "I couldn't find a bank account for you. Could your account be under someone else's name?"

"Account?"

"Savings account, checking account, investment account?"

He was amazed when I told him I didn't have one.

"Where do you keep your money?"

"A safe deposit box."

He looked really troubled. He leaned forward and whispered that I had a problem. It was weird. We were the only two people in the room, but he spoke so softly I could barely hear him. Who was he hiding from? I should have paid more attention. He said the safe deposit box might exist, but cash wasn't accepted for anything. I was going to have to explain where the money came from to have any chance of exchanging it for credit.

"What do you mean cash isn't accepted?"

"When the government emptied the prisons, they had to take stringent measures to fight crime. They track every credit you spend, what you spend it on, and who it goes to. Later on, if they suspect you of something, they know exactly who you've been dealing with."

"What about all that money I've saved?"

"Have you ever held a job?"

I admitted I hadn't.

"Had an inheritance?"

"No."

"Where'd the money come from?"

I couldn't tell him I'd stolen it. If I did, he'd either turn me in or ask for a bribe to convert it into credit. There was over fifty thousand dollars cash in that box. Enough for me to live comfortably for a few years even if I couldn't find a job. Now it was worthless. I also had lots of jewelry locked in there. If I could sell it, that would get me through, but what could I sell it for? Even more troubling was that the most marketable commodity in the world had ceased to exist. My job had just gotten a lot harder.

"Forget it," I said. "What else do we need to talk about?"

"We've got to create a budget."

I stared back blankly. He asked me how I planned my spending and I told him honestly that when I needed money I went to work. People with jobs or government checks had a regular amount of money coming in and they didn't have an easy way to get more. Living on that monthly check was the biggest problem in our house growing up. There was never enough to buy what we needed. Morris wanted to help me solve that problem for myself, even if I was convinced it didn't apply.

He pulled out a worksheet and prompted me through an estimate of what I spent on different things. I humored him, but the numbers didn't mean anything. I was just going through the motions, trying to get rid of him so I could be one step closer to going home. Then he asked me what I expected to earn when I finished the program.

"Fifty or sixty thousand," I said.

"Doing?"

I shrugged.

"Let's say forty."

"Where do you get that?"

"Everyone is guaranteed forty." He must have seen the disbelief on my face. "When they overhauled the tax code, the banking system, and replaced the prison system with reeducation, they decided the best way to keep people out of trouble was to guarantee everyone a good living whether they worked or not."

"I'm going to get forty thousand for doing nothing?"

"Minus support for your son, yes."

CHAPTER FIFTEEN

All these people came in and told me what it was like in the new America, but for all I knew it was a scam. All I had seen since waking up was my room in the prison infirmary and the treatment room where Debbie slowly taught me to walk again. I couldn't be sure how much time had passed since I was shot. After the stories they told me, I couldn't stop imagining what it would be like on the outside. Morris had just told me I'd get forty thousand dollars a year for doing nothing. I used to make more, but how could I complain about that much free money? Sure I had to watch all the DVDs Wendell Cummings and Dr. Blake prepared for me, but how hard could it be to watch that many movies? All I had to do was sit there.

One morning a few days later, Debbie brought me to the kitchen and showed me how to make breakfast. I'd never cooked anything before, but with her help it was easy. After that things started moving fast. I'd been lying in bed for years next to the old guy on the respirator, but after breakfast, I never went back to that room. Debbie took me to an apartment inside the hospital that had a regular bed, a desk, and even a television.

Four hours later I saw a shimmering head of red hair outside my new doorway. I stood up immediately and said hello. Charlotte came in, followed by two people I hadn't met. David Jones wore a suit as well tailored as Morris Farnsworth's, but David was a regular guy. He told me he was my employment counselor. He'd help me get a job when my training was finished, but he didn't have any urgency about the undertaking. I didn't need to either since the government would hand me forty K a year for sitting on the couch.

The woman behind him was a sexier, brunette version of Charlotte. She was young and enchanting with an amazing figure. She met my eyes and smiled devilishly, like she knew what I was thinking when I saw her long legs. Her smile said she considered it a compliment. Joanne introduced herself as my relationship counselor.

My mouth hung open. Wendell, Dr. Blake, Morris, Charlotte and now David and Joanne. Leaving prison was a major adjustment, but how could they afford to send all these people to help me? Were they trying to scare me straight? Or were they trying to make everyone earn their forty thousand?

Joanne wasn't pleased with my reaction. She was lowest on the totem pole of talking heads and assumed I didn't want her help. "No one wants to believe they need help finding a date, but there's a stigma associated with running afoul of our government's conformance policies. We're doing our best to help people see that's not right, but in the meantime, I'm here to help you find someone to share your life with. Someone who makes you happy." As hot as she was, she talked like she was reading from a policy manual. I tried to ignore it, but it wasn't easy.

"And I can't do that on my own?" I would have been glad to hook up with Joanne or Charlotte, but neither was extending an invitation.

"I'm an expert in relationship dynamics. I'll help you reflect on what qualities will mesh best with your personality, what traits a partner should have to join you as a successful mate."

"Do I need an ok from you to get the little red light turned off?"

"No." She wasn't happy about that.

She was even less happy when she saw me mentally writing her off. She jabbed her card toward me and told me she'd call when I got settled. That was the first indication I was leaving the prison and my first hint that my counselors could find me whether I wanted them to or not. In the next minute, David handed me his card and filed out behind Joanne. Charlotte opened a folder when we were alone.

"It's time to find you a place to live."

"What's wrong with my old place?"

"I've contacted the Berniers. They've decided to stop renting the apartment over their garage. Don't take it personally. Many people who used to rent rooms have stopped."

I'd never caused the Berniers any trouble. I'd helped Hank Bernier haul lumber for his deck and helped him take out the trash whenever I saw him making trips to the curb. I never brought anything to that apartment that could cause problems for him. And now he was throwing me out? And why was this woman contacting him for me? Did she really ask them about me moving back in? Or did she encourage them to throw me out? She seemed nice enough, but I wondered why Charlotte did what she did.

My stuff was in storage. Moving would be easy, but I'd been in that apartment for three years. I lived alone over the garage, but it was the happiest home I'd ever known.

Charlotte saw how frustrated I was and put her hand on my mine. "Don't take it personally, Michael. Lots of people rented rooms years ago to make extra money. It just doesn't make sense anymore."

I was baffled. "Why not?"

"Taxes," she said. "The government takes eighty percent of what you earn over forty thousand. For people who already have a job, renting the room doesn't really earn them enough to justify the hassle."

"Hassle?"

I didn't know much about taxes because I'd never filed, but I didn't consider myself a hassle. She told me not to take it personally for the third time and then she started showing me government apartments from her folder. She had four available units. Every one was about the same size as my old apartment, but they were in square brick buildings that reminded me of the projects.

CHAPTER SIXTEEN

Two days later I moved into my apartment. The place had an eerie, foreign feeling and I was even more uncomfortable than I had been at home after my mother put the gun to my head. The apartment looked empty, but eventually I learned how every inch of my place could be watched by Wendell and his people. My subconscious was warning me of the danger, that's why I was nervous, but I wasn't smart enough to listen yet.

The Berniers had thrown out my old furniture, so I had to buy a couch, a bed, and a television. I had some things in boxes, mostly clothes and a few amusements. I lugged them up the stairs, but the bulk of the moving was done by delivery people. I felt like a duke or something. Morris Farnsworth created an account for me and the government filled it with enough money to buy furniture and rent the apartment. All I did was collect my boxes from storage and unpack. Charlotte even drove me.

I made myself a frozen pizza, opened a Coke, and turned on my new television. Nothing but static. The delivery guys plugged everything where it was supposed to go, but I hadn't ordered cable because Charlotte wouldn't let me. I'd stolen a signal for years by paying a guy to splice into the Berniers' feed. I decided to see if I could do it myself, but the wall plate was locked down. It took me twenty minutes to pick the lock without my tools. I got it open, but the conduit had been cemented to stop me from fishing another cable up. There was no telling how much concrete was down there, so I didn't try breaking it up. The brick construction and the blocked conduit made getting service impossible unless I hung a cable out the window. Probably not a good idea on my first day.

I was still kneeling behind my television when Wendell Cummings walked in. He didn't knock. Didn't say anything. Just came right in.

"That won't do you any good," he said.

"What do you mean?"

"The way to your normal stations is through this case." He held up a black case filled with DVDs. He set it down on the center of the couch without waiting for me to get up. Then he walked over to the front of the television, plugged a little box into one of the ports and inserted the first disc. The television immediately came to life.

He motioned me to sit on the couch and pressed a few buttons on the remote control. "This is where I want you to sit whenever you are working on the program."

I didn't argue. Sitting on the couch directly in front of the TV made perfect sense. It was the only seat in the room.

"This first disc is easy," he said.

"It really is," came a voice from the television. The voice was coming from a miniature figure that looked exactly like me. It was dressed in the same jeans and Red Sox T-shirt I had on. If it was possible, the voice was mine, too. I don't know how he did it. He must have recorded my voice and image while I was in the infirmary, but I hadn't see him with any equipment.

A miniature Wendell Cummings appeared on screen, wearing the same boat shoes Wendell wore, but a different button-down shirt. "Since the real Wendell can't be here with you all the time, I'll be here, right in your television, to be your guide. Let's get started. What do you think, Michael?"

The real-life Wendell placed a keyboard on my lap and handed me the remote control. When he did, the miniature Wendell and the miniature Michael started telling me about the buttons on the remote control. They hopped on top of a gigantic controller exactly like mine and explained the buttons in such numbing detail a four year old could operate the system. The instructions took twenty minutes, and when they finished I felt like a moron for watching. Wendell stood three feet from me, glaring down.

I got up to go get a drink from the fridge and mini Wendell stopped me.

"Whoa, big fellah. If you need to take a break, remember to hit the pause key, like this." He jumped on the gigantic remote and playback stopped. The real Wendell hadn't moved or spoken.

I wondered if he had a button in his pocket, so I took two steps back toward the couch and watched him intently. Miniature Wendell said, "That's better."

I stepped toward the kitchen and he said, "Whoa, big fellah."

"Listen to them," real Wendell said. "They won't steer you wrong."

He left me there wondering how a television program knew I wasn't watching. The box didn't have any sensors on the front panel. I wasn't an electronics expert, but it had to have some sort of motion sensor or something to know where I was. Wendell had secured the box to the television stand so firmly it wouldn't even wiggle. The stand itself had been built into the floor. It was impossible to move. The fastener that held the box down was hidden underneath the box. I couldn't release it without moving it, and I couldn't move it without releasing it. I guessed it was important to Wendell that the box be placed exactly in front of my television and aimed squarely at me on the couch.

The outside edges were smooth. I couldn't find a single screw to open the cover and get a look inside.

"Please don't do that," mini Wendell said.

"What are you going to do?" I said to him as I rummaged through my boxes to find a standard screwdriver.

"The educator is an expensive piece of government electronics," mini Wendell said. "I cannot allow you to tamper with it."

There was a lip at the top of the box. I choked up on the screwdriver and worked it inside to pop off the top cover.

"I warned you," mini Wendell said.

I was actually glad for the warning. I got up and unplugged the television. The little box had to get its power from that wire so I went back

58

to work on the box, assuming I was safe. The instant the screwdriver tip shimmied inside, a painful current pulsed out of the tool, through my fingers, and knocked me flat.

Mini Wendell reappeared, this time floating above the black box.

"Hurts, doesn't it?" The hologram floated seemingly out of nowhere. The television was off and the solid black cover of the box seemed incapable of projecting anything. The most haunting part of the experience was that Wendell wasn't looking at the spot on the couch, he was looking at me down on the floor.

Holographic Wendell followed my retreat to the couch and then I thought I understood what was happening. The box was tracking the ankle bracelet. Prison may have been outlawed, but the government wasn't giving up that easy. They replaced prison cells with brick apartments, prison guards with ankle bracelets that kept you inside, and your time was measured not in years but with a bunch of plastic videos you watched like a kid in timeout. I couldn't imagine the whole thing fooled anyone. Did they really expect talking to a few counselors and watching a few videos—well maybe a bunch of videos—to change anyone?

Wendell Cummings wasn't my friend. He was the new prison warden, and from the moment that black box zapped me, I decided to get through the program as fast as I could and get back to my old life. I plugged the television back in and mini Wendell picked up where he left off just like nothing happened. I glanced at the stack of videos and realized I couldn't possibly sit through this drivel for three hundred hours.

I outsmarted the box the only way I knew how. I slipped off my ankle bracelet. Left it on top of four magazines, precisely where it would have been if I was sitting on the couch facing forward and paying attention. Then I walked out the door to freedom.

The world outside my brick-walled prison looked the same as it had before I'd been locked up four years earlier, but so many things, invisible things, had changed. People in this new world knew *what* I was even if they didn't know *who* I was, but I hadn't figured that out yet.

59

CHAPTER SEVENTEEN

Everything on the street looked the same, but drastic changes had been made while I slept. With every single felon released from prison, America was a dangerous place. People learned to protect themselves by using subtle clues to measure each other. Vocabulary, clothes, stride, they mattered more than ever. I couldn't see this as I walked down the sidewalk, but in a few days people would learn my face and when they saw me coming, they'd go the other way.

There was a Dunkin' Donuts around the corner from my apartment. I was glad to see it because I expected to visit every morning. I walked to the familiar pink and orange sign and went in. A tone sounded when I came through the door, a low-pitched ding to signal the door had been opened. No one came in behind me, but when I had taken a couple of steps, three higher-pitched tones played louder and clearer than the first.

The woman ahead of me stepped out of line and moved far to my left, pulling along a girl who was about three or four years old. The little girl yanked her mother's arm and started crying and stomping her feet because she wanted a donut. The woman whispered something in her ear and the girl straightened right up. The two of them walked out the side door and disappeared in a rush. I wanted to ask her what she said. Now that I had a son, stuff like that could be useful.

With them gone, I had a clear line to the teenage girl with long strands of dark hair escaping from her pink and orange hat. A teenage kid to my left looked really frightened. He pretended to talk into his phone while he aimed his camera at me with a shaky hand. When I stepped up, the girl behind the counter said, "What do you want? You can have anything."

She didn't offer to sell me a donut, she offered it free so I wouldn't hurt her. Why? And why was the kid so interested in my transaction at the donut shop that he'd waste his time filming me? Was I that popular? Had these people been warned I moved to their neighborhood fresh from prison? Maybe they put my picture on television. I looked down at my shirt and pants. There was nothing different about them. Nothing I could tell.

I asked for a Boston Kreme donut and a coffee. I hadn't had Dunkin's coffee in four years. She made my coffee and bagged a donut from the metal tray. I reached for my back pocket to dig for cash. I didn't have any. No one did anymore. The girl flinched when my hands disappeared. She must have thought I was going for a gun to rob her of a stinking donut and coffee.

I shook my head and asked her how to use the scanner.

I rolled my thumb over the top and magically the bill was paid. I didn't need a credit card or a plastic thingy. All I needed was my thumb and I brought that everywhere. It sucked that no one carried cash anymore. That would make my work a lot harder, but the thumb thing was cool.

When I turned around to look for a table I saw a cop standing inside the door. He hadn't been there when I came in and he wasn't there to buy breakfast. When I sat down to eat, he watched. When I trailed out the front door, he followed. It got even weirder after that.

Two blocks down, the cop turned back, but a black SUV with tinted windows paralleled me. The hybrid barely made a sound. I learned later that the FBI jumped on the green initiative to get these, not because they polluted less, but because they were so quiet.

Right then I felt like I was trapped in a reality TV program. Everyone around me was an actor. I could talk and people could hear me and see me, but the world around me was a fraud. Everyone was watching. They were keeping me locked up no matter what. Wherever I went, my cell expanded to accommodate. I tried, but I couldn't shake the paranoid feeling.

I stopped on the sidewalk to talk to someone from my old life.

I dialed Hank Bernier. He answered the phone all businesslike, but when he heard my voice he slowed down. Hank told me he was sorry. It had been a long time. Things had changed. They couldn't rent my room anymore. I didn't know what to think when I hung up. Maybe things had changed or maybe Charlotte and Wendell had told him what to say.

The whole time I was on the phone, the SUV waited at the curb. No one got out to shop and the dark windows made no excuses for following me. The donut shop was only ten blocks from my old place on Dent Street and my bank was somewhere in the middle. New England Bank had been a fixture in every shopping mall and on almost every block downtown. I hadn't seen a single ATM in six blocks. It took a while, but I realized people didn't use ATMs anymore. There was no reason to.

My old branch was still there with the familiar sign over the door, but above it was a larger sign for Govbank in red, white, and blue. I walked through the front door and over to the customer service desk like I did every time I needed to put something in my box. When I told the woman behind the desk what I wanted, she asked me to wait.

After three minutes, the lobby was empty. The glass doors at the front of the lobby must have locked because I saw a man come to the front door and push, but the door wouldn't budge. It felt like it had in the donut shop but on a much larger scale.

Eventually three men led me down the concrete stairs to an iron grate. The scanner verified my identity and again I waited. In two minutes a telephone rang. The man on the inside handed me the phone.

It was Morris Farnsworth. "What's going on Michael?"

I was stunned silent. Had my thumbprint summoned him?

"Aren't you supposed to be at home?" he asked.

"I went out for a walk."

"What are you doing at the bank, Michael? I'm here to help you, but I can't help if you're going to go around acting crazy."

"I'm just getting something out of my box. No big deal."

"What could be so important that you need to visit the bank? I see you've used your funds without trouble to buy coffee and a donut. What else do you require?"

I'd only bought the coffee and donut fifteen minutes earlier, and he already knew? Maybe thumb scanners weren't so great.

"I don't need your permission," I said and hung up.

I flashed my key to the guard and asked him to help me open the box. He shook his head grimly. Did he think I really needed Farnsworth's permission? I lost it. I poked my fingers into the grate and yanked like I could pull it off the frame and rip the guy out of his cage. "That's my stuff," I screamed. "I put it in there and I want it now!"

He shook his head again, with pity in his eyes this time. He had three buddies standing behind me and the grate to protect him. His eyes said I was the one in trouble. I didn't mean what I said. I wouldn't have hurt him. I was just angry they wouldn't let me get my stuff. Stuff I'd worked years to save.

I had no idea what was going on when the four guys in black came clomping down the stairs all knees and elbows. "Michael O'Connor," the lead man yelled. "Hands above your head. Turn and face the wall."

I'd heard the drill.

Gone, though were my Miranda rights.

Also gone was the deference previous officers had shown me when I was arrested. They smacked my face against the wall, then shoved me up the stairs and across the lobby.

"What's going on? What did I do?"

A baton caught me square across my gut. I had no way to protect myself while my hands were cuffed behind my back and I couldn't keep from folding and dropping to my knees. They yanked me up without slowing.

Like the citizens Double warned me about, the cops no longer feared the law they upheld. Years ago a prison sentence for a cop meant doom. With that threat of prison lifted, they were free to swing away. The baton drove home an important lesson. Don't dis the cops.

They walked me across the street and I got to see the inside of that black SUV with the tinted windows.

CHAPTER EIGHTEEN

I'd never seen Wendell Cummings mad until then. I really hadn't given him that much credit. He was a flimsy guy, hair hanging down, glasses hiding his eyes. Five minutes in my old neighborhood and he would have been stripped clean of anything worth taking. Here in the courthouse, people bowed their heads as he passed like he was a rock star or something. Everyone in a suit knew Wendell Cummings. Half of them stopped to shake his hand and congratulate him on this or that. I really didn't understand what was going on. I just followed him down the long hall and watched dozens of people fawn over him.

When no one was looking, Wendell glared at me through narrowed eyes. His jaw clenched so tight it was hard for him to speak. "You say nothing in there, understand?"

At that point I didn't know what was happening. I thought I'd been arrested in the bank for trying to open my own safe deposit box, which seemed ridiculous. Not knowing what I'd done, I just breezed along, but soon I'd find out that my visit was far more serious than I imagined. The court didn't take nonconformance lightly. Wendell less so.

What could they really do to me? No matter what they couldn't send me to prison. There was no capital punishment in Massachusetts. What were they going to do? Sentence me to extra videos?

I'd already gotten the worst I could expect from the baton, or so I thought. Unfortunately, I'd completely underestimated Wendell's creativity and that of his colleagues. Punishment helped society work. I was thumbing my nose at authority like so many on their way to the gallows. I couldn't know the danger I was flirting with. If I had, I would have acted much differently.

When I followed Wendell to the courtroom door I realized my cuffs had been removed and no one but Wendell really cared where I was going. I could have turned and ran out the front, but there were sixty police officers swarming around. I wouldn't have gotten far, and standing here in front of you, I can say I'm really glad I didn't run.

All the courtrooms I'd been in up to that point were large enough to hold a basketball game. This room was tiny. The judge sat behind a desk, not raised up on a platform to be worshipped. There was no jury and only a few rows for an audience. Two people sat behind the prosecution table. One was the officer who hit me with the baton. The other wore a dark suit and a smug expression.

I knew how these things went. This would be a pre-trial hearing. We wouldn't accomplish much. We'd talk about a trial date and the charges, and in about a month we'd select a jury and spend the day arguing. Between now and then I planned to figure out how to get out of this mess. I relaxed behind the defense table and wondered what maneuvers Wendell would use to get me off.

The judge motioned with his finger and the prosecutor went to the front of the room. Wendell didn't move to join them. I'd been in court. I'd watched trials on TV. Never had I seen the prosecutor talk to the judge without the defense listening. I wanted to ask Wendell why he wasn't up there, but he wouldn't meet my eyes. He glared until the men broke up their hushed conversation. The prosecutor laughed. Both men shook their heads in my direction, openly ridiculing me. I had no idea what I could have done that was so funny, but their mockery intensified Wendell's scowl.

"It seems your client has escaped his leash," the judge boomed.

"Yes, Your Honor," Wendell said humbly.

"Recommend we proceed to phase two," the prosecutor suggested.

"Objection," Wendell shouted from his seat.

"I'll hear it."

"It's only our first day on the outside with Mr. O'Connor, sir. It seems he's a little fuzzy on the ground rules and I'd like more time to get him accustomed to his new circumstances."

"That's ridiculous," the prosecutor hollered.

The judge waved him off and Wendell continued. "Mr. O'Connor has some extenuating circumstances, Your Honor. He's been in a coma for four years and has not had time to fully absorb the new rules."

The judge pondered this.

As I watched, it slowly hit me that my guilt had already been settled. We'd been in court four minutes. Wendell had barely said anything in my defense and they were already talking about sentencing. I was surprised, but what did it matter? They couldn't really do anything to me. Whatever phase two was, it would be an inconvenience and nothing more. I told myself I shouldn't be nervous about being ordered to watch more DVDs, but I was starting to feel queasy. I was annoyed at being caught for whatever I'd done. Even more annoyed that no one would tell me what that was, but at least I had the good sense to sit there and be quiet.

"Move to have this event stricken from Mr. O'Connor's record."

The prosecutor jumped from his seat. "Objection. We're already playing catch and release here. Don't take away my net, Your Honor."

"Denied. You may keep the relearner at phase one, but you must readmit."

"It's been one day, Your Honor," Wendell begged.

The judge pointed to a computer station at the front of his desk. Wendell walked sullenly forward, clicked several times on the keys, and scanned his thumbprint to sign for my release.

The judge banged his gavel and everyone stood. I was caught by surprise and rose last.

The prosecutor chuckled as he left the room. "This one's a winner."

Wendell was too angry to respond. He led me out of the room and to his car. He didn't say a word as we got in and drove through heavy traffic back to my apartment. Somewhere during the trip I remembered that he'd said, "My trouble was his trouble," or something like that. I felt it now.

When we were inside, he closed the door behind us.

The television was off. Holographic Wendell appeared. "Glad you decided to rejoin us."

Life-sized Wendell removed something that looked like a remote for a car door lock, clicked it, and holographic Wendell disappeared.

"Where is it?" Wendell yelled louder than I thought possible.

Maybe I was being thick, but I had no idea what he meant.

His eyes found my ankle bracelet sitting on the stack of magazines where I'd left it. He snatched it, threw the magazines fluttering across the room, and waved the bracelet in my face. "What are you trying to do to me?" His red face was inches from mine. He was even smaller than me. I wasn't afraid of what he could do physically. Then it really hit home. Wendell Cummings really cared about what happened to me. It wasn't because he liked me or even knew me. The system would reward him if I behaved and punish him, probably monetarily, if I didn't. All the counseling and the DVDs and the lectures were designed to earn Wendell his bonus. For a few seconds my world made sense.

"What's the big deal?"

"This bracelet signals to the world that you are obeying the rules. If you don't have it on, you are breaking the law. That reflects on you and, more important, that reflects on me."

I took the stupid thing from him, pulled my sneaker off, and slipped the bracelet back on.

"Happy?"

"Listen to me you useless little punk. I know you've never worked a day in your life. I know you've never been anything but trouble. I also have an idea why. I'm here to help you. If you take what I have to offer, you can have a better life than you ever imagined, but if you screw up, you're screwing up for both of us. I won't let you do that to me, Michael. I won't."

"What are you talking about?"

"My program helps people. I've spent the last ten years of my life trying to help convicts get back on track. The new laws finally gave me my chance. I've taught tens of thousands of people to read. I've helped them understand what happened to them when they were younger and how to rise above it. I've helped them understand that violence is wrong. But you, Michael, are putting that all at risk and I won't let you."

His eyes went wild behind the glasses when he talked about helping people. This was his crusade. He thought he was an electronically enhanced savior, rehabilitating wrongdoers by the stadium full.

"What did I do?"

"Can't you understand simple rules? You may not move three feet from that bracelet at any time. If you do, you are breaking the law."

"How was I supposed to know they'd catch me? Without the stupid thing on, I look like everyone else."

He wanted to tell me something then, but he didn't. Didn't or couldn't, I'll never know.

Going to the bank might have been a mistake. Maybe they knew I was a convict when I scanned my thumb. Maybe Morris told them who I was. If I had known how futile it was to try and hide by taking my ankle bracelet off, I never would have done it again.

"You have a lot to learn." He grabbed my chin and looked me straight in the eyes. The little guy was threatening me and if he hadn't just saved me in the courtroom, I would have slugged him. "Follow the rules. Keep the anklet on. Watch the DVDs. Do what you're told."

Even then I was thinking of ways to get my anklet to watch the DVDs for me while I slept.

"I know what you're thinking Michael, and you can forget it. The people won't stand for lawlessness. You'll have to pay and so will I."

That was the second time he told me how important my behavior was to him. If he had explained it all to me then, I might have been able to help him, but he didn't trust me with that information, not yet.

CHAPTER NINETEEN

All night long Wendell's angry face crowded my dreams. The next morning I crawled out of bed feeling sorry for the trouble I'd caused him. I should have been worried about my own trouble, but I didn't realize you could fail reeducation. I hadn't considered the consequences of my escape when I turned on the television and restarted the DVD from the beginning. I just wanted to make it up to Wendell in some small way.

I paid strict attention from the couch as mini Michael and mini Wendell showed me how to operate the remote control and the wireless keyboard. I'd never had a computer of my own but the system mostly ran itself.

When they finished teaching me how to interact, several six-year-old boys appeared on a school playground. They did a pretty good job acting out a story about bullying. One kid harassed another. The other little kids stood by and watched until they went back into the classroom. I'd had enough when the teacher started through the alphabet one letter a minute. I guessed it was a subtle way to reinforce lots of things, but I was pretty comfortable with the alphabet and more than a little hungry. It was a stupid decision, but I slipped off the ankle bracelet, propped it up on the magazines, and headed out the door. The teacher made K sounds as I left.

There was no sinister plan in me slipping out the second time. I already knew the alphabet even if I wasn't the strongest reader. Wendell might disagree, but I didn't need the review. I was insulted and I was hungry. I'd get a donut and coffee and be back in fifteen minutes, long enough to miss the alphabet and the crap about Johnnie losing his baseball cards.

I trotted down the sidewalk. I don't know why I was in such a rush. Maybe I was self-conscious knowing how angry Wendell had been when I got caught without my ankle bracelet. Maybe I was worried about being spotted. Mostly I felt guilty that I wasn't watching the silly movie, but I'd be back there fast and I wouldn't go anywhere near the bank.

When I opened the door to the donut shop and stepped in, I heard the same loud tone I'd heard before. I waited for the second, louder signal to play, but before it did, a man at a nearby table stood up and stepped quickly to the door. The crowd tensed in alert, then two different tones played, one high and one low. The tones let the pressure out of the whole place. The people in front of me in line had looked ready to scatter, but when they heard the low note, they turned forward and concerned themselves with items behind the counter, the speed of the cashier, and wherever they were going next.

I stood in the doorway trying to understand what had happened, then three fingers clamped down on my elbow. It must have been some kind of pressure point, because the pain from the claw grip was intense. The fingers pulled me to a table where I faced the man who'd gotten up when I came in.

"Sit," he ordered and he let go.

"I don't know what you want with me, buddy," I said loud enough to attract attention. The guy seated across from looked like he'd been through his share of trouble. Whatever he wanted from me, I wasn't getting involved. I had enough trouble and I wanted everyone in the restaurant to know.

"Quiet," he whispered urgently. "Cut the crap."

I stared back at him.

He pulled up his jeans and showed me the ankle bracelet with the familiar red light glowing. "Whatever you've got planned, wait 'till I'm gone. I've got enough trouble. I just want to finish my course and move on."

"What are you talking about?"

"You come in here without your leash. I know what you're up to. I don't know how you can be that stupid, but leave me out of it."

"I just want a donut."

"Bullshit."

"I left my ankle bracelet up there to fool the black box. I just needed—"

"You *are* an idiot, aren't you?"

"What are you saying?" Was he really afraid of the little black box?

"The bracelet is like your prison uniform. If you're wearing it, you're not trying to escape—or rob a donut shop."

"I'm not trying to rob this place."

"These people don't know that." He looked at me like I was four years old.

"They don't know I'm a con."

"Don't you remember what happened? Where have you been?"

I told him the story of the gunshot on the bus and how I'd been asleep for four years. He relaxed then and stopped looking at me like I was a raving madman. I was disconnected from reality, but only because I hadn't lived it like everyone else. The pity in his eyes said he knew I was headed for trouble and there was nothing he could do to help me. No matter how many people warned me, I couldn't understand how desperate my situation was.

He told me to listen very carefully. "Keep the bracelet on. Never take it off. Never."

I started to ask why and he held up his hand to keep me quiet.

"When everyone was let out, what do you think the rest of the people did? Do you think they waited around to get robbed? Do you think the cops sat by while these nutball judges let us all out with no way to know who we were or what we were doing?"

Great. The first guy I met on the outside was a paranoid freak who couldn't stand living outside prison. I'd heard some guys stay in so long they can't handle a life that isn't scheduled for them.

"You heard the chime when you walked in, right?"

I had.

"Some cop had the idea to mark us. They were smart about it, too. They put something in the drinking water back in prison. Gets into your bones and the cops can track you on the outside. Some electronics whiz realized what the cops were doing and invented these scanners. See it there by the door?"

The scanner looked like the inventory control scanners I'd walked through in hundreds of stores.

"They scan for this chemical. It's radioactive, I think, but I'm not sure. Anyway, the scanner dings when a con walks through. Then it scans for the frequency the ankle bracelets transmit on. If it picks up a transmission within three feet, it gives the all-clear."

"So that's how they found me yesterday," I said.

"Slow down, kid. That's just for the civilians. You see, when they opened the doors and let out two million convicts, they knew we were going to ransack the country. It was mayhem for two years. Those scanners are for the people in the store, that's all. They expect stores to be robbed every time one of us comes in. That's why they freak out when they hear the ding. Guys took their bracelets off, thinking they couldn't be tracked, and went out to hit the nearest gas station."

"That's why people left the store when I came in yesterday."

"Now you're getting it."

"What did you mean thinking they couldn't be tracked?"

"First you've got to realize how pissed the cops were about all this. They worked their butts off to put guys like us away. You know how hard it was back then to get locked up. When those judges decided to let everyone go, the cops did two things. They created the black box, which is supposed to help you. They also found a way to know who was up to no good and who was doing what they're supposed to."

"The black box is my babysitter?"

"No, it's worse." He reached up the back of his scalp and felt his hairline. "Feel around right here," he said.

I knew exactly what he meant. That spot on my head had been sore the day after I met Wendell Cummings. I found the tiny bump immediately.

"These guys are smart," he said. "Smart and angry. That's a tracking device in your head. That's why you never take off the ankle bracelet."

He let me think for a minute.

"They both transmit a signal. There are thousands of special police. Their job is to find you when you go off the reservation. Any time that transmitter gets too far from your ankle bracelet they know. It was awesome for the first year or so. The special cops rode around in black cars with tinted windows. They'd haul guys in and beat the crap out of them. They were right. They were always right. Anyone away from his bracelet is committing a felony. And as soon as you leave the bracelet, they send someone after you."

"They baited the cons?"

He threw up his hands.

I couldn't tell if he understood what they were doing or if he realized the futility and decided to go along.

"What about the black box? How can I beat that freaking thing?"

"Those things are evil. Trust me, don't mess with it."

"It's playing kid movies. Come on."

"You get zapped yet?"

I nodded and he laughed. He knew what I was up against and he wanted to help me, but it was like a father telling his kid not to play with fire. The kid knows his father is older and wiser, but he has to try things for himself. No matter how strenuously the father tells his son about the danger, the orangy red flames draw him in.

"Play it straight," he said, then got up. "I've got to go. They're going to be looking for you soon and I can't be within a block of you. I can't get hauled in again. I'm near the end of my rope."

I thanked him for his advice, bought my donut, and went back to the demon box in front of my television. I didn't understand what he meant then. Now I do of course. That's why I'm standing in front of you. I'm sorry I didn't listen. I guess I was like that little kid who has to get burned before he understands how hot fire really is.

CHAPTER TWENTY

I ran up the stairs and flung the door open. Holographic Wendell was waiting for me. "What do you choose?" he asked.

The DVD had been playing for the last half hour. Without watching the movie I had no idea what choice he meant. Miniature Michael was on the screen in a classroom. All the boys in nearby desks faced him. Underneath were three choices. Ignore. Assist. Report.

I clicked back and forth among the options. I didn't know what had happened while I was gone and I didn't particularly care. I chose Ignore. Holographic Wendell smirked then vanished. The movie played on.

The boys on either side of me were kids from the playground. As the lesson continued up front, I recognized the bully on my left and his favorite target on my right. The teacher spelled three letter words at an annoyingly slow pace. I couldn't believe I had to watch six hours of this.

The story stopped again.

The boy on my left lofted a sharpened pencil over my head. It stuck into the smaller boy's arm and he cried out. The teacher looked directly at me. The screen offered a choice. Ignore. Assist. Report.

I figured the best way to stay out of trouble was to let these two kids handle it for themselves. It wasn't my problem. I hadn't started it. The only reason the teacher was looking at me was because I was seated between aggressor and victim.

I pressed Ignore and the lesson continued.

In two more minutes I watched enough spellings and misspellings of cat, dog, box, fox, and hat to last a lifetime. The movie kept stopping and it took as much time for me to answer the prompts as to get through the DVD. Wendell said this would take six hours. If he meant six hours of movie time, all the stops and starts would keep me there all day. I decided to speed things up. Every time a choice appeared I quickly hit the Ignore key and the movie resumed. I didn't consider the choices. I wasn't learning anything from what was happening on the screen, but I didn't expect to. Wendell said I had to sit and watch and that's all I intended to do.

The last time I pressed Ignore, there were eight kids picking on the sad little boy next to me. He buried his face in his arms as they pelted him with pencils, gum, erasers and anything else they could find in the virtual classroom. The teacher looked to *me* every time something happened like I was in charge or something. If a child on the opposite side of the room picked up a book and hurled it at the defenseless little kid, the teacher looked at me for guidance. Wendell was trying to teach me that what happened around me in life was up to me, but I sat back and let the teacher run the class.

Suddenly the little boy was energized and armed with all the things that had been thrown at him. One fist held dozens of pencils and pens. The other held a few books and other assorted things he could only grasp in a computer simulation. I had done nothing to help him, but I'd done nothing to hurt him either. That's why I was stunned when he turned and started stabbing me with the pens and pencils. I had no control of miniature Michael. I grabbed the remote and pressed keys to try and fight back, but I couldn't.

When my virtual corpse slumped at my desk, the teacher came down the aisle and took the little boy away.

Wendell's lesson made it clear how much he really wanted to help people. Even though I wasn't participating, I heard Wendell telling me that what I did had implications. The boy was unfairly targeted. I could have helped him and because I didn't, others joined in. Interestingly, the losers in this simulation were the wrong people. I was killed. I hadn't done anything wrong at all. I hadn't helped either. The poor little kid who attacked me had been victimized so long he snapped. Did he deserve to be punished? Probably not. The bully walked free to start again with another victim.

I was all of these people. I'd attacked weaker kids to build my rep. I'd looked the other way to avoid retaliation. I'd been knocked off track by my mother's abuse.

At that moment I felt like lashing out at the little box, Wendell, anyone I could find. Holographic Wendell appeared in front of the television, his features brighter with the screen behind him switched to black.

"I'm very disappointed with you, Michael," he said. "You must complete one disc each day. Normally that takes six hours. Rushing doesn't help anyone, Michael. You can't cheat my system. You must pay attention."

Wendell waited a few seconds and then directed me to look outside my door. I found two cables, one short, one long. When I returned, a port on the black box opened and Wendell directed me to plug one of the blue connectors into it. I did. Then I connected the other end to a port that opened in the remote control. The shorter cable wrapped around my wrist.

I'd learn later that the apartment building I lived in was full of relearners. A small group of men serviced our special needs, like this cable that had just been delivered. The box summoned something and they brought it to my apartment. It could and would happen on a moment's notice, though in reality, the box made these requests well in advance.

Holographic Wendell explained that the program would continue only while I had the remote plugged into the box and the strap fastened around my wrist. When everything was in place and I was back on the couch, the movie restarted with the kids on the playground.

This time I paid attention to the bullying.

The bigger kid was nasty to everyone including me. While the movie was running there was nothing I could do. Soon enough we reached the scene where the bully threw the pencil over my head and hit the kid seated on my right. The prompt came again. Ignore. Assist. Report.

This time I chose Assist. I didn't want to be a rat. What was the worst this virtual kid could do to me anyway?

Another prompt came up immediately. Gesture. Speak. Retaliate.

I chose Speak. A picture of the keyboard popped up and a word bubble opened above my virtual head. Things were moving much slower this time, but I didn't even realize how long I spent thinking about what to say. I typed with one finger, one letter at a time, *give him a break. he didn't do anything to you. he's just a little kid.*

The teacher spun around. "Michael O'Connor. There will be no talking in my class."

At the same instant a shock jumped into my wrist, completely catching me by surprise. I jumped so high the blue connector popped out of the black box. I knew then what the guy in the donut shop meant when he called it demonic. I wish I had paid more attention. I had antagonized it by sneaking out and by rushing through the first lesson. There was no way back to the true beginning, and I was going to pay for every mistake from then on.

I hesitantly plugged the port back in, ready to pull it back out if the shock continued. Fortunately, the evil box was done punishing me. Maybe I should have gestured. Maybe if I used fewer words the teacher wouldn't have known it was me who talked. These questions weren't trivial. My battle against this box was about to get serious.

The onscreen action continued.

The bully gnashed his teeth. The little kid smiled at me. Another kid winked. The others all took notice.

CHAPTER TWENTY-ONE

I learned how to take a break from the automated lessons by pausing the action on the screen rather than taking off my bracelet and sneaking away. The machine stopped as soon as I disconnected the wrist strap, but I hit the pause button every time I needed to get up, in case the machine was keeping track. Several hours later, cheesy fireworks erupted on the screen.

Holographic Wendell congratulated me and announced that I had completed my first disc in forty hours. Average time was twelve hours. The record was two and a half. Wendell's six hour estimate back at the hospital included a fair amount of repetition for those who didn't get it right. I could do better. If I could finish my lessons early in the day, I'd have time to get outside and get on with my life. I'm not sure why I felt so good about finishing something so simple, but I celebrated with a steak dinner. The phone was ringing when I got back.

I picked up and Charlotte told me she had an appointment for me in two days. She wouldn't tell me where we were going only that I should be dressed and ready to go by nine-thirty that morning. When she hung up, I imagined her locking me in a room to confront my mother like I had the bully. Maybe Charlotte would charge her with neglect after all the things I'd said. I really didn't know what to expect, but my body surged with nervous energy. Even weighed down by the steak, I couldn't keep my eyes closed.

The next morning I was up at eight o'clock, earlier than I ever woke in the old days. I was jittery with nervous energy, but my thoughts were fuzzy and I needed a coffee to clear my head before I started my lesson. I went for breakfast without even turning on the television. All the way down the stairs and along the sidewalk I pictured my mother in one of those tent-sized flowery dresses. She was on the witness stand just as she'd been every time I closed my eyes that night. The prosecutor badgered her for the way she had treated me and I felt sorry for her when I saw how scared she was. She had done it to herself. I didn't blame Charlotte. I couldn't really blame myself either, but I still felt guilty.

The ding didn't surprise me when I walked through the door. Everyone stopped and listened once it sounded and then relaxed when the high note and low note followed. I looked for the guy who'd explained it to me the day before. I had dozens more questions for him, but I never saw him again. Graduates like him could really help the relearners, but when I suggested Wendell make mentoring a part of the program, he told me the counselors were more effective. They were educated professionals, but none of them had ever been to prison.

I ate my donut in front of the blackened TV. I finished eating before starting the next disc, so I didn't spill coffee on the deep blue carpet if I got an answer wrong and got zapped. To be honest, I sipped slowly because I knew I was headed for more shocks. When I emptied my coffee I had an idea. I rinsed the cup, cut out the bottom, and wrapped it around my wrist to insulate myself from the charges. I looped the strap outside the paper cup and started the black box.

Wendell appeared and asked me to fasten the strap around my wrist. I checked the connection and even tightened it, but the program wouldn't continue until I removed the cup and exposed myself to the shocks. Later on, I'd learn that the strap not only delivered shocks, but also measured the electrical impulses traveling up and down my arm. Wendell expected relearners to cheat his black box at every turn and he'd done a great job stopping us.

When the strap was tight against my skin, the schoolyard appeared. Kids ran and played on a sunny day. Miniature Michael just stood there motionless on the screen, watching the other kids. It took me ten minutes to realize that on this new disc it was up to me to move around my virtual environment. Wendell's program was brilliant in many ways, but it failed to provide even basic guidance. A little bit of instruction here and there would have saved me hours of puzzling over what he expected me to do. Maybe that was the point of the entire exercise, but I didn't give him that much credit. I'm not sure even now that's what he intended.

Once I figured I could move myself around, I started exploring the playground, watching the girls huddled in a tight circle and the boys playing tag. A boy ran by me and dropped something green in my path. The system prompted me. Ignore. Investigate.

I pressed Investigate and found a five dollar bill.

I tried to move and the system prompted again. Replace. Carry.

I chose to carry the bill and the system forced me to be so specific as to tell it I wanted to put the bill in my pocket. I was annoyed it asked so many questions. What I should have been was wary, but in the simulation or in life, if someone dropped cash in front of me I was going to pocket it.

The same boy came past me a few minutes later with his eyes on the ground. I steered away from him. A teacher crossed the playground and asked if everything was ok. After being jolted for my response in the classroom the day before, I chose a single word answer. I typed, *Yes*.

Recess ended and we went back in for a lesson. The boy sat in the seat next to me looking sad. Eventually the teacher came down the aisle and asked him what was wrong. He told her he'd lost his lunch money. The system prompted me and I ignored his problem. Then the teacher stood up in front of the room and asked if anyone had found anything on the playground.

"I'm not giving it to you, you ugly old bat," I said to the screen.

The simulation paused. Holographic Wendell appeared with a stern expression. "You must learn respect for figures in authority, Michael. Teachers, police, counselors, even me, we are here to help you. More important, we make our society work for everyone. When you disobey directions from someone in authority, you are taking from someone else. You may be putting them at risk. You may be taking an opportunity from them or depriving them of something tangible like you are doing in this

80

case. You will never graduate from this program if you do not learn to understand authority figures, their roles in our society, and how you can help them to be effective."

I couldn't believe he expected me to be a rat. Bad enough he wanted me to give the kid his money back. I'd figured that out, but he was telling me I had to help the cops? How could I do that?

Unfortunately for me, I missed an important part of the message. I heard Wendell talking, but I didn't make the connection that the program had heard what I said. It interpreted my words and was displeased. It took me a long time to realize that the box understood what I was saying, and until I finally figured it out I kept shouting whatever came to mind, just like I did when the Sox were on television. That only sped up my punishments.

The teacher asked again if anyone had found the boy's money.

It took the shock to wake me up to the lesson.

When the plastic strap stopped stinging my wrist, and that's what it was, a mild sting compared to what was to come, Wendell materialized and told me he was disappointed. He lectured about how wrong it was to take something that belonged to someone else.

My punishment was quite unexpected. The simulation started again. Two kids dropped money right in front of me. I avoided picking it up, but then kids dropped more and more things. I realized what I was going to have to do. I picked up an apple and followed the little girl who dropped it. I gave it back to her, expecting the simulation to end. She thanked me, but recess continued and as I looked around the playground, the kids were steadily dropping things all over. My hesitation to get involved cost me. I couldn't pick up the things fast enough and soon the playground was covered in various items. I could only pick up one item at a time and I had to find each child to return it. It was impossible to remember who dropped what. My second trial ended in a shock and another lecture from Wendell.

The third trial I did better. I raced after each item and returned it to the appropriate child. If the kids weren't moving in every conceivable direction, I might have been able to keep up, but the longer the simulation went on, the faster things were dropped. I returned forty-one items and then received my third shock and my third lecture. My real mistake was in the beginning. The longer it took me to learn the lesson, the harder my task became.

I caught my breath before starting again. I knew what I had to do, but I was missing something. Wendell wanted to teach me not only that it was wrong to take something that wasn't mine, but also that it was my duty to help those who had lost something. I understood, but the mechanics seemed impossible. Rather than start again, I took off the wrist strap and paced around thinking how I could possibly track down the kids to return the items. Somewhere between the refrigerator and the couch it hit me.

I started again. I immediately picked up a book a little girl had dropped and opened a dialog bubble over miniature Michael's head. I typed the word *teacher* and the teacher came to my aid. She took the book and from then on, rather than scatter like the children did, she followed me. I scooped up item after item and in about two minutes the playground was clean and the simulation once again went black. Fireworks exploded in front of me.

My victory made me surprisingly proud. Wendell was teaching me things I should have learned in kindergarten. This game couldn't change my thinking, but I finally understood what the black box wanted from me. If I conducted my virtual self like a saint, the simulation would be easy. Pretty soon I was going to learn that my ideas about sainthood might be a little left of center.

It took me three hours to finish the simulation, but had I understood the dynamics, I would have been done in two minutes. That was the record time—two minutes and five seconds.

CHAPTER TWENTY-TWO

I sat in front of the blank television feeling as proud of my performance in the simulation as if I had gone out and helped those kids in real life. Doing something good was like turning on a bright light in my chest that warmed me from the inside. I'd never felt like that before. The only thing I can compare it to is the thrill you get when you meet a girl and realize she feels the chemistry as much as you do. I was too jazzed to start another disc, so I rewarded myself with a trip outside to get to know my new neighborhood.

I left my apartment with no particular destination in mind. I soaked in my surroundings and began adjusting to my new life. The concrete landing and the heavy steel railings were meant to survive decades of abuse. Unlike the projects I grew up in, the stench of poverty had been removed from the stairwells. Climbing down, I wondered if the forty thousand was responsible. If everyone could afford life's necessities, there was no reason to squat in a cardboard box in the park or under some concrete stairs. I also realized I hadn't seen any kids running around. My mother had conceived seven kids to earn her living. Her life would be so much easier now. All she had to do was hold out her hand and she'd get more than she needed— without a single child to chase after.

I felt more hopeful at that moment than I ever would again. Out the window I saw a patch of grass enclosed by brick walls on all sides. A few guys sat at a picnic table. They had to be my neighbors, otherwise they couldn't have gotten out there. It took a while, but I walked down to the ground floor and found the courtyard door.

Every man at the picnic table eyed me suspiciously as I approached. When they saw my ankle bracelet the closest man stood and offered to shake my hand. Joel introduced himself. He was a hulk of a guy, tattooed with barbed wire up and down his arms. "What are you in for?" he asked.

"This the prison yard?"

The three of them showed me their ankle bracelets.

Until that moment I thought of this place as just another neighborhood. It wasn't tagged and broken down like where I grew up. Wendell had duped me into thinking I was living free and clear on the outside, but I was about to get an education. The three guys in front of me were tattooed, pierced, and pumped. All three were on edge, wary of every move, and ready to fight at a second's notice. Most people walked around so consumed by their own thoughts they lost track of their surroundings. These three predators lived off people like that. So did I.

One of the guys got nervous and stood up to leave, like I was a snitch.

"I'm just new at this," I said.

"Shitty luck. What'd you do?"

When I told them I stole a credit card and some cash they laughed out loud. When they stopped making jokes I told them that was before the thumb scanners made them useless and that I'd been in a coma when the courts unleashed chaos on the streets. They warmed to me then.

Deone, the smallest of the three, introduced the group. Joel was in for attempted murder after some guy started dating his chick and then taunted him. Tyrone was in for stealing from the grocery store. He just couldn't get by on his forty thousand. Deone and I had the most in common. He'd stolen a Lexus because he needed to get behind the wheel. He couldn't afford one of his own and his urge to drive a slick ride kept him here. You couldn't beat the new tracking devices, but he couldn't help himself.

Our building didn't have the amenities of a suburban apartment complex. There was no pool, no restaurant, and no game room. It was more like a school with private classes held in each student's room. We couldn't see the teachers, but Deone assured me they were there.

"If you guys have it all figured out, why are you still here?"

"Algebra," Deone said.

I didn't know what algebra was.

"What are you working on?" he asked.

I didn't know how to describe my progress other than to say disc three.

They laughed again. "Dude, haven't you figured it out?"

"What?"

"All you have to do is act like Mother Theresa."

I didn't know who that was. "Yeah," I said.

I didn't fool anyone. "Think of the biggest sissy you ever went to school with," Joel said. "Got it? Now when you turn on the box, pretend he's there and it's your job to act like such a fag that you make him look tough. Like you're helping him get a girl or something."

Joel's life revolved around women. A couple days later I'd learn that DNA testing for fatherless welfare kids was killing him. He was supporting eleven children and being stuck in here was bankrupting him, but he'd never finished high school and that was one of Wendell's new requirements. He couldn't work until he graduated.

I got tired of standing and walked around to sit next to Deone. A chalkboard lay flat on the table in front of him. I saw Wendell's name, Charlotte's, Dr. Blake's. All my counselors were there along with other names I didn't recognize. Obviously, they were using the chalkboard to signal each other, but why? These guys could teach me what I was up against and I didn't let the occasion escape.

"What can you guys tell me about getting along? I keep stumbling into trouble."

Deone said, "Don't do anything stupid."

At the same time Joel wrote, *Careful what you say* on the chalkboard and then pointed to his ankle bracelet.

I started to ask a question, but Deone shook his head gravely. It was important to him that I keep quiet, so I did. Deone then drew three rows of squares on the chalkboard and pointed to one in the middle of the top row. He drew an arrow to the wall at my right and when I looked over, there was a dark figure standing in the center window on the third floor.

"A crowd attracts attention," Tyrone said, meaning a crowd of relearners. Did they think we were planning a heist? Or a jailbreak?

"Not everyone is glad we're out," Deone said.

"No one's glad we're out," Joel corrected. "Except Wendell."

Everyone laughed except me.

"He thinks he can fix us," Deone said. "Thinks teaching us equations gives us control. We control ourselves, but he'll never understand that."

"That's a laugh," Joel said. "If you could control yourself you wouldn't be here. And you know you're never getting out for good."

All three seemed resigned to return over and over.

"Bad luck getting here on your first try," Deone said to me.

"What do you mean?"

Deone explained there were three types of programs. If you were lucky you got one of the easy ones. There wasn't much to them and you'd be out in a week or two. According to Deone, you never got one of those twice. Wendell's program was the hardest. He was nuts about helping people. He really believed that a relearner could walk out of his program and go straight for good. He worked day and night and made millions in the process.

"It could be worse, one of the cat baggers could have gotten you."

A cat bagger was a sadist who created his own program and had it sanctioned by the government. They tortured relearners to entertain themselves and made a living in the process. Most of the convicts in those programs went nuts and jumped out a window. Once you went to one of the cat baggers, you never came back. In the old days prisoners would sue if they didn't get the right kind of toast, but now the pendulum had swung the other way. People wanted protection from relearners and citizens were willing to close their eyes to get it.

CHAPTER TWENTY-THREE

For the second night in a row I went out to dinner alone, then spent the night staring at the ceiling unable to sleep. On this night I would have gladly replayed my nightmares about confronting my mother. The stories about the cat baggers wiped away any confidence I'd gained from my victory over the black box. The guys in the courtyard made me feel like an idiot for going so slow and that bothered me, but thinking about the cat baggers and how sinister they could be with Wendell's technology, that had me thinking about going straight. Wendell was trying to teach me something and that was frustrating enough. If the cat baggers were bent on tormenting me, they could create something infinitely complex or completely random where no matter what I chose or no matter how hard I tried, I'd be sure to fail. Strange as it sounds, I felt fortunate to be in Wendell's program and I didn't want him to kick me out. That was my first hint about how the system worked.

I had a sliver of hope Wendell would give up and send me to one of the easy programs. The stakes seemed trivial until I heard about the cat baggers. My new friends didn't know how the cat baggers worked, only that relearners who went to one of those programs were never seen again. The stories were probably dramatized, but I knew there were people in the world sick enough to do what Deone and Joel described.

If the threat of electrically induced psychosis wasn't enough to keep me awake, I could imagine Charlotte leading me onto the set of a talk show to confront my mother. She hadn't told me where we were going or what she hoped to accomplish. My only clue was that she told me to dress nicely. If our trip involved my family I wasn't sure why I needed to dress nicely, but I knew it wouldn't be pretty.

At nine I visited the donut shop in my newest jeans and the only long sleeve dress shirt I owned. I hoped I'd have enough time to finish my lesson when Charlotte was done with me because I was too tired to look at the screen before I left.

She arrived in a new Chevy hybrid, the car exhaling air and water as it reached me at the curb. She looked me up and down, unimpressed with my sneakers and jeans and, unable to see the ankle bracelet, she nodded toward my feet and made me show it to her. She wore heels and a black dress with a high neckline. She'd look at home wherever we were going. I looked like her needy cousin. Unfortunately, this was the top step in my wardrobe. The public defender's office had taken back the suit they loaned me for trial.

"Are you going to tell me where we're going?"

She pulled away and casually said, "To see Kathleen and Jonathan."

The words rolled out like she was taking me to the corner store for milk and bread. I reminded myself that Jonathan was my son. Using his name so casually, she made him what he was—a person. Until that day, he'd only been a vague recollection of frenzied nights a long time ago. I'd prepared for an argument with my mother where she was the bad guy and I was the wrongly injured, riding in to claim justice for my pain and suffering. The conversation with Kathleen would be exactly the reverse. If the people who administered the DNA tests could be trusted, I'd gotten her pregnant and disappeared. The ugly conversation I'd prepared for got a lot uglier in the car.

If I had been driving, the car would have slowed to a crawl, but Charlotte sped silently past block after block. She had nothing to fear except arriving late. I remembered how much I resented my own father as a kid. Jonathan wasn't old enough to be picked on by the other kids, but kids were smart. He'd have questions. I wondered if my accident would make any difference to Kathleen. I thought about Double and Cortez and the hassle they went through to build a family. Maybe I should have been doing the same. Maybe this was my chance. Maybe Kathleen would understand. Certainly she'd need help raising our boy.

Charlotte stopped in front of a house that was just a bit bigger than my apartment. There was a tiny lawn out front, big enough to need a push mower, but barely big enough to turn it around. The roofs were so close I could jump from one to the other if I wanted to slip in through an open window. Charlotte turned off the car and motioned toward the front door.

"You're not coming in?" I asked.

"You're a big boy."

"What exactly am I supposed to do?"

"Don't you want to meet your son?" She overplayed the dismissive tone. I knew she was warmer than that. Some days I thought I might even have a chance with her if I graduated, but on that morning she was the lead actress in the production taking place all around me. A play designed to teach me life lessons. The problem in this new world was that I never knew where the players ended and the citizens began.

The cement walk that split the lawn led me directly to the front door of the American dream. Hope surged through my spine to every muscle. Kathleen and I had been close if only for a short time. Maybe the black box had changed me. I'd lived alone for a long time, but there on the steps I imagined myself living inside, cutting the grass, playing ball, even kissing Kathleen before I went to work.

The broad-shouldered guy in dress pants and shiny shoes ripped that image from me when he yanked open the door and blocked my way in. He didn't even ask my name before he pushed me back onto the tiny concrete landing and faced me toe to toe.

"I don't care what those whack jobs over at reeducation say. I don't want you anywhere near my son. Understand?"

I was stunned. If Kathleen had come out and greeted me warmly I would have fumbled for words. I didn't know what I was doing there, and I couldn't have anticipated the confrontation at the door. I stood slack-jawed for a second, then shot a look at Charlotte for direction. Every lesson with

Wendell was the same. My expectations didn't align with reality, and until I figured out what they wanted from me I couldn't proceed.

What was he trying to teach me? I could think on my feet. I could read people. You had to where I grew up. But I felt as lost here as I did on the black box. I still don't know why he kept manipulating me. Maybe Wendell wanted to keep me confused so I couldn't see the truth. Or maybe he was trying to break me down and reshape the way I saw the world.

Charlotte waved weakly toward the door.

When I turned, a stern face topped with slicked, jet black hair met me. "I took the morning off so I could be here. You say one thing about relearning to my boy and I'll have you back in court so fast." His face was bright red, his voice loud enough to be heard in eight neighboring houses.

I'd had enough of this clown. "Is he my boy or yours?"

He cocked his arm and clenched his fist, but thought better of it.

"Careful," I said. "Hit me in front of my counselor and you'll be the one sitting in front of a black box."

He stepped close and lowered his voice. "I make one call and you'll be back in court this afternoon. I know every time you step into my yard, and I know what happens when they get tired of someone like you swinging in and out of that courtroom. Cross me and you'll end up in—"

"Nick?" Kathleen appeared at the door and her voice froze him instantly.

I wished she'd let him finish. He knew more about the system than I did, and if he had told me about this Plexiglass cage and what happens here, I would have applied myself ten times harder. I still don't know how such a thing can possibly exist. How it's been hidden from the government reformers and dogooders I'll never know. But knowing about this place would have completely changed my attitude. I would have been more scared of this room than Deone and Joel were scared of the cat baggers. That's the problem with these things. To be effective the punishment has to be so severe as to be frightening, ten times more frightening than whatever else is driving your actions. Citizens can't abide that level of punishment, and I understand now why the secret has been so well guarded.

CHAPTER TWENTY-FOUR

When we walked into the house Kathleen pointed Nick to a chair in the kitchen and he obeyed. My mother had ruled the house and demanded strict obedience, but we were just kids. To see a strong man bow to a delicate woman like Kathleen was a surprise. The curly red hair bounced at her shoulders just like I remembered. Before I met her I'd always liked blondes and girls with tans. The freckles hadn't done anything for me at first, but now they were a welcome sight as I followed her to the back of the house. It had been four years since I'd seen her. She'd given birth to my son and yet I couldn't see anything different about her.

When she reached for the door, a diamond sparkled on her left hand with a plain gold band snug against it. The rings redefined my trip as surely as if she'd punched me in the chest. I'd never be part of her life. Charlotte must have known Kathleen was married. Why hadn't she said something on the way over? Charlotte, Wendell, the program, they all sent me racing toward invisible roadblocks so they could see me stumble. I told myself it was a lesson, but I couldn't help feeling something special had been taken away from me.

Kathleen's backyard was closed in with white vinyl fencing that kept Jonathan in and the neighbors out of sight. He sat in a wooden sandbox. His tiny white sneakers were half buried and his jeans were dusted with sand in every crevice. As we came over he growled engine noises and pushed a yellow road grader back and forth. Several cars idled on the steep banks of his construction project. His dark hair matched mine. The fair skin he got from his mother.

When I saw the perfect little miracle there in the sand I understood why Charlotte brought me here. Cortez's struggles made sense. Part of me was in the little boy who played with trucks in a safe little yard where no one would come and poison him with drugs or throw a brick at him. Seeing him there so innocent left me without words. Love for something so unspoiled could make a man rush off to work every morning and sit in a corner when he's told. Charlotte taught me something I hadn't learned at home, something I couldn't learn anywhere but in that sandbox. I learned it in a single instant.

The lesson came with a price. I couldn't abandon the little guy, but staying connected with him would be difficult now that his mother was married to someone else.

Kathleen introduced me as Michael, not his father, simply Michael. I didn't argue. Rather, I squatted to his level and held out my hand. He slapped me five, his soft little hand not quite covering my palm. My heart erupted with pride and relief at being accepted.

The encounter wasn't as meaningful for him. He turned back to his grader and continued working his road toward the far corner of the sandbox where the even surface dipped into unruly dunes. I couldn't leave without offering to help. He thought about it a second, then looked right into my eyes as if he was about to entrust me with a very important mission and needed to make sure I was up to the task. He nodded ok, handed me a front-end loader, and put me to work taming the dunes. I raised and leveled them and he came along with the grader and smoothed out a racetrack for the cars.

Kathleen seemed pleased as she stood back and watched.

I built a level parking lot in the center for the cars and helped Jonathan build an excellent oval, complete with banked turns and a pit road. After that we raced around for an hour. Kathleen had shifted to a resin chair on the patio. She didn't interrupt and neither did Charlotte.

Jonathan wanted to build a sand castle and this disturbed his mother.

"We have to go inside and get cleaned up."

Jonathan protested and went back to playing, but he knew as well as I did that the visit was over. When I turned back to Kathleen I saw Nick standing behind her with a hand on each shoulder. I remembered what he'd said about staying home from work and I was sure the end of playtime had more to do with Nick's work schedule than anything Jonathan or Kathleen had planned. After five more minutes, she came over and brushed the sand off our son. Then she asked him to wait on the swings while the grown-ups talked inside.

I wanted to throw my arms around the little guy, squeeze him, and pick him up, but all he offered was another five. I took it.

Kathleen kept Nick and I separated. She sent him though the door first and took the chair between us at the round kitchen table. The remaining chair had a blue booster seat strapped to it. Seeing it, I imagined Jonathan playing with his food at the table and making a mess. Could I really take care of him at my place? How much stuff did he need? A crib or another bed? What did he eat? All these questions were rolling around in my head when I noticed Kathleen and Nick sitting nervously still.

"What's on your mind?" I asked, my eyes squarely on Kathleen's.

That's when I saw the folder. I knew it was horrible news by her tentative grip and her reluctance to say what was inside. She handed it over with a grim expression. The exchange would have gone better if Nick wasn't there. She could have shown some compassion, but a guy like Nick didn't want his wife alone with any man, never mind the father of her child.

"I want to adopt him," Nick said.

I'd only met him an hour earlier. I had no experience with adoption, so I didn't know what he was really asking. Until an hour ago I'd thought of children as a way to get more support from the government. That's why my mother had them and that's why my grandmother had them. The miracle of it all was brand new and Nick was already trying to rip that away from me.

"He's only thinking of what's best for Jonathan," Kathleen offered.

I couldn't say a word. I opened the folder and looked at dozens of words I couldn't pronounce. The details were a mystery, but the intent was clear. I was a handicap to Jonathan. Nick was a respectable man who would make a good father. Jonathan would be better off. They'd all be better off, if I disappeared from their lives.

"You wouldn't have to pay support anymore," Kathleen said.

"I don't care about the money."

Nick stood up. "You wouldn't! That's because they give it to you for doing nothing."

I shuffled paper and pretended to read the second page. I couldn't understand anything and kept flipping. The last page carried Nick's and Kathleen's signatures and had a blank line with my name under it.

I thought about Melanie Michaud and her baby. Then I thought about Charlotte out in the car. She'd never date a convict, not one she counseled. Was there another woman out there who would fit me better? Would they all turn away when they learned what I'd been through?

Nick sat back down and seethed at me across the table. I was an embarrassment to him. His wife had slept with a relearner. His child wasn't his. But it was more than that. Nick resented getting up and going to work every day. I'd never done it myself, but I knew it had to be a drag. That's why he hated people like me. He followed the rules while I did nothing. Eventually I could afford a tiny house like his without working a day in my life. He'd been taught all about fairness and justice. What he hadn't been told was that if you choose not to believe, these things don't exist. They were just ideas created to keep people in line. Sure, if everyone was like me and stole for a living, there'd be nothing to steal. We'd be fighting on every street corner. The world needed people like Nick, lots of them, but because of him, I could afford a very different life. Responsibility, integrity, and fairness didn't apply to me.

The injustice of it all made Nick crazy.

CHAPTER TWENTY-FIVE

Carrying that folder down that little cement path was more painful than leaving court in chains, destined for state prison. I didn't lift my eyes from the walkway until I reached the car. Charlotte was in the driver's seat waiting for me. She studied my face for any hint of emotion. She knew Nick and Kathleen wanted to take Jonathan away from me when she arranged our meeting. There was no sympathy in her eyes, just an assessment of what I might do about the papers and what that meant for my treatment. Treatment wasn't a word I'd use to describe what they were doing to me. Mistreatment, maybe. It wasn't completely random. There was a point under it all, but with every step forward they extracted the maximum emotional toll. Maybe this was what it took to evoke real change, or maybe Nick wasn't the only one out for justice.

I climbed in and she asked how it went.

"You know what happened in there," I barked.

She nodded to the folder. "And?"

"What do you expect me to do?"

"I don't expect anything. I'm here to help."

She was so beautiful I wanted to believe her. I was foolish. I imagined she was trying to save me from losing Jonathan to some administrative deadline. I wanted her to feel what I felt when I looked at her. Most of all I wanted to be with her. If she was tormenting me, any sort of a relationship would be impossible. Why did I hold on? I think it was her looks that kept me close while she reached into my chest and rearranged my insides.

"What other surprises do you have for me?" I asked.

"Like?"

"My mother? My father?"

"They're not as important as Jonathan. You needed to see him."

"And what about my father?" I didn't know why I was so upset about him. I hadn't thought about him since I left school. He was just the guy who got my mother pregnant. She was easy when she was ready for another kid. There was no connection. Seven men, seven kids. We didn't know who they were, though if the younger kids had asked, I could have given them some ideas. Maybe Jonathan awakened something in me, but I think I was just angry and wanted an excuse to vent.

"We haven't found him yet," she said.

"You found Jonathan pretty fast."

She went through a long explanation as she drove. Children of single mothers were all tested. Finding the mother was academic. Finding the father depended upon his DNA being collected after an arrest or when he applied to work in a sensitive government office. Not everyone was on file. Most law abiding citizens weren't. That was one advantage Nick's holier-than-thou lifestyle gave him over me.

"Are we done then?" I wasn't looking forward to the answer.

She said when I decided what to do about the papers, she'd be finished with my case and she'd turn me over to Joanne. Did I need a woman to help me find a woman? I'd never had trouble before, but I'd spent a few hours with Charlotte and she wasn't the least bit interested. Maybe the world had changed. Maybe the riots soured people to relearners so much that I'd need help to overcome the prejudice.

I couldn't decide what to do about Jonathan then. Even if I could have, I wouldn't have told her. I needed a reason to see her again. I needed hope. Even now that I've made my decision, I'm not sure I did the right thing. But I want you to know I did what I did because I had no other choice.

We drove on for several blocks without saying anything.

I asked if she wanted to go out for lunch.

She said she had an appointment.

When she stopped in front of my building I didn't want to get out. "Does this really work? What you're doing to me?"

She understood my meaning, but skirted the question. "I'm here to help you. I'm not *doing* anything to you. I'm helping you deal with things that need to be taken care of."

I remembered what they said about the ankle bracelets. Somewhere this conversation was being recorded. I had to assume that anytime we were together someone was listening, if not to weed out subversive counselors, at least to measure their performance. Maybe that's why she kept her distance.

"I meant the whole thing. Wendell, the black box, you, the others."

"Most times. Wendell's a smart guy."

"What happens when things go bad?"

"Wendell doesn't give up on people. He's one of the good ones."

"He is, isn't he? But what happens when he gives up?"

She pointed to the door without saying anything.

"The others are different aren't they?"

She folded her hands on top of the steering wheel.

"Do some people really go crazy?"

Charlotte wouldn't admit those other programs existed. She looked straight ahead through the windshield. No matter how many times I asked, she said nothing. Finally, she took her phone from her purse and pointed to the red button on the side.

"It's time for you to go. Don't make me call for help."

I imagined if she pressed that button, special police would be on us in minutes. Anyone listening to our conversation would be worried that I wasn't getting out of the car. She didn't want to cause trouble for me or for Wendell, but I couldn't tell if she was really scared because she hid her emotions behind a plastic smile. Other relearners could have turned violent. I didn't want to cause myself any more trouble. I got out of the car and she sped away.

97

CHAPTER TWENTY-SIX

It was a long lonely climb up to my apartment. I dropped the folder on the coffee table and stared at the black box in front of my television. It was lunchtime and I was hungry, but I wanted to finish the day's lesson so I could go wander around the neighborhood without worrying about falling behind. I grabbed a Devil Dog from the freezer, cracked a can of Coke, and sat down on the couch.

The folder kept drawing me away. I turned on the television and put the disc in, but before I snapped on the wrist strap and started the simulation, I opened the folder and studied the five typed pages Kathleen had given me.

I didn't own a dictionary or a computer to look up the words I didn't recognize, but I'd never been so intent on something written down before. I think that's what got me through all the gibberish. I'd never hired a lawyer. They'd always been given to me when I'd broken some law or another. That wasn't the case here. If I wanted to fight to keep my relationship, more accurately, to start a relationship with Jonathan, I'd have to hire my own lawyer. I decided to worry about that later and plodded through all five pages, guessing at the words I didn't understand. A few things were clear even to me. If I signed this agreement, Jonathan would live with Nick and Kathleen and I wouldn't be allowed to visit without permission. After seeing the anger in Nick's eyes, I was pretty sure he wouldn't let me near Jonathan if he didn't have to. There was only one benefit for me. The deductions from my bank account would stop.

I couldn't sign the papers, but I didn't tear them up either.

I took the folder to the kitchen table so I wouldn't keep looking at it. I'd never wanted a child or a family, but my hour in the sandbox had drastically changed my thinking. I understood why Nick wanted to protect Jonathan from me. Having me for a father wouldn't help the boy any, but I wasn't ready to give up my claim. It seemed Charlotte had taught me the most memorable lesson of all.

I connected the strap around my wrist and started the program.

A new scene showed on the screen. It was a young boy's bedroom, my bedroom. I don't say it was my bedroom because it was a seven-year-old version of me on the screen. The walls and the furniture matched the room I'd slept in, right down to the three other boys sharing the room. The graphics were good enough to show where we had pictures on the walls. It seemed Wendell could only spend so much time on each relearner because the images themselves were different. Even so, I was impressed.

By that time I was comfortable navigating the virtual world, though I hadn't put my own clothes on before. It turned out to be as easy as opening the bureau and picking a pair of jeans, sneakers, and a blue T-shirt.

Across the apartment and into the kitchen I met my mother. She was as large as I remember, dumping cereal into bowls with a snarl on her face. Maybe I imagined the snarl, but I remembered what the guys said about acting like a saint. I sat in my place, ate my cereal, and carried my bowl to the sink when I was done. My mother told me to have a good day at school and out the door I went.

A trail of green dots appeared on the sidewalk and I followed them. I assumed that green was good and that the line would lead me to school. I stopped half a block from home, remembering my previous failures. Should I have brushed my teeth? My mother didn't say anything about it, but I went back upstairs and brushed them to be sure.

Thinking myself Saint Michael, I continued after the green dots.

About a block later I spotted a little girl sitting on the curb, sobbing with her head on her knees. After my time in the sandbox I knew it was wrong to keep walking so I stopped and typed a question, *Can I help?*

She pointed to a tree overhead. Something round was caught high in the branches, a balloon or a Frisbee maybe. The graphics weren't clear enough to tell. It may not have been the point of the exercise, but I couldn't ignore this little girl's problem without expecting a shock.

It took a few minutes to figure out how to make my virtual self jump. In the process I found all sorts of useful things on the help menu, like opening doors and checking my pockets. Jumping though did no good. The Frisbee, I could see clearly that it was a Frisbee when I jumped, was too high. I tried climbing the tree, but it was too flimsy to hold me. When I got my leg up, the first branch snapped and I fell to the ground.

An old man came rumbling down the driveway and yelling at us to get away from his tree. My first impulse was to run and ditch the girl, but Saint Michael wouldn't do that. I held my ground and typed, *I'm sorry*.

The man was still upset, but he didn't say anything. He just looked at me and frowned. The three of us held there for a moment. I couldn't climb the tree and I couldn't jump up to get the Frisbee. The man was too old and too heavy for seven-year-old me to lift, so I pointed to the Frisbee and then the man. He led me to the garage and together we carried a ladder back to the tree. He climbed up and brought down the Frisbee.

The girl smiled and ran off, but there were no fireworks.

Saint Michael hadn't achieved his goal.

The green dots were long faded from the screen. I thought I should try to find the school, but something told me that wasn't the point. The old man stood by his ladder and I kept circling him. I wasn't sure what to do, but it seemed as long as I stayed close to him, he'd stay by the tree. Finally I had an idea. I typed, *Sorry about your tree. Can I do anything?*

Together we carried the ladder back and returned with a saw. He cut the branch off cleanly, thanked me, and went home. Fireworks lit the screen. It was the first lesson I completed without punishment. Elapsed time: forty minutes. Average time: twenty minutes. Record time: two minutes. Whatever. I was still proud.

CHAPTER TWENTY-SEVEN

The ding that announced my arrival at the burger joint didn't surprise me. It bothered me a whole lot less than the people in line at the registers. They held their breath waiting for the contrasting notes that signaled I was at least wearing my ankle bracelet and unlikely to attack unprovoked. The place was a few blocks further from the complex than I usually ventured. That's why the customers were so uptight. That's why I paused by the scanner until the tones signaled I was ok.

The burger and onion rings smelled like Heaven on my plate. I filled my Coke. Beyond the ketchup and napkins, I saw Joel staring down at an empty tray. I walked over and slid in across from him.

"You all right?" I asked.

He said he was, but I didn't believe him. There was a lot Joel could teach me, but he wasn't in the mood for conversation. My first day as a relearner I discovered how fast the cops could find me. If they wanted Joel, they would have picked him up already, so whatever was bugging him had to be personal. I didn't want lose one of my only relearner friends by going Dr. Phil, so I ate my burger and kept to myself until he felt like talking.

When I threw my trash away he still hadn't said anything.

"Want to go for a walk or something? I'm done for the day."

He asked me how many lessons I'd done and I told him one.

"You know you can do more than one a day, right?"

"Serious?" I assumed I had to finish one each day. I never considered starting a second one.

"Dumbass. You want to be in here forever?"

I felt like an idiot for all the time I'd wasted sitting on the floor bouncing an old tennis ball against the bricks. The television wouldn't work until I finished the program. I didn't think to try and speed things up and I didn't know what else to do to pass the time.

Joel led me outside, up one block, and down Broadway. I thought he was taking me to scope chicks so I tuned into the women parking their cars and dodging in and out of shops along the street. Every storefront had clean windows and glitzy displays. Vacant signs and broken windows dominated the street near our apartment complex. The only things around our place were the donut shop and a couple of other restaurants that catered to relearners. On Broadway we passed three stores that sold women's dresses, a hair stylist, a shoe store, and a jewelry store. This street was a haven for the ladies.

Several attractive women crossed our path. I checked for diamonds and got a few smiles, but Joel paid no attention. He was a huge guy and three women gave him a long looking over, but he just kept on walking like they weren't there. Even after a few of them said, "Hmmm" and "Oh Baby" he just kept on going.

"What's up with you?" I asked after he ignored an awesome pair of legs.

"Nothing," he said and pointed to a sleek brick building at the corner.

It wasn't a bunch of stores because there were no signs out front. The grass was cut in perfect stripes, so I thought it was an office building, one we might hit for laptops or something. Joel didn't say anything as we walked past and around back. The guys wore jeans just like we did, but they were different. I didn't see a single tattoo. Every guy wore short hair. None of them had that get-out-of-my-way swagger Joel flaunted.

I was trying to stiffen myself against going in with Joel to hit this place when we rounded the back side and walked onto the grass. Ten guys played Wiffle ball on the lawn and Joel walked over like he owned the place. The guys in striped shirts didn't seem to care. I followed him to a picnic table and noticed they had real bases set out and a net they used for a backstop. The lines were chalked. This was serious Wiffle ball.

Joel introduced me to Stephan, a white guy about my size. I was still trying to figure out what this place was when Joel said, "This is how the other half lives."

"You shitting me?"

There were guys all over, hanging out on the grass. The yard was ten times the size of ours and it wasn't enclosed by brick walls. Uniformed referees ran the game. Compared to this place, my apartment was like being back at the house of correction.

"How'd you get in here?"

Stephan misunderstood. He told me some guy grabbed his girlfriend outside a bar and he'd punched him out. A cop was standing there and hauled him in. I didn't really care what he'd done, I wanted to know how I could get out of my place and into this one.

He said it was the first time he'd ever been in trouble. That fit. All the guys playing ball looked harmless. The tension I'd seen in prison, in the courthouse hallways, and even around the apartment buildings I'd lived in, that tension didn't exist here. These were just regular guys at big boy summer camp. No one was going to get stabbed serving his time here, and they'd all stay out of trouble when they went back to their regular lives.

"Do you guys have to do the black box?"

"You're in Wendell's, huh?"

When I nodded, Stephan got closer. "The programs are all different. When I first came here, they showed us what you go through and they showed us bits of two other programs." He pointed at me then. "Don't tell anybody," he whispered. "The programs are supposed to be some big secret. The guys who run them are real competitive. No one is supposed to know what the other guys are doing."

"But they showed you?"

"Yeah. Man, losing my job was enough to keep me out of trouble, but when I saw how you guys live, I was sure I wouldn't be slugging someone else. When I saw the guy jump out the sixth floor window, I was definitely sure."

Joel and Stephan shared a look.

"We didn't see that program," Stephan said, meaning one run the cat baggers. "I think even the people who run this thing are afraid to try and get inside."

I asked him how he'd seen someone jump.

Joel broke in. "It's the end of the line. That's all you need to know."

It wasn't luck that got Stephan into this club. He was a first timer. Our records got Joel and I stuck into Wendell's classroom. That was the first time I was truly afraid of the new laws. In the old days we never believed we'd be sentenced to die, but then I knew if I kept screwing up I'd be sent to a place where lethal injection would be considered humane.

"You don't use the black box?" I asked to lighten the subject.

"We do, but ours plays video games. Some really good ones."

Stephan took us inside and showed us his room, the health club, and the restaurant on the first floor. The place was more like a resort than prison. It even had a bar. We couldn't drink outside our own apartments, but the bartender there assured us it was ok. Joel and I had a few beers. Stephan drank Coke and I noticed several other guys doing the same. I was so thankful for what I'd learned, I pressed my thumb to the scanner for the first two rounds. When we got to the third round, the bartender informed me I was out of credit.

Stephan paid.

Joel looked at me like I was the biggest fool he'd ever seen.

CHAPTER TWENTY-EIGHT

"It's Tuesday, brother," Joel said. "What are you going to do?"

I didn't know why it being Tuesday meant anything. I shrugged and followed Joel down the street away from Stephan and his cushy digs.

"You get eight hundred and seven dollars every Friday just like everyone else. What'd you do with it?"

"I needed stuff," I said.

"Like what?"

"Regular stuff. I went out to eat, and I needed a new television and some stuff in the kitchen, you know, regular stuff."

"What happened to your furniture allowance?"

"I spent it."

"Are you really that stupid?"

"I never did this electronic crap before. If I have money in my pocket I know when I'm short. These numbers in a machine somewhere and pressing my thumb? How am I supposed to know when I need money?"

"How did you spend eight hundred bucks in five days?"

"I made a lot more than that in the old days, and I if I ran out I could always get more."

"You're hopeless, man."

I thought about Morris Farnsworth. Maybe he could get me some of next week's pay a few days early. I'd be more careful then. When I suggested it to Joel, he stopped me there on the sidewalk.

"Don't do it, man."

"Why not?"

"There are four things they worry about. Four pressures you have to handle: sex, money, drugs, and education. Once you get past the kindergarten stuff you're working on, you'll see what's important. They test you until you can handle all four. Then you can get out."

"They can't do all that with the box." My voice cracked.

"Your education comes out of the box. Your money is tracked by computer. Everything you spend, they know. Sex, your dating counselor will keep a close eye on that. You find a girl you're ready to settle down with, you're close."

"And drugs? They can't possibly watch me every second."

"Don't have to. You use the toilet in your apartment?"

"Come on. That's bull."

"For real. Busted a friend of mine three times 'till he figured it out."

"Can you lend me a few bucks until Friday?"

Joel was agitated by the question. "What do you need before then?"

I admitted I didn't have any food in the house besides Devil Dogs and a few cans of Coke. He couldn't believe it, but I was used to eating out. I'd never cooked anything until Debbie showed me how to make eggs. Joel called me a fool. He said buying my own food and cooking it cost less than half as much as eating out. What was I doing all day anyway?

He was angrier than he should have been and I asked him why.

"I'm saving every cent," he said. "Got a girl who wants to marry me, but her mother says I'll never amount to nothing. Says I'll never be able to get her nice things. If I don't do something soon, she's going to quit me."

"My man, have I got a deal for you," I said.

I took the lead. Joel was puzzled. I didn't tell him where we were going, but he kept following down the sidewalk. When we got to the revolving door outside the bank he grabbed my arm.

"You're not going to rob it? You know there's no money in there?"

"I'm not that stupid."

With my ankle bracelet on, the security staff inside the bank was decidedly more cooperative, but when I got to the vault area, the attendant still waited for the call from Morris Farnsworth.

"What are you doing, Mr. O'Connor?"

"Just getting some personal items. Is that ok with you?"

He gave his permission. I took Joel's advice and skipped the questions about getting my pay early. Morris didn't ask why Joel was with me at the vault and I assumed he didn't know we were together. That was a huge mistake.

They showed us to a viewing area and I opened the box and started pulling out things to show him. It was a big box, packed with cash and the high-end jewelry I'd clipped. I'd been hitting the ritzier suburbs of the city, so most of what I had was higher class than anything Joel could afford. I felt like I owed him for his help. That and I really needed him to feed me for the next two days.

"This stuff is hot, isn't it?"

I pulled out a pair of diamond earrings. They were about a half carat each. "These have been chilling in here quite a while." I pulled out a necklace, but it was way too much. It had to weigh five or six carats. No way she'd believe he bought it himself.

I spread out a deep-red cloth like the ones they had at jewelry stores and arranged the pieces. He was amazed at the stuff I was taking out. My heart sank when I saw the useless stacks of cash. Even the jewelry would be hard to sell. I didn't have one of those thumb machines, and unless I bought a jewelry story there was no way to sell this stuff and make it look legit.

Joel's eyes jumped from piece to piece. He kept shaking his head like he was trying to talk himself out of taking anything. I put the really high-end stuff away. We wanted his girl to be impressed, but not suspicious. Eventually he settled on the earrings.

"What do you want for these?"

"A cart full of groceries," I said. He stuck out his hand to shake and I said, "And some help getting them home."

He didn't flinch. He kept the earrings, then we put the rest of the stuff back and headed for the grocery store. He told me how he met his girl on the way. Inside, he showed me to the frozen section where I could take most of the stuff and cook it in the microwave without too much work. I grabbed an armful of frozen pizzas, another few boxes of Devil Dogs, and a bunch of other stuff I wasn't sure I liked, but Joel assured me was pretty good and easy to make.

On the way to the checkout I found a whole box of donuts made in the bakery. I didn't have a coffee maker, so I couldn't make coffee at home, but that was about the only thing I had to do without for the next two days.

Joel pressed his thumb on the scanner and found out the earrings cost him a little over a hundred and twenty bucks. Not bad. They were probably worth two thousand retail, judging by the size of the diamonds and the house I took them from.

All the way home he talked about his girl. How hot she was and how into him she was. They were going to get married. As soon as he finished the program, she was going to move out of her mother's house and in with him. He was going to get a job and have kids. The whole American dream fairytale. It was the happiest I'd seen him all day. Even though I'd screwed up and spent every cent, I was happy with the way the day turned out.

CHAPTER TWENTY-NINE

The chocolate frosting on the donuts didn't taste quite right with orange juice. I don't usually drink orange juice, but what do you drink in the morning if you can't afford coffee? I was sitting at the kitchen table feeling good about what I'd done for Joel the day before and thinking about what torment Wendell's lesson would bring, when someone banged a fist hard against my door.

Only cops and jealous husbands knock like that.

Even before I got up, I knew I was in trouble.

I left my second donut half eaten and a little juice in the bottom of my glass and went to the door. When I opened it, two cops spun me around and clamped cuffs on my wrists. Again no Miranda warning, no hint of what I'd done or what they were charging me with. They hustled me downstairs, one in front, one behind.

In fifteen minutes I was at the courthouse. Wendell hadn't arrived, so they put me in a room and handcuffed me to a heavy pipe. I sat on the bench and waited. This was my second time here and I was beginning to understand that life in this new era wasn't that different from the simulation. Wendell and the police knew everything I did. The next few minutes were weird. I don't know if Wendell was smart enough to have planned this, but I was thinking about my life and what I'd done. It was the exact same way I thought about working my virtual self through the simulation. I evaluated every step I'd made in the last day and thought about what I could have done wrong. Could the black box lessons have hit me that hard? If it was the lessons, Wendell was a genius.

Wendell never came in. A court officer in a white shirt escorted me to the courtroom. When he led me up front toward Joel at the defense table, I thought I was being brought in to testify against him, but the officer didn't bring me to the witness stand. He brought me to the defense table on the opposite side of Wendell.

Joel hung his head low and I knew we were both in serious trouble.

Wendell looked flustered. Tufts of hair stuck out on both sides like he'd been pulling at it all night. His bloodshot eyes focused on the judge. He didn't tell me to keep quiet, but he didn't need to. My comfort with courtrooms had disappeared somewhere between Joel telling me about the cat baggers and Stephan telling me he'd seen one of their torture videos. I didn't know how much tolerance Wendell had left for me. Joel had told me the transfers to the cat baggers were unofficial so they couldn't be invalidated by some judge. If Wendell decided not to take the heat for me again, my records would disappear and no one I knew would ever see me again. I could only hope I'd be headed back to my apartment after court. Wendell had problems and I was making them worse. I only wish he'd told me the whole story sooner.

Even if I had my own apartment and the freedom to walk around the city, I was still a prisoner deep inside the belly of the system. I was no freer than I would be in a cell. The scenery and the food were just nicer. I wondered if I'd ever be free again. The cops could track me wherever I went, so it wouldn't be hard for them to put me back in.

The judge stopped reading at his desk and called the proceeding to order. Joel and I were being tried together. After my last trial, I was ready for things to move fast.

The prosecutor opened by reading a statement from a woman who had been Joel's future mother-in-law until her daughter came home with the diamond earrings. She was the one who called the police. The investigation that followed was partially automated and amazingly thorough. Joel's recent transactions were scrutinized and at no time had he legitimately purchased diamond earrings.

The prosecutor directed us to the monitors mounted into each desk. Wendell shuffled some papers and we saw a green line and a purple line that snaked around a map of our neighborhood. The purple line, I quickly realized, tracked everywhere I had been in the last three days. The prosecutor narrated where the green line, Joel, joined me in the courtyard just days earlier, and how we'd gone to lunch, to see Stephan, to the bank, and to the grocery store.

I knew I was in deep trouble then.

Joel didn't even look at the screen.

Next the bar bill was displayed along with the rejection when I tried to purchase the last round of beers. Our trip to the bank was shown on video, complete with the call from Morris Farnsworth with perfect audio coming through the speakers at our table.

The prosecutor opened a metal box and started digging things out. It was my safe deposit box! Only I was supposed to be able to access that box. That's why I kept everything there. What happened to my rights? Soon the prosecutor's table was covered in jewelry and stacks of cash. Wendell didn't say anything. All I could do was watch.

There was no video of Joel taking the earrings from the box, but it wasn't a difficult leap for the judge to make. If there was any doubt, it was removed when the judge saw him buy my groceries and help me lug them home to my apartment. The video from my kitchen clearly showed all the items going into my refrigerator and onto my counter.

The next part really blew my mind. They couldn't prove the earrings were stolen because I'd done such a good job covering my tracks. The victims would remember being robbed, but they weren't attuned to police activity enough to know their items had been recovered. The cases were so cold, they would never be found deep in the files at police headquarters. Ah, the old days of paper files. The police couldn't afford to dig through their files long enough to find the rightful owners, so they couldn't prove I'd stolen anything. No matter. The prosecutor argued that it was impossible for me to legitimately have so much cash, or the jewelry appraised at seventy-five thousand dollars, because I'd never had a job.

He went so far as to analyze my mother's and my grandmother's assistance from the state and the fact that neither of them had ever held a job. The judge was convinced that I couldn't have inherited the items in the box. It was common sense, but in all my experience with the law, the burden to prove every element of a case fell on the government.

They gave me a chance to explain where the jewelry and cash had come from. What lie would cover five years of breaking and entering? I couldn't hatch one that quickly. If I had, Wendell would have gone postal.

They prodded. Could I show receipts? Could I produce witnesses?

No. I said nothing. Wendell and Joel didn't even look at me.

The contents of my box were confiscated to pay for my care. I wouldn't learn until later that cash actually had value. The bio payment devices only worked within the United States. If you left the country, you had to bring cash or credit cards. I could have gone to another country and lived well for years had I known, but it was too late.

The prosecutor asked Joel if he'd taken the earrings from the box.

"Yes, sir," he said.

"Prosecution rests, Your Honor."

CHAPTER THIRTY

Sitting in that defendant's chair waiting for the judge's decision, I had a bitter realization. Any kid who'd been to the principal's office more than once would know Joel and I had lost our case. The outcome was assured, but my revelation was deeper. Everything I'd taught myself about how to survive was useless. I could stand in a man's house while he made dinner, wait for him to go to bed, and then take what I wanted, but that didn't do me any good any more. I couldn't sell what I took and I wasn't about to start wearing the jewelry I lifted. Even worse, the most lucrative commodity of all had been wiped away by the financial wizards who tracked every dollar, every purchase, every penny of interest and profit. They had put me out of business.

I had no choice but to change. In a few seconds I'd learn how close I had come to missing my chance.

The judge pronounced Joel guilty of receiving stolen property and committing fraud by buying my groceries to pay for it. I was found guilty of selling stolen property. The thefts of the jewelry and cash were long past. They didn't bother to prosecute those, because without prison a conviction was a conviction. There was no prison term to be made longer by adding charges. What I'd done so far hadn't even changed the program as far as I knew, but then I was still naive enough to think the entire program was stored on the discs in that black carry case.

I watched the judge's every movement. Joel had his head hung down as if he knew what was to come.

"The relearners must remain separated by fifty yards at all times."

"They're living almost that close," Wendell protested.

"No longer," the judge ordered.

One of the court officers went to work typing something into a computer. If we came within fifty yards of each other after we left the courthouse, we'd both receive an electric shock from our ankle bracelets. The shock would continue until we separated. It would be cruel for us to live in the same complex.

Wendell stared at the judge. He knew immediately what that meant. Joel did too, but I had to hear the judge's words to understand.

"Choose," the judge ordered.

Wendell's fingers ran a well-worn path through his hair. He looked from side to side and then said to me, "You better not screw up again."

Joel's head dropped. His hands caught his forehead before it slammed against the table. He didn't see Wendell walk forward and click the computer screen. When he pressed his thumb on the scanner, Joel's fate was sealed. He'd been so close to making it, to marrying and settling down. In the end it was the girl's mother who unraveled things for him. The pressure pushed him to me, and my ignorance dug a hole too deep for him to crawl out of.

Joel's loss meant I had been saved.

Wendell led me out of the room and that was the last time I saw Joel. I asked about him in the yard and even walked back to ask Stephan what happened, but no one could ever tell me. I tried not to think about what they could do with the black box and a man confined to a small apartment, high in a building. Whatever it was, they were far beyond electric shocks and childlike computer simulations. He couldn't escape with a tracking device implanted in his skull. The only way out for Joel was the window. He knew it and I knew it. The only question lingering in that room I'd just left, was how long it would take for him to hurl himself through the glass.

Bad as I felt for him, I had my own problems.

Wendell led me into a room a few doors down from the courtroom. The door sealed like a refrigerator and when I sat down at the small table,

Wendell exploded into a rage of insults that went on and on until he was out of breath. He kept grabbing his hair, like it was a stand-in for my neck. His wild eyes looked like he'd been working for days without sleep. The mild-mannered guy who'd been so calm the day we met in the hospital almost lost control. He could have pummeled me. What would they do to the state's most successful reeducator if he attacked me? They couldn't punish him. He couldn't become someone else's lab rat. A thin line of self-control was the only thing that kept Wendell's rage from turning violent.

I didn't say a word and I'm glad I didn't. He might have wanted to argue, but I was beginning to understand how completely Wendell controlled my fate. Eventually the yelling and the lack of sleep tired him out and he sat down.

"What am I going to do with you?" he mumbled.

"You could try explaining things."

"You didn't know it was wrong to sell stolen jewelry?"

I should have, but I'd had that stuff a very long time. I believed it was mine, not those ladies I'd taken it from. They'd never have found me, never have realized I had what they'd lost, not without that old lady ratting out Joel. That was the point Wendell had been trying to make all along. Right and wrong mattered even when no one would ever find out. It was the basis of those silly simulations that kept shocking me. But simulations and reality are different. I had been surviving on my own for ten years. Sometimes survival required bending the rules.

"I'm sorry." I wanted to tell him I was positive no one would ever find out. That I was helping a friend. That I was scared of being hungry for two days, but none of those things mattered to Wendell. He only cared about his program.

"I need you to stay out of trouble. How am I going to get you to do that? Do I need to pay a counselor to babysit you day and night?"

He was desperate. He'd just saved my life and I owed him my best. I felt like crap for causing him so much trouble. I'd never felt that way about any cop or guard before, but when things went bad for me, they went bad for Wendell, too.

"Tell me what to do."

"Sit in your room and finish the program before you get in trouble again."

"That helps you?"

I don't think a relearner had ever asked about his interests before. He looked at me sideways, like I was messing with him, but I wasn't. He'd saved me and I wanted to help. My problem was that the system I'd taken advantage of my whole life had leapfrogged me while I was sleeping. I couldn't learn the new rules fast enough. It seemed like the cops were watching me with night vision goggles while I fumbled around in complete darkness. The person I kept stepping on was Wendell Cummings.

He thought a long time before speaking and I knew he only trusted me because his situation was so dire. He had been working on an early reeducation program when the Supreme Court decision came down. He was the foremost authority on prison reform and his relearners were the most successful in the country. He got millions for research and his company boomed. Soon he had a monopoly and others wanted part of the exploding market. He sold his black box company and went back to running a program for relearners. It's what he loved. It's what he did best, but in the last several months Wendell's program had begun unraveling.

The programs were scored, he told me, by how many relearners were judged non-conformant. That was the new word for a conviction. Every time he had to reeducate a former client, his effectiveness rating was lowered. Lately, he'd had a terrible string of non-conformers and his program was close to being shut down. There was more to it, but basically, if I kept getting into trouble, he'd be forced out of business.

CHAPTER THIRTY-ONE

"I know what you did for me in there," I said. And I meant it. I was terrified for Joel. Wendell knew what it would be like. I wondered how he could let it happen. He cared about the people he taught. He'd dedicated his life to reeducation even before there was money in it, but there were things even he couldn't control.

He shook his head as if I couldn't know how horrible a death Joel was about to meet.

"How can you let it go on?"

"It's not up to me." He told me the best thing he could do was to help the relearners that came to him. Eighty percent of his first timers stayed out of trouble once they were released. Even some of those who came through a second time were helped. It was an amazing improvement over the old way when a third of prisoners wound up back in prison within three years of finishing their sentence. Relearners went on from his program to productive, normal lives. His eyes were full of pride. He was helping people like me who'd been gypped by the genetic lottery. The things my mother failed to teach me were stuffed into Wendell's program. I could reshape my world if I tried. It was a nice idea, but changing the way I fit into society was a massive undertaking. Even trying my absolute best, I kept falling down.

I couldn't blame Wendell. He was doing everything to help. But why was he standing aside and letting the court officers deliver Joel to some barbarian? "Can't you do something? Couldn't you go public?"

"Are you kidding? The people would applaud."

I was stunned. Would decent citizens celebrate Joel's torture?

Two million felons were let out of prison all at the same time. I was in a coma then and I missed what happened on the street. The sheer numbers overwhelmed the police. Society changed. Ordinary people shuttered themselves inside. Then one day it all threatened to come undone. The Supreme Court had voted five-to-four that extended prison sentences were cruel and unusual punishment and must be abolished. Six months after the mass release, the chief justice was gunned down during a robbery. His face was plastered all over the news, but what made a bigger impression was what happened to the non-conformer. He was enrolled back in his program, where he collected a government check that was larger than what many citizens earned.

Every news station and every talk radio show screamed for changes.

The changes started, but something surprising happened first. Over the next week, the remaining four justices who voted for the release were shot to death. The guys who killed them didn't even run. They were cheered and after they were reeducated, they walked out of the programs free and clear. The government had to go underground then. Unpopular officials risked being murdered by anyone who disagreed with them. By removing real punishment, they had unwittingly made themselves assassination targets.

That's when the big changes started. Local police forces across the country had already swelled. Their numbers tripled. That helped, but the real control didn't come until the money disappeared and the welfare system changed. That took away the biggest motivator for most relearners. Once they realized they couldn't make a living burglarizing homes and stealing cars, they stopped. They got enough money to live comfortably even if they didn't work. I realized that myself. Only when I spent myself out of money did I resort to selling the jewelry. That was a mistake I'd never make again.

"You think if people knew relearners were being tortured they'd look the other way?"

"Look the other way? No. They'd volunteer to help."

I couldn't believe decent people would line up to torture someone like me, but I remembered how Nick treated me and how hard he was trying to keep me from seeing my son. "Really?"

"Imagine how powerless you'd feel if you were attacked and the relearner was simply moved a few blocks away and set free. Decent people want blood."

"Is that why you take all the tough cases? You trying to save the relearners from jumping out a window?"

"It doesn't work that way. Each program is assigned new non-conformers in a defined order based on when the non-conformer is arrested. Once someone is in a program, he or she returns to that program until expelled. Every program gets its share of hardened criminals and its share of first timers."

He told me that there were special cases. Some program managers volunteered to take tough cases because they earned triple credits for convicts like Joel that were expelled from another program. The credit was only good if the relearner didn't non-conform again. If that happened more than once, the benefit of getting the troubled relearner was erased.

"You don't take those people?"

"Some people don't want to be helped, Michael. Some people will never change. They are hardened criminals and there is only one way to deal with them."

"And?"

"I'm not willing to do what those cases require."

CHAPTER THIRTY-TWO

As smart as Wendell is, he has a bad habit of assuming I understand what he means even when he gives me little more than a hint. He tells me half the story and expects me to figure out the rest. I wonder if he's done that with you, too. Don't get me wrong, I'm good at understanding people. I get what people are about just by watching them for a few minutes. But there is a big difference between understanding someone's motives and understanding complex rules you can't see or touch. Wendell told me the government went underground, but he didn't tell me that special measures were taken to protect officials—and that he is one of those officials. That simple message would have saved us both a tremendous hassle.

Then there was the small matter of punishment for hardened criminals. Joel had made mistakes. I was somewhat responsible for his latest problem with the jewelry, but before that it was attempted murder. That wasn't his first arrest either. Wendell had to decide which of us was more likely to get into trouble and sacrifice that relearner to the cat baggers. Until I learned about the cat baggers, I thought the new laws were gutless. Sure, the program was annoying and the counselors were irritating, but you couldn't go to prison and you couldn't get the death penalty. Now that I knew about the effectiveness ratings and how much our mistakes cost Wendell, I understood that he controlled my fate with a few clicks on a computer. Wendell had given Joel his chance. Now he was as good as dead. If I didn't turn myself around, I'd end up on the concrete next to him.

I spent my adult life perfecting my craft to put myself beyond the law's reach. I never believed I'd be seriously punished until I met Joel and Stephan. I was terrified that day in court, but still couldn't comprehend my vulnerability. How could people close their eyes to torture and murder? I was afraid to imagine the sort of man who would torture people he didn't know. In my heart I knew it wasn't the money, but I had to bury the knowledge that I could be delivered to men who reveled in their despicable task. You know I'm not like that. You've been watching me for weeks, years as far as I know. If you've been paying attention, you know I could never take pleasure in hurting anyone.

Wendell believed I could make it. That's why he took me home.

He may have been watching me then, but I didn't care. I was glad to be alone at home where I couldn't be arrested for breaking a law I didn't know about. I made myself a frozen pizza and sat down on the couch with a six pack of Coke and a box of frozen Devil Dogs. I chained the door closed and from then until Friday afternoon I did nothing but eat, sleep, and battle the evil little discs I fed into the black box. The idea that a lesson would take six hours and I would be free after doing one a day was forgotten. I lined them up one after the other and I struggled, really struggled, to do my best. That I was out of money and couldn't really do anything on the outside helped somewhat, but the thing really driving me was the short walk from the defense table to the conference room—the moment when I'd abandoned my friend. I'd gotten him arrested and I'd left him to die. For days when I slept I imagined volunteering to take his place, but that was a pipe dream. I couldn't offer myself to be killed. I was barely beating the box. I was in no shape to deal with the cat baggers and I knew it.

With the strap around my wrist, I saw a man lose his wallet. I maneuvered myself to pick it up, then found a policeman to help me return it. I met a lost little boy wandering the park and helped him find his mother. I turned off leaky faucets, righted spilled garbage cans on the sidewalk, and stopped traffic when a child darted into the street. Disc after disc I did the most righteous deeds I could imagine. And as time went by, the wrongs became harder and harder to identify.

In my final challenge, there was a group of men playing basketball on the playground. I walked by them a dozen times before I realized one of them was selling drugs out of his bag. When I told a police officer, the men scattered. The wrist strap gave me a shock, but it wasn't particularly painful compared to what Joel was dealing with. Early Friday morning I remembered what I had seen in the donut shop when I set off the alarm. I bought myself a virtual camera and went back to the playground. At four o'clock in the morning, I recorded the man selling drugs from his bag. Minutes later I was at the virtual police station with my camera. When I placed it on the counter, the screen lit up with fireworks like never before. Did they really expect people to walk around with cameras and turn in their neighbors? It was easy in the simulation, but in real life there would be consequences.

In three days I completed forty-nine discs. It was as easy as Deone said it was, but I had forgotten what he said about the other half of the lessons. Deone was stuck on algebra. I didn't even know what algebra was yet. That morning I fell asleep and dreamed things my old self would have dismissed as ridiculous. In my dreams, I acted like the virtual Saint Michael. Maybe it was because I had done so many lessons all at once. Maybe it was because the painful shocks made the consequences real. Whatever the reason, I was becoming the person Wendell wanted me to be, in my dreams at least.

When my eyes cracked open at ten o'clock, I could still see the faces of the people I'd helped. Wendell would have been proud of what he'd done to me, but honestly, I'd been trying my best all week. I wasn't ever trying to get in trouble, I'd just been unlucky. Some part of me would always be the boy stealing peaches from the grocery store.

I want you to know I have never really hurt anyone. I don't know if Wendell can look past who I am. Regardless of what he thinks, I need you to believe in me. I need you to know that I had to do those things to survive. You would have done the same if your mother put a gun to your head.

CHAPTER THIRTY-THREE

The euphoria of finishing forty-nine discs wore off the first time I thought of the agony Joel was enduring. I strained against the weight of my eyelids and the dull vibration in my head that scattered my thoughts. My tongue tasted like cotton. I could barely focus on the television, but every time I closed my eyes my subconscious played images of Joel in intense pain and reminded me of the hollow, breathless feeling I had when I left the courtroom without him.

I needed to press on. To finish this course before I caused any more trouble. Little did I know how naive that idea was. I'd left school in the middle of eighth grade, but I'd fallen behind long before then. I had to drop out when I left home, but that decision helped me avoid the truth that I just couldn't keep up. Years without trying stunted my education. I thought I could sit in that little apartment and complete four and a half years of school, but I'd forgotten how hard it was.

Boldly I started the next disc, expecting to tear through it like I had Wendell's psychological and moral lessons. The introduction droned on and on about the requirements to complete high school equivalency. I would need to pass dozens of tests in math, English, social studies, and science. Fortunately, once passed, I didn't have to worry about that subject anymore.

Miniature Wendell told me that this was an adaptive environment. The system determined what I knew by measuring how long it took to answer a question and how many consecutive questions I answered correctly. Then it focused on what I needed to learn and not things I already knew. What he didn't say, and what I would eventually learn, is that the system tested many things I wasn't aware it was testing.

The first subject was math. Miniature Wendell said we were going to work on my digit span. This would improve my memory. We'd work on it until I had an average digit span. I had no idea what he was talking about until he said three single numbers one after the other and asked me to type them in. That was easy. We graduated to four numbers, then five. I made my first mistake at six and Wendell told me we would try again.

I paused the program by taking off my wrist strap, ran to the kitchen, and came back with a cereal box and a knife because I didn't have a pen or a pencil in the entire apartment. When I refastened the wrist strap, Wendell started calling out numbers again. I carved them into the cereal box and when Wendell asked for them back, I typed them without fail. We reached seven, eight, and nine numbers without trouble. I was waiting for the system to tell me I'd passed and wouldn't need to do this silly exercise anymore. Looking back, I should have stopped when we got to eleven numbers, but I kept going through fourteen and fifteen. Wendell congratulated me and then there was a long pause. He began again by calling the number six. The instant I touched the knife to the cereal box, the wrist strap jolted me.

"You're only cheating yourself," Wendell said. "And I won't allow it."

It would have been better for both of us if he had. I would have finished the program and he would have had another graduate.

He started over.

I shifted the knife to my left hand and kept my right hand, the one with the wrist strap, perfectly still. He called seven and then nine. I paused then carved. Soon as I touched the box, a spark jolted me. The knife flipped from my hand and landed handle first on the couch.

"How many times do we need to do this before you realize I'm watching you?" Wendell asked.

"If you're watching me, why don't you come up and teach me the lesson in person?"

"I'm not a teacher. I'm in the security room. What rock did you crawl out from under?" Miniature Wendell was this man's puppet.

Fitting, if not entirely accurate.

I learned several things in that exchange. There were security people, probably there in the apartment complex somewhere. They could see and hear me and zap me if they chose. I also guessed they could type things for Wendell to say. That meant they could tinker with my lessons just to irritate me. By this time Joel probably had a dozen characters talking to him. None of them would be as polite as the security guard.

I went back to work and honestly failed the digit span test.

The machine began math from the very beginning. It asked me to add single numbers in my head and type in the result. I did so without using the knife, but I did use my fingers. I didn't get any more shocks, so I assumed that was all right. After a bunch of those, Wendell asked me to subtract simple numbers. I did so and typed in the answers. The numbers got bigger and were displayed on the screen. It took me longer, but I worked through dozens of problems.

I tried to remember what grade we worked on addition and subtraction. It wasn't eighth. It might have been fifth. Was the black box really asking me to make up eight years of math? I was glad when we moved on to multiplication and division, but it took me hours to pass the exam on the basics.

The unimpressive fireworks started me thinking about what separated a guy like Nick from me. Was what he learned in school really that important? He'd probably gone to college. If he was locked up in here, he'd only have to stay long enough to finish Wendell's fifty-two morality tests, then he'd go back to his job. What work could I do if you let me out of here? Would math and English be important? I learned to pick locks and start cars. Those were useful skills. Would the black box teach me anything useful on the outside? Or would I have to find someone like Double to teach me to survive all over again?

CHAPTER THIRTY-FOUR

What a bonehead I was, locking myself in my room until I finished the entire program. I can handle hard work, but I totally underestimated the time it would take. Funny, estimation was on the list of math subjects the black box would eventually try to teach me. Deone was stuck on algebra. The black box hadn't mentioned that yet, but I remembered doing fractions, long division, decimals, and number lines in school. All those things came before algebra. Wendell announced we were going to add columns of numbers. What was that? Third grade math? It was an insult. How much school had I missed? Dozens of hard lessons lay ahead and math was only one subject.

I dropped the wrist strap and walked to the kitchen window.

I would have run then if not for the tracking device under my scalp. I was sure the pile of lessons would crush me before I finished three years laboring away in this room. Even if I could stick it out, the government would get tired of paying me for doing nothing. My slavery to the black box would be cut short. I just couldn't know who would bring it to an end.

As I'm standing here, we all know two things. First, the government gave up on me before I quit. Second, three years was ridiculously optimistic.

The living room window was big enough to jump through. From the third floor to the cement walk wasn't quite enough to kill me, but for a moment while I looked down, I saw a simpler end to my problems.

Did every citizen walk around with all this math in their head? If they did, how did I get so far behind? Did I sabotage myself? Was it my mother or my teachers? I thought about Joel and how close he was to jumping. I had no one really. Double and Cortez had it right. I hadn't even started down that road. I was going to lose my son to Nick and Kathleen. I was twenty-five and I had nothing to live for.

My feet moved back until I could only see the street through the window. As easy as it would be, I couldn't throw myself out. I didn't want to end up mangled on the sidewalk and live only to be tethered to a ventilator for the next twenty years. I stared at the glass and a few times I looked to the door like it would open up and offer another path, one where less work would lead to a comfortable life, like the one Nick and Kathleen were making for Jonathan. The program beckoned, but that was hopeless. I sat and stared until the knock sounded on the door.

Dr. Blake stood on the landing in a jogging suit.

I hadn't heard from him since the prison hospital, so for him to suddenly show up the day I started his portion of the program was too much of a coincidence. The program had called him just like it had ordered the cables delivered to my apartment. Maybe Wendell knew I'd be thinking about jumping at this point. Maybe someone was watching. I couldn't be sure. After our talk, Wendell should have been rooting for me to jump.

Blake looked fresh in his suit, like he'd been on his way to the gym and gotten an urgent message to come to my place and keep me away from the window. Based on the bulge around his middle, I guessed he wore the jogging suit because it was comfortable, not because he planned to mount an exercise bike. The brand new running shoes seemed to confirm this.

He sat down uninvited on the couch and put his feet up on the coffee table. I would have done the same if not for the keyboard, the remote control, and the wrist strap for the black box.

"You had a tough day, didn't you?" He asked the question with a smile, reveling in my difficulties.

I told him I'd plowed through a bunch of Wendell's discs, but he saw through my rosy spin.

He said math was one of the toughest parts of the program. I just nodded. Then he told me I was at the fifth grade level and that completing the math component was going to take years regardless of what else I

127

worked on. That was the first time I thought he was trying to shove me out the window.

"You don't appreciate what's going on here, do you?" he asked.

Appreciate was exactly the wrong word in my mind.

"You're getting a major opportunity here. A chance to grab hold of your life before you get flushed. While you're sitting in here learning things you should have learned when you were ten, the government is paying for you to live pretty darn comfortably."

"Prison is prison."

"You have no idea how lucky you are?"

"Lucky?"

"What should society do with people like you, Michael? People who for whatever reason threw their lives away? Is it our responsibility to pick you up and dust you off? Is it my responsibility to save you?"

I wanted to tell him to screw. That I'd be fine on my own, but by then I knew that was a lie. Blake knew it, too. I was a thief, an excellent thief, but the government took that away from me. It was impossible for me to make a living and Blake took great pleasure in having control over me.

"The world is at a crossroads. Common sense is returning and you are one of the first beneficiaries. Why don't you appreciate that?"

Did he really think I should be thankful for being stuck here?

"Listen, when you went into prison, the system was broken. Anytime a system hangs around long enough, you get people pecking away at it from all sides and eventually it doesn't work anymore. The guilty hired more and more expensive lawyers. Trials took forever and judges let men they knew were guilty go free. So more and more work by the police was accomplishing nothing. Trials work much more efficiently now, don't you think?"

"And this helps me?"

"Sure. In the past, convicts sat around watching television. What did they learn? Nothing. Were they really being punished? I think not. We tried a few feeble efforts at rehabilitation, but now we understand the truth."

I couldn't help myself. "What truth?"

"To rehabilitate someone, to truly help them lead a useful life, takes a mammoth effort. We can't afford to waste that effort on just anyone. We need to pick those who are deserving and weed out the rest."

"Which am I?"

"You're a guy with a chance. You doomed yourself by quitting school. We are giving you a chance to save yourself. We're offering to teach you all the things your parents and your teachers failed to make you understand. That's a massive effort. A massive effort."

For some reason I went back to his revelation that I was learning fifth grade math. Was my mistake really that big? Could I stay in this apartment another six or seven years to learn what I'd missed? He was right that it was a massive effort, and I was doing all the work.

"Don't be discouraged."

I didn't say anything.

"You're in the best program there is. Wendell is a genius."

I still didn't believe I was lucky.

"There are seven programs in Massachusetts. Five are reeducation programs, but a few employ questionable methods. You were lucky to draw Wendell's program. It's your best chance to turn things around."

"What good is this crap?" I waved toward the black box.

"You still don't get how monumentally you screwed up by dropping out of society, do you? You've figured out that you can't run. Let me show you your alternative and then you'll see how lucky you are."

CHAPTER THIRTY-FIVE

I climbed into the passenger's seat of Dr. Blake's BMW, feeling guilty about what I'd done to Joel and nervous that I might actually see him. I was also morbidly curious to see the place where I might eventually die. Blake was my teacher and I believed he was trying to help me however painful the lesson was. I'd never really thought about the man himself until he started the car and rushed off into the dark. Why did a man like Dr. Blake teach in a reform program instead of taking a professorship in a prestigious college? Did he get some special satisfaction from teaching relearners? Or was he unable to secure a position with a more respectable clientele? The answer turned out to be one and the same, but as he zipped along, I was intent on what he was about to show me.

Blake took back roads south and west, away from the city. He kept me talking, I assumed, so I wouldn't know how to get back to wherever he was taking me, but our destination was only fifteen minutes from my apartment. When we pulled up to the guardhouse, I had visions of breaking in and helping Joel escape. I kept telling myself that the tracking devices would never let us get away, but to be honest, it was the sheer horror of the place that cooled my ideas about sneaking through the woods and helping Joel.

The car stopped and the guard came to the window. He recognized Dr. Blake immediately. "We weren't expecting any new residents tonight."

Blake explained that we were there for a tour and the guard said, "Lucky you," in my direction. After what happened later, I still wonder how much that guard knew and what he meant by lucky.

The former prison building had been renovated, but it still retained its bland cement face. Windows were added and barbed wire was removed, but the residents inside were locked in tighter than when the building advertised itself as a home to violent criminals. Given the choice, the relearners inside would gladly return to the days of common rooms and televisions.

"This is your other option," Blake said as he parked the car in the far corner of the vacant visitor parking lot. He killed the lights. "If you can't finish your education. If you can't stay out of trouble. This is where you will wind up."

He was trying to scare me. I stiffened, determined to keep my cool, but Joel and Stephan had already convinced me to do anything to avoid coming here. Earlier I'd been thinking my choice was to jump or to finish studying. It had been a close one. What Blake was about to show me was more gruesome than anything Joel and Stephan described.

Blake pressed a button and my window buzzed down into the door. Animals called to each other. They could have been birds or bugs, I wasn't sure. If an animal didn't live in a park, or walk on a leash, I probably hadn't seen it, and didn't really care to. The noises were a bit spooky, but they weren't what Blake wanted me to hear.

It took a minute or two, and then I heard a man scream as if he were in horrific pain. I imagined his fingers were being crushed in a vice as he wailed on and on. Blake explained that at night they keep the upper windows open so the relearners who've been here longest have an opportunity to jump. He wanted me to hear what was happening inside this remodeled prison. We had to come at night because the windows were closed during the day in case anyone wandered through the woods. According to Blake, the screaming continued day and night.

I asked Blake why we needed such a place. And if people knew about it, why hadn't it been shut down. Blake didn't answer. He seemed angry that I hadn't asked what was making the men scream. He asked himself the question and proceeded to answer.

He told me they couldn't have relearners die off too soon after they came here, so they toyed with them a while. They didn't kill anyone, but once a relearner came through these doors, he never caused trouble for decent citizens again. A few men ran the entire facility. They locked the relearners in their apartments and used Wendell's technology to keep track of their clients.

The black box was a warm up. They showed recordings of other relearners nearing their breaking point. All the rooms were identically decorated, so no matter which room they showed on television, it appeared to be the room the relearner was currently in.

They got the name cat baggers by trapping feral cats from suburban colonies, riling them up, and releasing them into the relearners rooms at night. Even wild as they were, the cats perished quickly. Some of the more violent relearners enjoyed smashing the cats with whatever was at hand. The guards removed everything heavy from the rooms, but then the relearners began to whip the cats with towels and belts. Finally, the guards found a drug that caused temporarily blindness. That was a spectacular success. Imagine waking up blind in the middle of the night with five hungry wild cats gnawing at your arms and legs.

That was just the beginning. They released colorful gasses into the rooms. Some were harmless, others simply irritants, still others rendered the relearner paralyzed while a guard came into the room and abused them. They used street drugs, dart guns, and poison. They even tried pumping in exhaust fumes from cars in the parking lot.

I'd heard enough. I'd do anything to avoid this place, but Dr. Blake wasn't finished. He told me about a young man they pumped full of appetite stimulants. They fattened him up until he couldn't move and then they let in the cats while he was fully aware of their attack but could do nothing to defend himself. Blake had made his point, but he didn't start the car. We sat there another twenty minutes until I heard something awful. It was nearly midnight when I heard the half-hearted scream and then the collision of bone and flesh against concrete. The crunching and cracking made me shiver, and I knew a man had just jumped to his death.

"I get it. Why'd you bring me all the way out here?" I asked.

"This is what's in store for you. You've been judged non-conforming twice since you left prison. You're headed here if you don't shape up. If you don't finish your exams before you get arrested again, you'll be in one of these rooms."

This was punishment. The men who ran this place took pleasure in tormenting relearners. They had no one to answer to and they never would as long as their clients kept leaving in body bags. This was no alternative, but the black box in my apartment held years of work I just wasn't prepared to complete. Blake knew this, that's why he took me here. He wanted to impress upon me how hopeless my situation was.

"What do you want from me?" I asked.

"I'm here to help you," he said.

My stomach started churning. Something was wrong and I hadn't figured out where this was going yet.

"I can help you get through your lessons or I can make them supremely difficult. It depends how cooperative you are."

"Cooperative?"

He pulled the waistband of his sweatpants and there staring at me was an erect mushroom with a chubby little stalk. He wasn't wearing underwear because he'd planned this from the very beginning. He told me if I was willing to do him a favor a few times a week that he'd make sure my progress went smoothly. These things happened in prison. His other relearners did what was necessary to graduate. I wanted to vomit.

Charlotte came to mind. I'd fantasized about her since the first time she swished into my room. Was my interest in her any different than Blake's disgusting move here in the car? At least my advances were subtle. Sitting there I learned something important. Now that cash was gone, sex was the new currency of the underworld.

CHAPTER THIRTY-SIX

The next morning three flat gray pads arrived at my doorstep, courtesy of Dr. Blake. If the screams, and the suicide weren't enough to keep me awake all night, Blake's sleazy request certainly was. I hadn't finished walking home until three o'clock and didn't open my eyes until the knock on the door prompted me to go out and find the pads.

I was too tired to go back to math problems, so I ate a donut from the kitchen. They were getting a little hard around the edges, but Joel had taught me something important about finances. Too bad my mother or Morris Farnsworth hadn't given me that lesson earlier. I went down to the donut shop for coffee, now accustomed to the reaction when the door notified the masses that a criminal was in their presence. They didn't think of me as a relearner. Only Wendell bought that crap.

My mind wasn't clear enough for math problems even after coffee, so I went straight from the donut shop to the courtyard and found Deone and Tyrone alone at a picnic table in the sun. They grunted when I sat down. I thought that was all the conversation I was going to get until they asked if I knew what happened to Joel.

I told them about the girlfriend, the earrings, and the mother-in-law.

"Damn," Tyrone said. "He was through. Just a few weeks and he was out of here."

Deone couldn't believe Wendell sent Joel to the cat baggers. I didn't tell them I sold Joel the earrings. They would have shunned me, so I changed the subject by asking what they were studying. They were both in their senior year. They were close to getting out, but not as close as Joel had been. That was why they stayed here in the courtyard. The walls kept the relearners away from trouble. It was a safe haven for relearners even if it resembled a prison yard, or maybe in some ways because it did.

"Have you guys ever been to see the cat baggers?"

"You didn't get in the car with Blake?" Deone laughed.

"How was I supposed to know he's a homo?"

"You're a bigger fool than I thought," Deone said.

"We going to be seeing him around your place?" Tyrone asked.

"Screw you guys."

"You walked home, huh?"

They didn't wait for me to nod. Good thing, because I wasn't saying anything. "Did he do the whole thing about the police chasing you?"

"Dude, you've got to smarten up."

I hope you are as disgusted by Blake as I am. He had his scam down and I'm sure he netted more than his share of friendly favors that way. The pressure on relearners came from every side. People don't care what happens to us. I honestly think most people would rather send relearners to the cat baggers than let Wendell train them and set them free. I know what happened while I was sleeping was tragic, but that kind of prejudice isn't right. I'm sure none of you has been in my position, but you must know in your heart that we don't deserve to be tortured.

At that point in my conversation with Tyrone and Deone, I was looking for any distraction to clear away the image of Blake's open jogging pants. I told Deone about one night when I boosted four cars from the same neighborhood without anyone getting wise. Deone and Tyrone shared some stories about times they'd gotten away and times they'd gotten locked up. As we were sitting there in the sun I remembered what Wendell said about how much non-conformers hurt him. Deone, Tyrone, and I had made our living taking things from other people. It's all we knew.

Those guys back at Stephan's seemed like the country club set. They screwed up and decked some guy and got into trouble, but they'd be out quick and they wouldn't be back. What did it really take to teach some college grad banker to stay out of trouble? Whoever was running that place had it down and Wendell was getting screwed. I thought about how much I would have to learn to get my GED. Wendell had worked hard to create all those lessons and to assemble the counselors to help me. That was a lot harder than picking teams and refereeing a Wiffle ball game. I wondered what else they did over at Stephan's.

I asked Deone and Tyrone who else they knew around our courtyard. The group looked rough. Maybe it looked rougher to me because there were only six or seven white guys. Back in prison where racial gangs dominated, the six of us would have been dead. There was no threat of serious violence here. No one got stabbed because everyone was afraid of the cat baggers. But everyone in that yard had an edge. They were survivors like me. Tattoos and funky hairstyles were everywhere. We were nothing like those homogenized campers who lived with Stephan.

Tyrone and Deone knew bunches of inmates from the old days, guys who'd done serious time. Some of them stayed out here in the courtyard because they felt jittery being on the street. They liked the walls. Others had been in and out five and six times each.

I didn't believe many of them would make it on the outside. Wendell would give them his best shot, but in the end, most of them were going to be locked in a room like Joel's. It was inevitable. Sitting there watching the guys around the yard I got angry. Wendell was trying to help me. He'd saved me from the cat baggers twice already. He was getting screwed by the system, mostly because he was trying to do the right thing. He thought he was getting a fair shot at whoever came along, but it was obvious that someone was tilting the odds. Whoever ran Stephan's program was making easy money while Wendell was killing himself to help people and getting nowhere.

I should never have gotten involved, but I couldn't help myself.

CHAPTER THIRTY-SEVEN

The only person I knew in the whole complex was Stephan. I didn't have his phone number, so I walked over and waited on a bench that faced the Wiffle ball diamond. From there I watched the sidewalk headed east and anyone coming out to join the game. If I had known Stephan's last name I would have asked around, but I didn't want to raise suspicion and be sent away, so I acted like I was waiting for him to join me.

The first thing I noticed was that the men in this building only walked to get from place to place. Where I came from, guys added all these extra movements, like animals showing off to attract a mate. Arms flapped, heads bobbed, knees and hips flew. It was a lot of work to walk in the hood, that's how we kept in shape to run from the cops. Personally, I walked with minimal motion, not to separate myself from the gang bangers, but to keep from knocking things over when I moved through a dark house.

I couldn't help watching these guys shuttle back and forth. It was like their big jobs and fancy educations weighed them down so much they didn't have the energy to show off. There was no tension when two guys passed. They nodded to each other and they moved on. If a guy didn't nod back, it was no big deal; the other guy didn't give him a second look.

There was a whole lot of normal walking around that place. They wore collared shirts to play Wiffle ball. They kept their hair short, not as short as mine, but my shaved head was a bit extreme. I didn't see a tattoo or a guy with his hair dyed or spiked up into a Mohawk. Normalcy wasn't evidence of anything, but I knew when I finally talked to Stephan, I'd have something real to bring to Wendell. Something that would get me away from Blake.

That wasn't my goal in going there. Once I realized what I was doing might earn me a new counselor, I was excited about the idea. Still, deep down I wanted to help Wendell. That was what got me started on this journey, and that was what saw me through until I came to stand before you.

So I sat on the bench another two hours. In that time I saw Dr. Blake make a giddy rush through the double doors. He wasn't wearing his jogging suit, but I guess he didn't need it if he was going into a guy's apartment. I wondered if he could really be collecting a favor here. These guys didn't feel the pressure like we did, and he must have been worried about being caught on camera when he pulled down his pants. Maybe he didn't care. Maybe he watched the tapes. He could have been hitting up the one guy in this building who was on the edge of being shipped to the cat baggers. Balding and pudgy with a job none of his peers respected, Blake might count himself lucky to get what he could, cameras or no cameras.

I thought about following Blake inside and recording him in the act, but I couldn't risk angering him again. If he caught me I might look back fondly on the shocks from the wrist strap. I couldn't risk the conflict, especially since he might be innocently doing his job.

Another half hour passed and Morris Farnsworth walked from a shiny black sedan to the back corner of the building. He entered through a rust colored door that blended with the brick exterior. Morris looked like a lot of other guys from a distance, but I hadn't seen anyone else wearing a suit and a bow tie. I was surprised that two of Wendell's counselors were working here in this program, too. I thought the business was a whole lot more competitive than that.

When Stephan finally showed up I had a dozen questions rolling through my mind, but I tried to keep it low key. Blake shouldn't have told me about the cat baggers, but since he did, I wondered how much Blake and Morris Farnsworth shared with the guys over here.

Stephan headed for the Wiffle ball game in shorts and a golf shirt. I jumped up and met him on his way. When I told him I was a lefty, he offered to show me a few pitches so I could join his team. I'd only played catch on the sidewalk and in the park two blocks from the projects, never anything organized. I didn't tell him and he didn't ask.

When the game I had been watching ended, Stephan went out to the pitcher's mound to look for an opponent. He got one and after we loosened up, our five-man team faced off against another. These guys might not have been aggressive when they walked, but they were maniacs on the field. They laid out and dove for the ball, sliding on their chests after making a catch. The other team identified me as the weak link and pretty soon balls started coming my way. When I got up to bat, the first pitch blew my mind. This guy with a flattened nose threw the ball an inch off the grass, then it climbed up into the air and hit the metal plate hung behind the batter for a strike zone. The next two pitches made impossible curves from places I couldn't hit them to the outer edges of that plate. I knew I had no chance to help my team.

The rest of my Wiffle ball career was strikeout after strikeout and balls whizzing over my head into the outfield, but while we were batting I learned some interesting things about the guys on my team and even the spectators.

When you asked these guys what they did, they had a legit profession. They were bankers and lawyers and insurance men. They worked in offices or computer rooms in tall buildings. They frowned when you asked them what they were in for. They weren't proud of the DUI charge or the punch they'd thrown at their boss at a party. I counted fourteen guys on the field after the game. Not one of them had ever been to prison and they all had a job to go back to. These guys weren't coming back. This was a bump in the road for them. Someone was making a killing by letting them play ball instead of punishing them for their crimes.

CHAPTER THIRTY-EIGHT

When the game was over and I was done talking to the guys around home plate, I knew the place was a sham. I was working my buns off to finish ridiculously difficult lessons and these guys just played ball. I wanted to scream about how easy they had it. You might be thinking I was angry because I made our team lose. You're right, I didn't help our team, but losing that game didn't matter to me. The other guys were intense about Wiffle ball and maybe that's why they were so good. For me, the game was a way inside, nothing more.

Afterward I asked Stephan if there was more to the reeducation program than athletics and he offered to show me what he was doing upstairs. On our way to his apartment he pointed out the security room like it was common knowledge. It was the same room I'd seen Morris Farnsworth go into.

When I went back home later, I checked the layout of my building and found our security room in the back corner of the first floor away from prying eyes on the street. I knew my apartment was being watched but I had not known from where. Because our exercise area was enclosed and because we had no reason to walk around behind the building, I'd bet most relearners who lived in my complex had no idea the security room was tucked back there. The building was designed to discourage us from ever finding this room.

We took the elevator up. Another convenience unavailable at my place.

Stephan's apartment wasn't as grand as I expected. His furniture looked a lot like mine. He told me he'd bought it from the guy who was there before him. He had the same black box, but without the wrist strap and gray pads that had been delivered to me.

When he showed me what he was working on, I laughed. He had a week left in the program and three discs remaining. His discs were what I had originally expected. They were kids' movies.

We watched several minutes of some boys picking on another kid because his shirt was different than the others. The whole idea seemed childish to me, but Stephan's eyes never left the screen.

"You like this crap?"

He paused the player. "No. But I've got to answer the questions at the end. I pay attention so I only have to watch the thing once."

He restarted the movie and instantly refocused on the screen. I asked him what he did for work and he begrudgingly told me he made computers talk to each other or something like that. The whole tech world was foreign to me. I watched a few minutes, more curious about how feeble the questions at the end would be than anything.

Stephan was really into the movie.

I checked the characters for one that looked like him, but none of them did. I guessed they hadn't stolen that trick from Wendell.

Stephan blinked twice. I'd noticed it before, but for some reason I perked up. I asked him to back up the movie. We watched it again and he blinked in the same spot.

Three more times we replayed this bit about one kid hitting another. Every time Stephan blinked.

I asked him if he had a Coke. He said they were in the fridge, but I nodded to the kitchen where we had a better chance of talking unobserved.

He followed and handed me the soda with a curious look.

I spilled a handful of sugar, spread it over the table and scratched, *That movies f'd,* in the granules.

He just shrugged.

I carved, *You keep blinking at the same part*, with my finger.

He carved, *Tap when I blink.*

141

That wasn't necessary. Once I'd told him, he realized how much he was blinking at the violent images on the screen. He tried slowing them down, but the player had only very basic functionality. He thought for a minute, disappeared to his room, and reappeared with a camera.

We made a good show of watching the next ten minutes of the movie.

"I've got to get back," I said for the benefit of our audience downstairs.

He let me keep the Coke and walked me out into the hall. There he played back the images from his camera. The movie showed in super-slow motion, and what we saw explained why Stephan was so riveted to the action and why he was troubled by the violence.

Twice a nearly naked woman appeared for a single frame or two.

Then, when the boy in the movie was punched, Stephan himself appeared in a single frame, getting stabbed by a much larger man.

The men in this complex were learning more than they knew. I couldn't believe this was happening in America. Professional men were brainwashed to stay out of trouble. Teachers were extorting sex from relearners. Men were being tortured to the brink of their sanity. I knew then that if anyone could help me tell the world about this, Wendell could. Stephan gave me the camera and I promised to come back after I'd shown the movie to Wendell.

He thanked me absently when I left. I knew he was wondering about the other lessons he'd watched. What else had they implanted in his mind while he thought he was watching a harmless story about a bunch of children?

CHAPTER THIRTY-NINE

As I rode the elevator down I realized that using children's movies was an ingenious way to get the men to let their guard down. The Wiffle ball culture reinforced their ease, the naked women held their attention, and the violent images drilled the lesson straight into their subconscious. The other thing that struck me as I walked into my apartment was how slick the programs were. The government handed complete control of the relearners to Wendell and his peers. Competition between them polished the primary programs, but the lack of supervision allowed rampant abuses. Maybe the abuse wasn't a mistake. Maybe that was the only way the government could control us now that the prisons were empty.

Wendell wouldn't torture anyone or stoop to using subliminal images. I knew he'd be outraged when he saw what was on the camera, but I didn't know how to find him. With Blake and Farnsworth working for both programs, I wasn't sure if I could trust any of my counselors. I certainly wasn't telling Blake anything. After our disgusting encounter in his car, he had it in for me. That made sneaking home with the camera especially tough.

I went straight for the kitchen, opened a box of microwave popcorn, and slipped the camera from my pocket to the bottom of the box. Once I rearranged the packets on top and pushed the box to the back of the counter I felt better. I even microwaved a bag to complete the rouse even though I wasn't hungry. With the bowl on the coffee table, I arranged the business cards my counselors had given me. They were my only real contact with the outside world. I pushed Blake and Farnsworth to the left, knowing I couldn't trust them. If Wendell had given me a card, I would have found a payphone and called him, but I guess he was too important to be bogged down by every relearner. Too bad. If he had trusted me with his number, it would have made both our lives easier.

When the knock came, I had my finger on Charlotte's card, tapping it like she was the only one I could trust. When I opened the door, there she was in a skirt and heels, like I'd summoned her by touching her card. She took a seat on the couch and when she crossed her legs, her skirt rose well up her thigh. I reminded myself that I was a relearner—her client. I was sweaty from the Wiffle ball game and the hike to Stephan's. As much as she smiled at me across the upholstered divide, she wasn't interested. She was the pretty face on the reeducation machine.

I offered her popcorn and a drink. When she refused, I picked up the bowl myself. I couldn't help thinking about getting together with her. Even sweaty and dirty as I was, I wanted to believe she was interested. That's why she had this job. Every relearner wanted Charlotte. The legs and the hair were bait to get me to do what they wanted. We were being filmed. Nothing would happen. I tried to get control of myself by imagining she looked like my mother, but my eyes refused to be tricked.

She noticed the grass stains on my pants and asked what I'd been doing.

I told her about the game, still wondering why she showed up when she did. We hadn't spoken since the encounter with Nick and Kathleen a week ago. Maybe she'd given me a week to think about things and put this date on her calendar, but more likely she was here to help out her colleague.

She fished for information about Blake. She asked how I was doing with the program and I told her everything was going fine. She asked where I was and I said I was working on math.

"Are you having trouble?"

"Everything's fine. It's just like being back in school. That's all."

She pointed to the gray pads on the floor. "That's not a good sign. You sure you're not having trouble? I could call Dr. Blake for you."

I had yet to be tormented by the gray pads, so I didn't know what unpleasantness they held for me. Clearly this was a step up from the wrist-strap shocks, but at least they weren't plugged in. I hadn't thought about them much. I knew Blake wanted to punish me for refusing to service him. I almost asked Charlotte what they were for, but I didn't want to give her an excuse to send Blake to my place.

"What brings you by?" I asked to change the subject.

"Nick and Kathleen have been calling me. They are very anxious to move ahead with the adoption."

"Of my son." I said it more forcefully than I'd expected. Was something really being taken away from me? If Charlotte hadn't told me about the DNA test, I never would have known Jonathan was mine. Would I have been just like my father and the other men my mother knew? I didn't want to be, but here was Nick, offering, no insisting, to take on my responsibility. The pregnancy didn't change anything between Kathleen and me. She was married to him. Did I want to be the third leg of this parenting trio?

"They'll make him a good home," Charlotte said, as if I couldn't.

I knew it was true. I didn't even know why I was protesting, but I felt like something was being stolen from me and I wanted to fight.

"You won't have child support deducted from your pay anymore."

The more she pressed the more determined I became.

"Nick has a good job. It'll be very difficult for Jonathan growing up the son of a relearner. After the adoption he won't have to know. He'll never be teased on the playground."

Any thoughts I had about sleeping with Charlotte vanished. She thought my son would be better off if he didn't know I existed. She looked at me sincerely, but I was below her. She came here and she seemed unafraid, but to her I was an animal in obedience school. If I needed proof all I had to do was look down at my ankle. I told her I'd think about the papers.

She left in a hurry.

CHAPTER FORTY

That was the first time I felt out of balance with the world. Would I always be repulsive to Charlotte? I would have worked hard to impress her. I was already doing my best to finish Wendell's program without getting into trouble, but that wasn't enough. She would always see me as a relearner. Would everyone on the outside see me that way? Could I ever buy my own small place and settle down? Would my neighbors hate me? Would they protest outside my door? Could I get a job? Or would employers refuse to hire me because I couldn't be trusted?

I might have been a bit emotional after Charlotte thrashed my pride, but I seriously considered staying inside the apartment forever. I wondered how long the government would keep paying. Would they kick me out if I didn't show the potential to finish? The counselors and all the technology they used to watch me had to be expensive, but I never believed Wendell would throw me to the cat baggers.

There was one thing I needed to do if I wanted to stay. I clicked the button on the remote control. The television lit up and Wendell appeared above the black box and chirped right into a lecture. "If you have any hope of finishing your GED you need to work much harder. You must spend at least five hours a day attending to your studies."

It was Blake talking through Wendell. After learning about the control room from Stephan, I guessed Blake had been downstairs waiting for me to begin a lesson so he could harass me.

I chose to continue working on math.

A long division problem popped on the screen. That wasn't surprising in itself, but Blake was asking me to divide 6,809,775 by 735. The last time I used the program I was dividing even numbers by ten or twenty. I knew he was making it as difficult as possible for me, but I also knew I couldn't afford to quit. I needed to show effort and that's exactly what I did.

I worked and worked at the problem, constantly multiplying 735 to try and find the right digits for my answer. I was getting close when Wendell popped up and said, "You're out of time, Michael. You really need to try harder." Blake was watching and making sure I didn't finish.

Nine more problems came, each one as difficult as the first. No matter how organized I got, I couldn't finish the problems in time. I wasn't sure if Blake was manipulating the clock, but I knew for sure he was watching me. If he could speed up the clock, he would.

After the tenth problem, holographic Wendell returned.

"You missed ten out of ten. You must do ten push-ups for each wrong answer."

He couldn't make me do a hundred push-ups.

"Spread the gray pads on the floor. One for each hand at shoulder width and one for your feet."

I tossed the pads on the floor.

"Michael, you are five feet, eight inches tall. The pads are too close together for push-ups."

I arranged the pads appropriately and the machine instructed me to get into position. I held myself there and the machine ordered me to begin. I tried doing tiny push-ups and the wrist strap zapped me.

"I can see you, Michael," holographic Wendell said.

I pressed out fifteen push-ups and my arms ached. Sixteen was a struggle. I managed to get to nineteen before I collapsed. My chest hit the floor and when it did, the strap zapped me again.

It took me nearly an hour to finish the hundred push-ups because I needed to rest so long in between. My arms and shoulders ached. I was covered in sweat. As soon as I finished, another impossible long division problem appeared on the screen. The box didn't even give me time to get to the couch.

What I needed was a calculator and a way to hide it from the cameras. With that thought, I stood and started checking the walls and ceilings to see if I could find tiny lenses. I spent half an hour walking around the living room shaking my arms as if they hurt. It wasn't acting because they did, but in all that time I couldn't find a single camera.

Little Wendell jabbered at me. He didn't like the delay and like a fool, I put on the wrist strap and had another go at the problems. I did my best work and got two correct out of ten. Wendell ordered eighty push-ups and I spent the next hour completing them. After that there was no way I could do more math. My arms couldn't hold me anymore and I couldn't take the shocks when I rested.

Blake had me in an impossible situation and he knew it. I had to keep studying or get thrown out of the program. The only other program that would take me was impossible to survive. At that moment I had a fleeting hope that Wendell would help me if he knew what Blake was doing, but who was Wendell going to believe, a relearner or his teacher?

I decided to go outside and wait for Blake to leave the security room. Then I would try some of the other programs and see what I could learn when he wasn't there to interfere. I needed to rest my arms and a walk outside was just the thing.

CHAPTER FORTY-ONE

The front of the building emptied onto a busy commercial street. At least it had been busy before the relearners moved in. There were a few shops still in business and plenty of cars parked along both sidewalks. I had no idea how far the cameras extended, so I walked to the donut shop and leaned against the bricks for a while. I wanted to wait long enough for Blake to lose interest and go home. What I forgot was that he could track me anywhere I went. He didn't have to wonder where I was. He could find me electronically and so could anyone connected to Wendell or the police.

I thought I was being smart walking the long way around two blocks and circling back to the control room from the opposite direction. Blake couldn't know my intentions, only where I was at any particular moment, but I'd forgotten that. The street-side wall continued well past the rest of the building, forming a leg that jutted out. That leg housed the control room and also hid a fair-sized nook along the back wall where Blake parked his car. The men working for Wendell could bring things, or people, in and out of the building without being seen because the enclosed courtyard concentrated the relearners in the center of the building. Wendell kept us contained where he could monitor us easily without our knowing what he and his counselors were doing.

The parking lot behind the building was home to cars with sagging tires, leaking fluids, and rusty panels. I settled low onto the curb where I could look past a fender and see the control room door while staying hidden.

Sitting there on the granite curb, I felt my biceps and pecs tighten from the push-ups. Pretty soon my butt hurt from the granite and I pushed back onto the tiny strip of grass and stretched my legs out in front of me.

If I was smarter, I would have realized Blake was probably in the control room watching my little dot on a screen somewhere. As I waited and waited for him to finish, he was probably waiting for me to get sick of sitting outside and come back in where he could torment me. Eventually it got dark and Blake waddled to his BMW and drove away.

I laid flat and waited for the car to disappear. I didn't move even after it was gone in case he could track me from his car. I gave him almost five minutes and then I stood up to go back inside.

I hadn't heard a single movement around me. I made a living by knowing my surroundings and blending in, but that night in the dark I allowed myself to focus only on the door, the car, and Blake.

Nick sprung up when I reached the hood of the rusty Chevy. He cornered me at the worst possible time. My arms were sore from all the push-ups and Nick outweighed me by fifty pounds. My hiding place among the old cars was good because almost no one came back here. That meant no one was coming to my aid either. Nick, on the other hand, was ready. Tight leather gloves covered his fists. Long sleeves protected his arms as he grimly blocked the path back to my apartment.

I thought about running, but my legs were stiff from sitting on the granite. I had a better chance to talk my way free than to outrun the brute.

"What do you want?"

"What do you think I want, moron?" Nick growled.

He wanted my son. There were so many things I could have said to put him over the edge. I'd gotten to Kathleen first. Jonathan was my son and he couldn't have him without my permission. But I didn't feel powerful in the narrow space between the cars. I could have threatened never to give up my rights if he touched me, but I kept quiet. Nick was beyond negotiation. He was ready to force his will, and Kathleen wasn't here to reign him in. I wondered what would happen if we went to the police. Was my word as valuable as Nick's?

If I reported this encounter and the last, maybe I'd have some credibility, but after being arrested three times, I was a bit short.

Nick tired of the long silence. He poked me in the chest and said, "Sign the damn papers."

"You can't force me to give you my son." Honestly I hadn't thought about the papers since Charlotte left. I didn't know what was holding me back. I didn't know Jonathan. I hadn't intended for him to be born, but it felt wrong leaving him and it felt wrong for him to be stripped away like this.

Nick twisted a handful of my T-shirt and lifted hard enough to prove he could hold me in the air with one hand and pummel me with the other. "I'm done waiting," he snarled.

When I didn't answer, he said, "I work inside Govbank. I can make things miserable for you in a thousand ways. I can make it look like you're stealing credits one day, selling them to foreigners the next, and I can bankrupt you the next. No one will ever know what I've done."

The threat took me by surprise. Could Nick really be that powerful? I'd grown up surrounded by angry faces. Reading people saved me hundreds of times. Nick wasn't bluffing. He worked in the bank and he believed he could ruin me.

"We both know where you'll end up then," he said.

"What?"

He couldn't know about the horrors Blake had shown me. Impossible. But he didn't mean reeducation. My mouth hung open and he backed away knowing his point was made.

"Sign," he said.

He rounded the Chevy, stopped, and turned to meow in my direction. I was stunned to be at the mercy of yet another man. I couldn't look back into my past and ask myself where I'd gone wrong because I'd never really been on the right track.

CHAPTER FORTY-TWO

The ceiling barely faded from sight that long night in my apartment. Wendell, Blake, Charlotte, and now Nick were all pressuring me to be something I wasn't. Every move I made, they were there. It seemed they were inside my head, reading my thoughts before I had them. How could they know what I'd do, where I'd go, and which tests I'd fail? They had dealt with hundreds of relearners before. They knew everything about me. Maybe from behind a video monitor it was easy to know what my options were and which one I'd choose. It wasn't emotional for them. The choice to give up Jonathan or build a relationship with the boy and his mother was a checkbox on their list. To me it meant passing judgment on how I was raised and whether I was able to become something more than my father had been.

For a while I felt like they were all, every one of them, herding me toward destruction. Wendell was responsible for everything that happened. Blake wanted blowjobs and who knew what else. If he couldn't get what he wanted, he'd gladly flunk me and move on to the next relearner. Charlotte seemed too cold for someone so beautiful. I had no idea what she was capable of. Nick wanted his boy and he wanted to cleanse any memory of a relearner sleeping with his wife.

I watched the slow march through the numbers on the clock radio until the morning light prompted me to get up. Showering was painful. I couldn't reach my back and I knew the next day would be even worse.

Pulling on my jeans and sneakers, I thought about signing the papers to get Nick and Charlotte off my back. She might force me to see my mother, but that was an argument I could handle. Blake was a nightmare. Just thinking about what he did made me sick to my stomach. There was only one person who could help me with him. My biggest problem was finding him.

I felt a little guilty heading for the donut shop after Joel's grocery shopping lecture, but it was easier to buy my coffee than to make it myself. My coffee wasn't terrible. I needed the caffeine in the morning and I wasn't looking for much more than that, but the donuts were much better fresh even if they did cost double.

I didn't even give the black box a second look on my way out the door. The gray pads seemed harmless at first, but I knew why Charlotte looked so grim when she saw them. They were the beginning of the end. No one could satisfy Blake's ridiculous demands for problem solving speed, and the push-ups made it impossible to work very long. If things didn't change, I would never complete another lesson.

On the sidewalk I had a whim to go buy paper and pencils so I could make up my own problems. Practice might help me get better, but beating the machine was hopeless. I plodded along with my eyes on the concrete until a black blur in the street came even with me and stopped short. I was thinking about pencils and how I'd sharpen them when I turned and saw a long Lincoln blocking traffic. The window buzzed down and the wide black mouth of a twelve gauge poked out. I immediately dropped to the concrete behind a neon blue fender and a new-looking tire.

The gun blared.

Glass shattered and a few pellets ricocheted back and smacked against the car not far from my head.

The pump worked back and forward to chamber another round.

The gun blared again. This time the pellets hit the car I was hiding behind, deflected over my head, and crashed into the lower part of the window. The car took the worst of the second blast. Stray pellets cracked the glass in a dozen places but it didn't shatter.

The car door creaked. The shooter came out after me.

I jumped up and ran past the donut shop, against the flow of traffic. The Lincoln couldn't back up through the cars stopped behind it. I crossed into the street and the gun boomed again. I couldn't tell what they hit. I heard glass and metal banging all around me, but none of the pellets hit home.

I kept going full out for three blocks. When I couldn't run anymore I caught a taxi and headed north toward the city. I'd never heard three shotgun blasts since I moved to town, never mind during the morning rush on a crowded street. The gunman didn't care about witnesses. There must have been forty people in cars or on the sidewalk. He could have killed any one of them with a ricochet.

I was in more trouble than I imagined.

The cab dropped me at a grocery store. I went in and stayed near the back where I couldn't be seen from the street. I hadn't gotten a good look at the guy with the twelve gauge or the driver. My first suspect was Nick, but Blake could have hired someone just as easily.

There was only one person who didn't pop up on my list of suspects. He was the only one I could trust and right then I decided how I was going to save myself. I did a little shopping, ducked into an Internet cafe nearby, and hurried home.

CHAPTER FORTY-THREE

I dumped the packets of popcorn all over the counter and found the camera at the bottom of the box where I'd left it. I slipped it into my pocket, grabbed the shopping bag from the table, and rushed out the door before anyone could stop me. Instead of going right to my destination, I made a quick stop in the park near my old place on Dent Street. The basketball game had grown considerably in the five years I'd been gone. It seemed lots of people had free time on their hands during the week. Men in shorts lined both sides of the court waiting for the next game to start.

The man with the gym bag was in the same place by half court. "Got any percs?" I asked.

"I could use a new iPod. A red one," he answered and pointed to a store across the street. I went over and paid for it by scanning my thumb. They had dozens of them in the glass case and I was pretty sure this was another currency that had replaced cash.

Back across the street, I traded the iPod for my purchase and hopped back in the cab. I wasn't sure I needed the pills, but the man I wanted to visit discouraged unexpected company. I stopped the cab two blocks from the house and when I saw the place I knew I had made the right choice.

An eight-foot concrete wall rose up from just off the sidewalk to surround the entire property. It was still early, so climbing the wall anywhere along the front was out. I walked past a few times, then crossed the street and checked out the house from there. Someone with huge money had built this place a hundred years ago. It was six thousand square feet.

Three floors with a slate roof. I didn't see any people, but I did see three Rottweilers roaming inside the wall. I'd done this hundreds of times. I never would have picked this house because of the dogs, but I didn't have a choice. I needed to see Wendell. I could have gone to the front gate and pressed the buzzer, but he would have sent me away and things would have been even worse. I decided not to ask permission.

I walked around the block, cut through a yard that looked like no one was home, and climbed a tree that leaned near the wall. My sore arms struggled to lift me and the three pounds of hot dogs stuffed down my shirt, but I pulled myself up and crossed from a heavy branch to the top of the wall. When I ripped open the first package and started breaking the hot dogs into chunks, the dogs came running. I poked a Percocet into the center of each chunk and tossed them on the ground. I kept breaking, poking, and tossing and the dogs gobbled down the pieces greedily. When they had eaten five pieces each, I stopped adding the pills and used the meat to entertain them, hoping they would pass out. I threw the pieces left and right, letting the dogs chase after them and fight over each morsel. I broke smaller and smaller chunks as I ran low, but the dogs showed no sign of tiring. When I finally ran out, the dogs looked up at me cockeyed. There were enough trees to hide me from the house, but that wouldn't matter if the dogs started barking.

I waited and waited, expecting them to tip over, but they didn't. They looked woozy, but stood firm. Finally, I got impatient, reached out for a branch, and climbed down a tree inside the wall. The dogs watched like toddlers entranced by a television program. Their limbs were too uncoordinated to move aggressively. I stepped away from the tree nervously, but the dogs didn't follow. They tilted their heads and took a few longing steps then laid down in the grass.

It probably wasn't smart to walk past the dogs smelling so strongly of meat. If there was another dog inside, it would have torn me apart, but I wasn't thinking of that as I trotted across the lawn toward the back corner of the house. I didn't stop until I was inside the overgrown rhododendrons.

From there I was sure I was safe from the cameras, and I took my time inspecting the lower windows that led down into the basement.

I was just about to start working on a window when I clearly heard a grandfather clock chime inside the house. The window directly over my head was wide open. It was one of those old windows, double the size of the ones they put in new houses, and it sat low on the wall. All I needed was a short boost to get inside. I found a garbage barrel someone had been using to collect leaves. I tipped it over, popped the screen, and in seconds I was inside the largest dining room I'd ever seen. The table could seat fifteen or twenty. That one room was bigger than my entire apartment.

I stepped into the shadow of a large cabinet filled with dishes and stood motionless against the wall to get in tune with the sounds of the house. Nothing moved. I was glad not to hear the padding of another guard dog, but it was strange not to hear anything moving in a place so big. Across from me was a huge portrait of Wendell with a woman as wide as my mother. It was made to look like a painting, but it was definitely a photograph.

I spotted two motion sensors and moved slowly to the staircase without setting them off. I turned a corner and heard the click of a sensor activating. It had me, but the alarm didn't sound. Lucky it was off. In front of me, a matching staircase led up to the second and third floors. I placed my sneakers quickly and quietly so I could get out of the huge open space before someone wandered in. From the second floor landing, I moved down a long hall of closed doors, pausing at each to listen for activity on the other side.

If I had called out at that point, everything might have been fine. I was unarmed. Yes, I came in uninvited, but someone left the window wide open. I should have said something to let Wendell know I was there, but I stalked the entire second floor without a sound and continued up to the third. At the far end of the hall, I heard shuffling behind the door. I'd opened a few and found mostly empty rooms, but this one had been waiting for me since I scaled the wall.

CHAPTER FORTY-FOUR

I closed the door behind me and the four computer screens at the far end of the room went blank. There was a metallic thunk at my back, like a dozen deadbolts ramming home at once. I grabbed the door handle, but it wouldn't budge. Trapped, I spun around. The front half of the room was completely empty. The wooden floorboards and bare walls led to the U-shaped desk where Wendell sat facing the windows with his back to me. My arrival hadn't surprised him at all.

"What did you give my dogs?"

"They'll be ok."

Wendell turned around. "How do you know? Did you ask them if they were allergic to narcotics? Did you weigh them to get the proper dose?"

What was his problem? I hadn't hurt the dogs and I really needed to see him. Why couldn't he understand that my message was more important than his dogs taking a nap?

"What if an assassin climbs the fence? Can my dogs protect me now?"

The dogs would be out for hours, but was he serious? Was he really scared of assassins?

"What gives you the right to climb through my window and come traipsing through my house? Do you know how expensive that carpeting in the dining room is?"

"No, sir."

"Well? What gives you the right?"

"I needed to see you." I felt like an eight year old being scolded for tracking dirt into the house.

"Maybe I didn't want to see you. Did that cross your mind?"

"I have something important to show you."

"Important?" he scoffed.

"I had to come. I needed to see you and you're seeing me. I did what I had to do."

"And who's choice is that? That I'm seeing you, I mean."

"Mine," I barked. I was angry and I was tired of being manipulated. He was going to listen to me and there was nothing he could do about it. I took two quick steps forward. I would have marched to the desk and grabbed him by the neck, but a floor board six feet away popped open and a glass partition shot up to the ceiling. In a blink, the room was divided into two. My side was considerably smaller than Wendell's.

"Would you like to rethink that Mr. O'Connor?"

Why was he nitpicking? Couldn't he see how important my message was? I wouldn't have broken in otherwise.

"In a polite society when we need to see someone, we ask permission."

"What does that have to do with anything? I found something important and I need to show it to you."

"Ah. Exactly my point. You need. You need. You need. That's why you're here, Michael. You only think about what you need. You're willing to sacrifice what someone else has or wants to satisfy whatever whim has your attention. In a civil society we don't take from others without asking. That applies to dogs, and houses, and even time."

I lost my cool. His flat tones were so irritating, I couldn't take it anymore. I ran to the glass and started pounding.

He was completely unfazed by my rage. So was the glass. Wendell frowned as if I were failing another test on his black box. He casually clicked a button and six ceiling vents started pouring blue smoke. With nothing to stand on, there was no way to prevent the smoke from blanketing me. Wendell's side of the room remained clear. He snickered through the haze as I tried to wave away the smoke.

"What I'm about to give you is as harmless as what you gave my dogs."

"I'm not a dog."

"Clearly not. But those dogs provide a valuable service. They earn a living by protecting me. Just how have you earned your living these twenty-five years, Mr. O'Connor? You're a career criminal who has never done anything worthy of the food you eat or the air you breathe. Some might say the dogs are more valuable than you. What do you say to them?"

At first I couldn't believe he really wanted an answer. Was he insane? Of course I was more valuable than those dogs. I went back to the glass so I could see his face. He looked right back, waiting for me to explain myself.

"I'm a human being, for God's sake."

"You're smarter than the dogs. I'll give you that. But what service have you ever provided, Michael? Tell me. It's an easy question. What have you done to help support your fellow man? Why should we keep feeding you?"

The question had never been put to me that way. I needed to eat. I deserved to eat. That's all there was. Was he serious? Why wouldn't he feed me? I was human. It was my right to live and be healthy. He couldn't take that away from me.

Locked inside the glass or even on the street I was completely under Wendell's control. I started to think how unfair that was when a realization hit me heavily in the chest. Wendell created the black box and assembled the counselors to teach me something, however misguided that effort was. He made something that hadn't existed before. Even with me here in his house, he was at work, or at least interrupted by his work.

I had never done anything useful to anyone else. I was good at what I did, but that served only me. That was Wendell's point. To rejoin society I had to earn my keep. Wendell wanted me to follow rules I'd abandoned long ago, but I needed more time than Wendell was willing to give if I wanted to learn how to follow those rules.

I couldn't answer his question. There was no defense of my last ten years, but what I did have, I pulled from my pocket and held up to the glass.

"What's that?"

"It shows how your competition has been cheating you."

Wendell pressed a few buttons. Heavy duty fans blew air up between the floorboards and the smoke slowly disappeared through the ceiling vents. A compartment opened in the wall near the divider. I walked over and placed the camera inside. When I removed my hand, the compartment shut and its twin opened on the other side of the glass. Wendell collected the camera and went back to his desk. When I tried to explain how to view the images frame by frame he waved me off.

"Nice work," he said when he was done watching.

"Thank you."

"That's not what I meant. Did your friend watch the videos?"

"What's—" Wendell wouldn't let me continue.

"He learned the lesson? Didn't he?"

"Yes."

"So what is the problem?"

"This is wrong. They can't plant ideas in someone's brain. Didn't you see the guy with the knife?"

"Excellent work I'd say." He saw how flustered I was and kept on. "The stakes in our business are incredibly high. We are the last line of defense for decent people. The lesson is what counts. Your friend Stephan was doing fine until you got in the way."

He knew I had been to Stephan's.

"Oh yes," Wendell said. "Nathan Farnsworth, my friend who runs that program, he was quite upset with you yesterday. Had to start all over with Stephan to make sure he got it right. I'm sure when you see Stephan, he's not going to be particularly happy with you either."

CHAPTER FORTY-FIVE

Wendell knew about the subliminal messages and he didn't care. When I heard him applaud the technical work, I wished I had been smart enough to check my own videos for hidden messages. Those children on the playground were probably a cover for Wendell to pump something more ominous into my head. I'd never know because Wendell kept the camera.

I was trapped on the wrong side of the glass. Wendell looked at me like a troubled goldfish that kept leaping from the safety of its bowl. Was he really trying to protect me? He needed me to stay out of trouble until his ratings improved, but that was for his benefit more than mine.

Did Wendell know who had tried to kill me that morning? If he wasn't such a patsy I would have suspected he was involved. Being worth more dead than alive made me question everyone. Even worse, I was causing trouble for a man who could push a button, fill the room with carbon dioxide, and watch me slowly suffocate, or pump in some neurotoxin and watch me drop. I was glad it was Wendell holding the button.

"Aren't you upset that he's cheating you?" I asked.

"Subliminal messages aren't cheating."

"It's more than that and you know it. What are you? Some kind of hero? Is that why you take the impossible cases?"

"What are you talking about? Criminals come in and go to the next program in line."

"Haven't you looked at the relearners your friend Nathan is getting?"

"That's not allowed," he said, then waggled the camera at me. "This is the most I've seen of what they do over there."

"Haven't you looked around?" I told him about the people I talked to in both apartment complexes. In Wendell's program, most of the relearners had offended over and over. That made it look like he was failing, but in reality, they had offended over and over before they arrived. The people who lived with Stephan were mostly first timers with trivial offenses.

Wendell ran his fingers through his hair as I'd seen him do in court.

"Think about me," I said. "Who is set up to fail more than me? I still don't understand the new laws. I've never had a job. I didn't finish school. Is it a coincidence that you got me? All this trouble you've got now, it isn't by accident."

Wendell perked up and asked how many people I had talked to.

"Thirty at home. Twenty at Stephan's. All you have to do is walk around. They look different. They act different. You're teaching hardened criminals. He's running a country club."

He thought a long time and said, "Telling me this doesn't change anything. What do you want? Why are you helping me?"

I hadn't wanted anything when I came in. I was trying to do the right thing. Maybe the lessons were getting through, but his question awakened a thought. "How about this," I said. "I help you prove that you're getting screwed by Nathan Farnsworth and you keep Blake off my back."

Wendell looked disappointed. He must have thought I was looking for a way out of math class or something. He couldn't have known the truth. At least I hoped he wouldn't let Blake victimize his relearners.

"Blake knew I was having trouble with the program. He came and took me to see the cat baggers."

Wendell tried to interrupt, but I just kept talking.

"He told me about the cats, the drugs, the weird surgery. I haven't been able to sleep since. When I heard bones crashing into the ground and the horrible pained screams coming from the rear windows, Blake had me where he wanted me."

Wendell assured me that such a place didn't exist.

"I was there. I saw it. And I saw something else, something mushroom-like that should have stayed in Blake's pants."

Wendell bolted upright. He leaned over his desk, measuring me as if I were making up a story to escape my work, but he seemed to know I was telling the truth. I felt like he could read my mind when he wanted to. It was usually disturbing, but in this case I was glad to have him on my side.

He went to the monitor and I saw my silhouette appear in something like an X-ray. Then he pressed a button and the glass wall retracted into the floor. I waited for an invitation to move closer, but it didn't come.

Sirens sounded at the front gate and Wendell flew into a panic.

What could he be doing here that was illegal?

He pointed at me and said, "Downstairs. To the dining room. Now!"

I left the way I had come. Soon after, I heard him running downstairs for the front door. When it opened a group of heavy feet tramped in. Four men came my way. The man in the lead held a notebook sized screen. He followed it until he was looking directly at me where I stood against the wall by the cabinet.

Things might have been easier to explain if I had just taken a seat at the table, but I didn't know the police were interested in me.

I heard a conversation in the hallway.

"You know you need to register any relearner coming onto your property. How many assassination attempts have you survived?"

"I forgot to send notification. I'm sorry," Wendell said.

"That's crap and you know it. Your dogs are passed out against the back wall. We found three empty hot dog packages thrown into your neighbor's yard."

"I'm sure the dogs are fine."

"The law is the law, Mr. Cummings."

Wendell came into the room, bowed his head, and the cops cuffed me.

CHAPTER FORTY-SIX

How was I to know it was illegal for me to go to Wendell's house? Yes, I'd broken in. And yes, when I was led out in cuffs I understood why Wendell was so upset about the dogs and that I climbed through the dining room window. But would he have let me in if I had walked up to the front gate and buzzed? I don't think so.

It would have been easier standing outside the gate wondering what to do next than riding in the back of the police car to drive-through court. I'd been tried and convicted there twice in less time than they could have scheduled a pre-trial hearing in the old days. The cops always had the evidence they needed by the time they drove me there. Every case was rock solid. The efficiency was startling. I thought about that for a long time. Sure, they could track me everywhere I went, but the real difference was the lack of theatrics for the jury. Even more than that, the judges only cared whether you were guilty or not. There wasn't a lot of wrangling about admissibility of evidence. When they were trying to put me away for stealing the DA's Mercedes, the lawyers were constantly wrangling over technicalities. The word admissibility hadn't been uttered in the next two trials. The facts were the facts and the judge knew whether I was guilty or not. They didn't spend a lot of time convincing him. The judge knew I was guilty of robbing the DA, too, but back then it took nine months to do anything about it.

We arrived in the building and were stationed in the hallway outside the courtroom for about ten minutes before Wendell escorted me in. I wasn't surprised by the speed of my trials anymore.

The prosecutor presented the case in less than ten minutes. He showed the judge where I had been that day. How I'd climbed the wall and entered through Wendell's dining room window. They even showed pictures of the dogs sleeping off the drugs. There was no time to establish what I'd given them, but they guessed exactly where I'd gotten the pills. The guys at the basketball game were going to have a nasty surprise in the next day or so. I hoped they wouldn't connect it to me.

I just didn't understand the new world I was living in. I was stumbling around in the dark and stepping on everyone around me. Joel, Stephan, the drug dealer, and especially Wendell. If I didn't figure out how to stay out of trouble and how get through the program soon, I wouldn't last.

The judge asked for our defense. Wendell stood up and said that I had come to him with some important information. Or at least I believed it was important enough to rush inside without permission. The judge asked for this information and Wendell approached the bench and whispered it to him.

The judge chuckled in my direction, and I knew even before Wendell sat back down I was going to be found guilty again. I raised my hand and asked permission to speak. The judge allowed my request, but glared at me skeptically. Wendell could barely contain himself in the seat next to me, but I stood up anyway.

"Someone tried to kill me this morning, Your Honor."

He motioned me to proceed.

"I assumed it was related to the information I collected the day before. I didn't think it appropriate to bring to the police. Not knowing who else to ask for help, I went to Mr. Cummings' home."

"How exactly were you assaulted, Mr. O'Connor?"

"I was walking in front of the donut shop about two blocks from my apartment. A car stopped, a large black sedan, and someone from the passenger seat fired a shotgun at me."

The prosecutor started clicking away at his computer. I started to speak, but the judge held up his hand to silence me. We waited for the prosecutor to project a short video on the screen. The camera was inside the shop, but it caught me in blurry form, walking down the sidewalk, then ducking for cover behind the blue car.

"That's me," I said. "By the tire."

Somehow the prosecutor projected a red dot on the image. It fell right on top of me. I can only assume it was a signal from my tracking device caught at the instant of the gunshot.

"Did you question Mr. O'Connor about this incident?"

The prosecutor conferred with the lead officer who'd taken me from the house. It seemed the new court system left no time for stories to be fabricated on either side. The officer admitted he had not and the judge was not pleased.

"Our technology does not excuse shoddy police work," he boomed.

The prosecutor and the officer seemed surprised. I guessed they hadn't lost a case against a relearner in a long time. Armed with indisputable facts, why would they? What I didn't know was that this was a court for relearners only. Citizens who had never been convicted of a crime entered the old system of juries and admissibility and free passes. When the officers came here they expected to win, just like they expected to be whamboozled when they stepped in front of a jury.

The judge called Wendell up front and the two whispered. The rest of the room fell silent and I heard bits and pieces of the conversation. "You've done great things... This one isn't going to make it... You're on the edge. I'd hate to see that happen to you."

They got quieter, but I knew what was going on. The judge was offering Wendell a chance to dump me, to send me to the cat baggers where I couldn't give him any more trouble. It was the easiest path for Wendell. One of his biggest problems could be solved with a few short clicks. I thought I heard Wendell say he didn't mind that I'd come to his house, but it was so soft I couldn't be sure what they were saying.

He came back to the table.

The judge pronounced me innocent of the charges.

The prosecutor was in shock, ditto the officer behind him. They shot me dirty looks as the prosecutor went up front, clicked the screen a few times and pressed his thumb to the scanner. I didn't know what the thumb print was doing. Maybe it was charging him for the court time because he lost. Whatever the penalty was, he blamed me for forcing it on him. I was collecting enemies every day. If I was looking for an ally, I wouldn't find one there in the courtroom.

Wendell and I filed out solemnly, but when we reached the conference room, he shook my hand vigorously. He told me he was glad to finally win a case. It was like a great weight was lifted. Like he was about to be closed down and those few words from me had kept him in business.

He sat across from me and said nothing for several moments. He was probably thinking about how lucky he was. If his funding were cut off maybe he'd lose that huge house. Maybe he'd be vulnerable to all the relearners he'd tormented over the years. He nodded as if he were talking to himself and then he said, "I can help you with Blake."

He didn't say he knew what Blake was doing, didn't even say he believed me, but my spirit lifted. Until I got my delivery the next morning, I didn't know how generous Wendell's offer was.

I was surprised at what happened next. The whole time I'd been telling him about how he was being cheated, he shrugged it off. I didn't even think he was listening, but there in the conference room, he turned angry. For once he wasn't angry at me. He said he wanted my help. If I could collect convincing proof that Nathan was gaming the system, he'd make sure I never had to see Blake again. He promised I'd get all the help I needed to pass the program.

I agreed without considering what I'd have to do. It was the most hope I'd had since waking up with the oxygen mask over my face.

CHAPTER FORTY-SEVEN

I barely slept that night. Never did I sleep well in that apartment. Maybe it was because I was being watched. Or maybe it was something they were doing to keep me awake. After hearing about the cat baggers and the drugs in the drinking water, I didn't trust anything in my apartment. They always knew where I was. They could tamper with my soda or my food whenever I was a few blocks away. The longer I lived there, the more paranoid I became.

I thought a lot about helping Wendell and how great it would be if I never saw Blake again. My first plan was to gather the names and criminal histories of the men in both complexes, but that wouldn't work. Nathan Farnsworth would explain away the differences by saying his program was better. I didn't want to cause any more trouble for Wendell, so I decided I had to figure out who was cherry picking the easy cases for Farnsworth and directing the tough cases to Wendell. I had to prove that person was cheating the system. First I had to find him.

Doing that was going to take time. I decided to head to the donut shop, have some breakfast, and think about the best way to get started, but when I opened the door to my apartment, Wendell was standing there with an armload of books. He hadn't knocked, but he knew I was coming.

He invited himself in and placed all of the books but one on the coffee table. He told me that when I started the program again, I was to go to the English section. It would ask me to start reading, *The Adventures of Tom Sawyer*, which he handed me. Then he did a surprising thing. He picked up the gray pads and tucked them beside the television. Next he unplugged the wrist strap, wound the cord around his hand, and stuffed it next to the pads.

"You won't need those anymore," he said, but he cautioned me to read the book carefully, then read it again before answering the questions on the black box. "If you don't understand a word, look it up."

I told him I would.

"You'll need this." He showed me what looked like a pen with two buttons, one red and one black. He pressed the red button and pointed the pen at my face. I winced, but nothing happened. When he held the black button, my face appeared on the television, looking awkward and nervous. The pen held hours of video, adding to what was recorded each time the red button was pressed. There was no way to delete what was captured.

He shook my hand, thanked me for my help, and left.

There were five other novels on the coffee table and an unabridged dictionary. I was glad to have the wrist strap and the gray pads gone. I didn't know how Wendell removed the punishments from my lessons and I didn't really care. I could never have finished if I had to do push-ups every time I made a mistake. Actually, as you are listening to me here in this hall, you're hearing the improvement Wendell helped me make by giving me those books and forcing me to read them over and over. My vocabulary blossomed and as I talked with educated people like Nick and Charlotte, I understood more of what they said and even what they only implied. If Wendell had brought me before you when I first awoke, I'm afraid this entire speech would have sounded like it came from a fifth grader, which, I guess, is what I was—a fifth grader with highly-developed vocational skills.

With Wendell gone, I walked downstairs without the book for fear of losing it on the street. I walked the sidewalks on alert, watching everyone who approached and every car that drove by. None appeared threatening. I wished I knew who had attacked me the day before. My two candidates were Nick and Nathan Farnsworth. No one else wanted to kill me, except maybe Wendell.

Nathan had the most to lose. His program could fall apart if the relearners knew it was full of subliminal messages. He had big money on the line and he'd already proven he couldn't be trusted. I had to go back there and I'd have to be careful to stay clear of the cameras when I did. When I returned to see Stephan, no one in that control room could know I was there. That was going to be a challenge since I couldn't find the cameras in my own apartment.

The other possible assailant was Nick, but I ruled him out right away. He had threatened me, but that was just a bunch of hot air. He wanted his kid and I couldn't blame him for that. He couldn't afford to have me shot and besides, he was all about law and order. That's why he hated me so much. A guy like Nick can't pick up a shotgun and start blowing out display windows. Nathan was my guy, but for the next few days, I'd stay away from both of them.

I reached the donut shop alive, had my coffee and Boston Kreme, and thought about how I could use the pen to help Wendell. I'd never tried to catch a criminal before and it took some time to get my head around the idea. The closest I'd come was sending junkies into neighborhoods I'd been hitting hard. That had worked for me in the old days, but this was different. I couldn't walk away and let the cops do everything. I had to see where the case went every step of the way. The guy I really needed to catch worked inside the system. Busting a criminal in the act was just my way in.

I left the donut shop, thinking about who I could go after. One name came to mind: Cortez. I owed him after what he did to me. He was the one guy I could feel good about putting away.

As I stepped outside, I noticed the neon blue sedan parked in front of the display window. The window had been replaced and the area was so clean you couldn't tell I had almost been killed there a day before. The sedan didn't show a single scratch from the pellets I heard hit the fender. I should have suspected something then. I hadn't checked the license plate while I was running for my life, but I knew it was the same car. It should have had a bunch of dents and scratches, but it didn't.

CHAPTER FORTY-EIGHT

I went back to my apartment because I didn't know where to start my investigation and I didn't feel safe hanging around on the street while I decided what to do. I knew how to get into almost any home, what to take, and how to sell it. Catching criminals was a whole different mindset, and ideas didn't come easy. I sat on the couch and thought about Cortez. He probably still worked nights at the hospital and I could pick him up there and follow him home. This time of day he was probably home sleeping. I didn't know where he lived. I didn't even know his real name.

Maybe I was stalling because I didn't now where to start, but I picked up the book Wendell had given me and set to reading. It was rough at first. I didn't understand what I read, so it was a chore that moved at a dreadfully slow pace. There were ten or twenty words on every page that I didn't recognize and I fumbled in the dictionary to find them. Even the definitions used words I didn't know, so I ended up looking up words to understand the words I'd looked up, to understand a book full of gibberish that hadn't been used in a very long time. It was frustrating, but it was easier than push-ups and impossible math problems.

A few times I set the book down and thought about giving it up for the day, but there wasn't much else to do in the apartment except bounce the tennis ball against the brick wall. That accomplished nothing. When I thought of quitting, I remembered the night Blake took me for a ride. The memory of bone and flesh meeting concrete and the screams echoing out into the trees was enough motivation for me to find a way to understand the story.

I never thought I'd take reading so seriously, but I opened the notebook I bought to beat Blake's insane math problems and I wrote, *Tom Sawyer*, at the top. From then on, every time something important happened or a new person joined the story, I wrote it down. The notes were a shortcut to what was happening. I couldn't find anything in the pages of the book, but if I needed to know something, it was probably in my notes.

The craziest thing I did helped the most. After I finished a chapter, looked up the words I didn't know, and took notes, I went back and read the whole chapter again. To my surprise, it got more interesting. When I read the chapter a third time, I understood what was going on and even how the characters felt about what was happening to them.

Hours passed. About the time my eyes started to hurt I realized Wendell was telling me something by giving me this particular book. Tom was clever to get other people to do his work, but tricking others and shirking his responsibilities was wrong. Wendell saw a lot of Tom Sawyer in me. I should have finished school. I should have gotten a job. I should not have taken things from other people. Wendell was telling me to change in every way possible. I was already working at it, but I'm not sure that was enough for him.

I was really hungry that afternoon, but I kept on reading. Every time Tom took advantage of someone or told a lie, I felt guilty. I didn't know how Wendell did it. I hadn't eaten anything from the apartment in a long time and I hadn't turned on the television, so it wasn't drugs or subliminal messages. Wendell couldn't be manipulating my feelings except through the words on the page. Was that possible? However he did it, I was changing. Maybe it had been happening for weeks and I was just realizing it then. Or maybe this was how everyone felt when they read this book. For me it was a new experience.

It was well past two o'clock when I put the book down and went into the kitchen. I was still wary about eating anything from my apartment, but I wasn't afraid of Wendell. He didn't need to pick out that book for me. He could have poisoned and tortured me if he wanted to. Wendell was a dogooder. If I had any doubt, it vanished when I saw the sleek black computer on the kitchen table. A note said the computer was to help complete my errand.

I microwaved a frozen pizza without a second thought to what might have been surreptitiously injected into the package. (That was one of the words I looked up from another book.) I washed it down with a Coke and turned on the computer. I'd used computers in the library to check baseball scores, watch videos, and search for music. I'd never had one of my own before and couldn't help checking it out. I ate most of the pizza while I checked the weather and how the Sox were doing.

I don't know where the idea came from, but I realized the computer might be able to help me find Cortez. I typed his name into Google, but all I got was a bunch of stuff about some guy who invaded South America a thousand years ago. For the next twenty minutes I mostly stared at the computer and sipped Coke. I found some interesting stories, but none of them were any help.

Finally, I read a newspaper report about a guy who got shot outside a bar downtown. They mentioned a few people connected to the case and I knew what I needed to do. I searched for my name and stories about my arrest and trial five years earlier. I spent a long time reading articles that made me sound evil. Someone who used computers every day might have found it in five minutes, but half an hour later, I followed the links about my trial to Cortez's real name: Carlos Mendoza.

When I typed his real name into the computer, it listed addresses all around Boston. I narrowed it down to West Roxbury and Hyde Park, and in another ten minutes I had an address that was close to the hospital. I wasn't sure if this was what Wendell expected me to do with the computer, but I had my first target and I was ready to step onto the other side of the law.

CHAPTER FORTY-NINE

As excited as I was to get started, I forced myself to go to bed early so I'd be alert at four o'clock the next morning. The donut shop wasn't even open when I hopped a cab for the hospital. What I had planned wasn't illegal, but if Cortez saw me following him he'd know what was up. We both know he ratted me out. My following him could only mean I'd come to get even. So I hunkered down in the dark at the edge of the parking lot where I could see everyone coming and going from the hospital. I sat there for two hours and the only movement was the sunrise and an ambulance that pulled in at six o'clock. It wasn't until almost seven that cars started pulling into the employee lot.

Fifteen minutes later, people dressed in scrubs, some blue, some white, some with little patterns on them, all marched out toward their cars like zombies headed back to their tombs for a day of rest. One lady headed for a Volvo two cars down from me. I pushed back onto the grass and opened *The Adventures of Tom Sawyer*. I wasn't sure why I'd brought it along, but it convinced her I wasn't there to cause trouble. Strange as it was for someone to be up this early, reading on the little strip of grass at the edge of the parking lot, she backed out without revealing my hiding place.

Two minutes later Cortez drove by in a Toyota and I recorded the license number in my notebook. I didn't run for a cab. I knew where he was going, at least I thought I did. I let him get out of sight then took a cab to the address I'd found online. It only took a few minutes to find the Toyota with the plate number I had written down.

I didn't have the fancy gadgets Wendell used to spy on me. All I had was my notebook and the slender camera. It was enough, but what I didn't think through was that after working all night, Cortez would be tired. Neighbors started coming out of their houses. Parents drove off to work. School kids stood on the sidewalk and waited for the school bus. People walked their dogs. I was in the middle of it all trying to blend in.

After about an hour, Cortez's wife came out with a little girl in blue farmer jeans and a white shirt. She got on the last school bus that went by. The poor kid had to lean forward as she walked to balance the heavy backpack. The woman was young with black hair. She was dressed up in pants, like she worked in an office where she didn't want to hear comments about her legs. She went inside for a few minutes after the bus left, then pulled an old Honda out of the driveway and drove off. I assumed she went to work. And when she didn't come back for the next several hours, I guessed I was right.

That left me on a bench a block and a half from the Mendoza's house. When Cortez didn't come out in the first hour, I realized he was probably sleeping. Women kept coming out to walk their dogs and my only disguise was my book. I read and they left me alone.

I was on that bench all morning. I hadn't brought anything to eat and by lunchtime I was starving. My throbbing bladder forced me to sit still. I was dying for a Coke to keep my eyelids from drooping, but that would have forced me to go looking for a bathroom. I kept nodding off in spite of the pain and finally had to stop reading. I held the book open and pretended to read while I looked over the top of the pages at Cortez's house. A dozen times I wondered what I was doing there. I needed to go, but I couldn't leave. I kept hoping he'd come out to meet someone and then I'd have him, but I knew it was a fantasy.

Cortez sold credit card numbers in the old days. He did it on his computer and on the phone. Sitting outside I'd never see him sell anything. And to make things worse, credit cards didn't exist anymore. Everything was done through the bank and I wasn't smart enough to catch him cheating the bank. Even if I knew what he was doing, I was helpless sitting outside his house. He was sleeping in there and I was wasting my time. I didn't know anything about catching criminals. What I did know was that Cortez got me into this mess. If he hadn't ratted me out, I wouldn't have the ankle bracelet, the black box, and the little camera in my pocket. Best of all, I would never have met Wendell Cummings and Dr. Blake.

For a moment I thought about crashing through the door and bashing Cortez's head in. That's what he deserved. That's what the guys back in the old neighborhood would have done. But it wasn't the old neighborhood. Every step I took was tracked by the cops. If something happened to Cortez while I was within three blocks, I'd be blamed. I needed to stay outside and stay out of trouble.

When I couldn't wait anymore, I walked down to the corner and bought a sandwich and a soda from a convenience store. What I needed above all was the bathroom, but I really enjoyed the roast beef and American cheese at the small table in the corner.

Cortez walked past the window. He didn't look inside the dark store, but I saw him clearly through the glass. He looked better than he had in the diner. He'd been shifty-eyed back then. Maybe that was just him working. Breaking the law, knowing he could be caught at any time must have made him nervous. He looked completely at ease, but I was pretty sure his wife hadn't stopped buying things and making him crazy. Cortez was cutting corners somewhere. If I could catch him, I could put things right for Wendell and for myself.

He went into the barber shop but didn't get a haircut. He talked to the barbers and the customers for half an hour instead. From there he walked to a little outdoor produce stand and talked with the owner for twenty minutes. For the next two hours, I followed, Cortez talked, and I realized I would have been better off at home reading my book.

When the little girl in farmer jeans stepped off the bus, I walked over a few blocks and hailed a cab home.

CHAPTER FIFTY

My first day as a crime fighter would have been a total ruin if not for what happened next. I was exhausted after getting up at four o'clock. I barely dragged myself out of the cab and down the walkway to the long brick building. Even tired as I was, I stayed alert for anyone moving nearby. It wasn't long ago that someone tried to take me out with that shotgun, and I hadn't done anything to smooth things over with Nick or Nathan Farnsworth. I had to be ready for another attempt. Getting a gun would have been like buying an express ticket to the cat baggers, so I was ultra alert whenever I walked in public, especially near the apartment.

That's when I saw the scraggly-haired guy lugging a box down the concrete path parallel to the one I followed. If this was one of Wendell's videos, I would have trotted over to help him no matter how tired I was. Maybe that was the right thing to do, but that wasn't why I offered to help.

It was the flat nose.

When he nodded my way, I remembered that white ball whizzing along the top of the grass only to pop up and hit the strike zone. The man moving into my building seemed to have control over the laws of physics. I started over to him to talk about his pitching, but by the time I reached him I realized he was a resident in Stephan's building and didn't belong here. If he was in trouble again, it should be costing Nathan Farnsworth not Wendell Cummings. Why was he moving in?

I wanted to grab the pen camera and get a shot of him, but I knew I could do better. I bided my time, lugging boxes up two flights of stairs until he was as tired as I was. He didn't have any food whatsoever at his place, so I invited him over for a Coke and whatever else we could find. It turned out to be microwaved pizza and Devil Dogs.

The food brought me back to life and having the flat-nosed pitcher there in my apartment gave me hope. When he turned to throw the plastic Devil Dog wrapper in the trash, I set the pen camera on the table, pressed the red button, and pointed it at him. I did it carefully even though he had his back turned in case one of my counselors was watching. They'd sell information to Nathan no matter who they hurt. Wendell was too focused on saving the disadvantaged to look out for himself and he was too naive to realize his own counselors were taking advantage of him. That made getting the evidence in my own apartment dangerous, but I had no choice.

"Think you could show me how to throw that riser?" I asked.

"Sure." To my dismay, he got up and stepped over toward the oven. He pretended to hold a ball and make a low arc with his arm, releasing down near the floor. The holes had to be down to make the ball rise and with practice you could make it rise and curve at the same time by tipping the ball to one side or the other when you released it. The camera caught none of it. Turning it would have been too obvious.

The pitching clinic took several minutes in front of the oven, which I had never used the whole time I'd lived here. I stopped asking about Wiffle ball and soon he sat down again. I'd really enjoyed my time over at Stephan's, and if things had worked out differently, I would have been back to play again. I would have enjoyed learning to throw that riser.

"Did you like living over there?" I asked skeptically.

He caught the implication in my voice and hesitated. He knew he shouldn't have been transferred. I could see the guilt in his face and Wendell would see it, too, when he played the recording.

"It was great," he said with finality in his voice.

"Why move here?" I asked as innocently as I could.

He shrugged and pushed back in his chair to get up and leave.

I ducked down close to the table and whispered, "It's not that bad here."

We both knew it was much better where they had Wiffle ball games and movies instead of a walled courtyard, impossible math problems, and electric shock therapy.

"You screwed up, didn't you? What'd you do?" I asked.

He didn't want to say, but I prodded him a few times and he finally opened up to me and the camera. "I lifted a fifth of Johnnie Walker."

I didn't get it at first. Everyone had enough cash to buy whatever they needed if they were careful. Johnnie Walker wasn't cheap, but it wouldn't break the bank. He told me he was in for DUI and couldn't buy booze. I remembered seeing him drink soda in the bar. The thumb scanners stopped him from buying alcohol anywhere just like Stephan.

"I made it three weeks, but I couldn't take it anymore."

I felt bad for him. He told me he'd been drinking when we played. He wasn't addicted, but it steadied him. He lied to me and himself. Neither of us believed it. He couldn't stop and his trouble with law enforcement wasn't over. That's why Farnsworth dumped him.

I whispered again. "Aren't you supposed to go back to the program you came from if you get into trouble?"

He leaned close and said, "Not me."

I didn't understand what he meant.

"They weren't going to take me back. They said I could come here or I could go to the cat baggers. At least here I've got a chance. If I stay clean I'll get out in a month or two."

"They can't do that, can they?"

He looked nervous. He whispered so the ankle bracelets under the table couldn't pick up his voice, but the recorder was right in front of him. He told me they had erased his record. It was like he'd never been there. Like he never screwed up. It worked for him. It worked for Nathan Farnsworth. The only guy getting shafted was Wendell Cummings.

He left me with a recording that should have secured my freedom.

CHAPTER FIFTY-ONE

I was pulled in two different directions. I wanted to get the pen camera to Wendell as fast as I could, but I knew someone was always watching and if that someone was working for Nathan Farnsworth, he could already be plotting ways to get the camera away from me. It was getting late. After the attack outside the donut shop, I felt safest behind the brick walls, especially at night, but there in my apartment I had no place to run if they came for me. They could find me anywhere, thanks to the tracking devices, but if I hid the pen somewhere outside where they didn't have cameras, it would be safe until I got it to Wendell.

I had my hand on the doorknob, but detoured back to the phone. Wendell had given me his card after I was caught breaking into his house. He'd want to know what I'd found no matter how late it was. I called his house. The phone rang ten times. No answering machine picked up. I imagined the weak electronic buzz in that sprawling place of his. I imagined the dogs perking up to alert him to the call. I imagined the fat lady struggling to get up from a low recliner. But no one answered. After fifteen rings I hung up.

A glimmer of hope hit me on the stairs. Maybe Wendell was in the control room and that was why he didn't answer. Maybe he was holding out hope that I'd save him so he was staying nearby to help. The butter knife in my pocket argued otherwise. If I believed I'd find Wendell in the control room, I'd have no need to jimmy the lock. I rumbled down the stairs. My hope dimmed the closer I got to the bottom, as if my mood were tied to my elevation. When I reached the ground floor, I decided I couldn't go to the control room with the pen camera. I had to hide it first in case Morris Farnsworth or Dr. Blake was in there. I really had no idea who else might be working in that control room, but if the person inside could lead me to Wendell, I could stop hiding.

I went the long way around the building, following the sidewalk to the corner opposite the control room, and then around back to the parking lot. Most of the cars here never moved and any one of them would make a good hiding place for my pen. I chose one with tires so deflated the rims rested on asphalt. I remembered the big display in court that showed exactly where I went and when I stopped somewhere. I didn't linger around the car. I chose my path to look like I was crossing through the parking lot to get a view to the control room door. When I got near the car, I sped up. I only hesitated by the back tire long enough to balance the pen on top of the worn rubber treads, and then I sped my pace again. To the computer it would look like I kept a steady pace across the parking lot to the clump of trees I used to spy on the control room.

I waited there long enough to make it convincing to those watching me, but it was hard to stay still. Behind that door I'd find a man eager to save me or any number of men eager to silence me to save themselves. I was strangely drawn to that room despite the danger. Could Wendell really be there at this time of night? He should be out to dinner with his wife or home watching television. Still, as soon as I'd been in place for ten full minutes, I crossed the parking lot with a stealthy walk that was more show for the cameras than anything else.

There wasn't a single window into the room. No way to tell if there were twenty men inside with machine guns, or if Wendell was there waiting to help me, or if this was some urban paradise built to reward those who sought it out.

I banged the door with my fist. Banging alone wasn't a problem. Seeking Wendell out, reaching out for help was a good thing. It was what I did next that caused me big trouble.

No one answered the door. Nothing moved inside no matter how loud I pounded. I swiveled around, looking for anyone who'd seen me knocking. I knew what was going to happen next. It was automatic. I didn't even think about it. I should have. I needed help, but I needed to know what was behind that door even more.

The butter knife slid from my pocket and was between the door and the jamb instinctively. The lock worked open in seconds. It was too easy. I should have known it was a test, but I was only thinking about busting Nathan Farnsworth and getting out of this program. I knew when no one responded to my pounding that Wendell wasn't inside. If someone was there, they would have at least come and shooed me away.

I stepped inside and closed the door behind me.

I called, "Hello," as if the door had accidentally been left open and I'd stepped inside to make sure everyone was ok. Of course it wasn't true. Coming in here with my ankle bracelet on was dangerous. Someone somewhere would know what I was doing was wrong. I'd tell them I was looking for Wendell. It had worked for me in court last time, but that ploy wouldn't work twice. I knew bullshit and excuses didn't play in the criminal justice system anymore, but I couldn't admit it to myself.

The lights came on when I stepped forward. It wasn't a new trick. I'd seen motion sensitive lights before. The work area was tiled with monitors set into a wall in columns of three, six across. The countertop housed banks of pushbuttons that corresponded to the monitors, but they weren't labeled to show what they did. There were three keyboards on the desktop, too, but I ignored them to focus on the single chair and the myriad buttons. Someone sat at this desk and rolled back and forth on the tiled floor, watching what happened on the monitors.

I sat on the swivel chair and thought for a moment as if I worked there. I reached up and pushed a button trimmed with red at its base. Nothing happened. I pushed the button to its right and the monitor on the top row came to life. It showed an empty apartment much like mine, but it wasn't mine because this one had a solid brown couch. Mine had a faint pattern to it. I tried the button beneath and to the left and the camera moved left. Then

I started pressing all sorts of buttons. The camera moved right, up, down, then zoomed in. Then the picture changed altogether and I realized I was looking at the same living room but from a different angle. If the layout was exactly like mine, this camera was hidden somewhere in the window trim. I played with buttons all over. I saw guys sleeping. I saw one guy get mad at whatever he'd made on the stove and sling a pot against the wall. Sticky white goo sloshed all over his rug. I enjoyed myself until I realized that someone could come in and catch me any second. By then I understood how the buttons were arranged. I clicked off the three monitors I had been watching and stood up.

Even alone in the room I felt like I'd been caught. I didn't remember really wanting to get in here. Yes, I was curious about what went on here and finding Wendell was a good reason to come down, but I felt like I'd been tricked into sneaking inside. I didn't believe they could manipulate my thoughts and make me do things against my will. But at that moment part of me wanted to run out the door and back to my room. I knew I was being watched. I knew it was a trap, that there was a more sophisticated room built to watch this one. Part of me was too curious to turn for the door and go. I'd come this far. The damage was done.

The walls were blank, cement block painted a light creamy yellow. The ceiling was stark white plaster, swirled, but in patterns too fine to hide a camera. If there was a camera watching me, it was hidden in the panels that housed the monitors. There were two many crevices for me to check. It didn't matter. Just stepping inside this room was damning enough. I hadn't meant any trouble. Anyone watching the video would know that, but intentions didn't seem to matter to the judges. My fate was predetermined, I was only acting out Wendell's script.

I explored the far end of the room, expecting to find a way to get behind the monitors to see the tangle of wires that connected everything together. What I found was a hallway, *this hallway I'm standing in now*, hidden by the angle of the rear wall and the monitors. The long hall ended in cement blocks. There were two doors, one on either side. On my left was a large glass window. I stepped up, but stopped short of a dark line in the floor. It was a plate glass wall, like the one Wendell had used to trap me in his home office.

There was another thick black line beyond the window. Common sense was telling me I was walking into one of those animal-friendly traps, only I was the animal. I told myself I was alone, that no one was standing ready to spring the trap. Still, I expected it to close on me as soon as I crossed that first black line. It didn't. I cupped my hands against the window, but couldn't see anything beyond.

I shifted along tentatively, mindful that any step could send the plate glass partitions jutting up to the ceiling to lock me in. The door was ten feet away and I couldn't resist it. I hopped over the black line. As I did I imagined it flashing upward to cut me in half from below, like a dull, upside down guillotine.

I stepped safely to the door, opened it, and did a double take.

Inside were two rows of chairs facing the window. I leaned far enough inside to see that anyone inside could clearly see the hall even though from the outside I could see nothing of the room.

There were six chairs in the front row, seven in the back. Twelve jurors and one alternate. I dodged back into the hall. The two partitions would force anyone caught between them to stay in view of the window.

You know that of course because I'm trapped between the partitions now. The doors beyond the partitions are for you, so you can come and go without worry about what I might do once you've judged me. And of course the glass walls keep me right in front of you where you can see me, but I can't see how you are reacting to my story.

That first time I stood here I realized the program that had me trapped was merely an accessory. What you decide is all important.

CHAPTER FIFTY-TWO

I rushed out the door to the broken down car and felt the bald tire for the pen-shaped camera. My fingers found only the crown of rough tread. I got down on my knees and stuck my head underneath the bumper, thinking the camera had fallen behind the tire. The streetlights didn't reach back there, so I leaned in and swept the rough pavement. It wasn't there. Flat on my stomach, I felt the axle, the shocks, and even inside the rim. Someone had taken the camera and disappeared in the fifteen minutes I'd been inside the control room. I came away with greasy hands, a dirty shirt, and no record of my conversation with the Wiffle ball pitcher.

I ran all the way around front and up the stairs to my apartment. I shut the door and wedged a chair under the knob so no one could get in without me knowing.

On the couch I tried to separate the charade from reality. I knew I was being watched. My every movement was being tracked and there was nothing I could do about that. But why? If they wanted to ship me to the cat baggers, why hadn't they? I didn't even know who's decision that was. The judge they kept bringing me to? Wendell? Or was it someone else entirely? I couldn't be sure if I was swimming circles around a fishbowl waiting to be flushed, or if Wendell was really watching me, even counting on my help.

I wanted to believe Wendell needed me. I collapsed on my bed, thinking about the battle between Wendell and Nathan Farnsworth. There was only so much money coming from the government and they both wanted it. Nathan was stealing it even if they didn't call it that. I felt good about helping Wendell, but I still couldn't sleep. Instead I spent hours picturing every face I'd seen since coming here. Everyone I'd spoken with. With every recollection I wondered if our meeting was an accident or if it was staged to teach me something.

Sleep finally did come. I only know that because I woke to pounding on the door. I could barely open my eyes and shuffle to the door. Pulling the chair away made a ruckus, and when I opened the door Charlotte stood there with a puzzled look on her face. After losing the camera the night before I saw beyond her gorgeous face and wondered if she was here to occupy me so something could happen while I was gone. She never told me where we were going and I got the feeling her unannounced visits had more to do with Wendell's agenda than helping me. Living through it like I was, I couldn't connect the dots and figure out where she was steering me, but at least for the first time, I was looking ahead and trying to catch up to the other actors in this play. If I couldn't see the puppet master, at least I was looking for the strings.

Charlotte waited while I showered and dressed. She was standing when I left the room and when I returned. I assumed her choice to stand was more a revulsion for my furniture than something stealthy she was trying to do while I was in the shower. My furniture was new enough, but I think she felt everything about me was dirty. Whenever I was around she got antsy. I felt stupid for ever being attracted to her.

I looked out the window while she drove, not at the scenery, I just wanted to be turned as far away from her as possible. I wondered where she was taking me, but I wondered more what was happening back in my apartment.

We arrived at a small house similar to Nick and Kathleen's. It was on a side street of connecting chain-link fences, tiny green lawns, and curtains pulled open enough to see what the neighbors were doing.

Charlotte led the way to the door and I followed like an obedient puppy, turning my head to everything that caught my attention. When the door opened, I couldn't believe who I saw.

"Who's that, Dad?" a little voice asked from behind him.

187

Double barely filled the doorway. He'd lost sixty pounds.

He flashed a knowing look to Charlotte. He expected us. What was she trying to do by bringing me here? Was Double supposed to be my role model? It was early for that. I was a long way from finishing my studies. I'd been carrying that book everywhere, and I'd read most of it, but it would be years before I was done with my work. The dating counselor hadn't even called yet. The life Double was leading here was way out of reach.

The door thumped closed and I saw Tannia breeze in from the back of the house. I was drawn away from the elegant lines of her face and the contrast between her slim figure and Double's bulk by a little hand tugging at the seam of my jeans.

"I'm Manny," the little boy said.

I bent lower and introduced myself. His smile was unstoppable. Embarrassed, I righted myself and scanned the adult faces in the room. Double, Tannia, Charlotte, they all watched me greet Manny. Self-consciousness gripped me and my limbs felt stiff as I imagined this too was some test designed to measure my ability to have children of my own.

No words were spoken, but Charlotte and Tannia slipped away into the kitchen. Double didn't turn to watch them go. He was focused on me. The surprise was coming as he stepped forward. I wanted him to just blurt it out, to tell me what Charlotte was pressing him to say, maybe even paying him to say, but he looked as uncomfortable as I felt.

He motioned me to sit. I took the corner of the couch and he faced me from a faux leather recliner from someone's garage sale. He told me what a great thing he had with Tannia and little Manny. I couldn't help but smile thinking about the boy's little white sneakers and the innocent way he looked up to me, like I was just as important as anyone. Charlotte didn't look at me that way. Neither did Tannia and pretty soon Double wouldn't either.

He showed me his ankle and rubbed the base of his skull where the tracking device had been implanted and later removed. He told me how hard it was for little Manny and that if he were still a relearner how much harder it would be. I saw it coming then, but I couldn't stop it. I didn't even try. He told me I should give Jonathan up. Maybe he was right. Maybe I should have. But I didn't see the lesson in giving up my responsibilities or my rights. The more Charlotte pushed me, the more I wanted to hold onto little Jonathan with all I had.

I told Double to stay out of it. He'd done his job and I wasn't going to hear it anymore. He looked frightened. For himself or me I couldn't be sure. I believed he'd been threatened. Maybe he was one of Wendell's graduates. Maybe Wendell still owned him. Double didn't know what to say after that. We both knew my ankle bracelet recorded everything. I did have one question I needed answered.

"What happened to Crusher?"

"Same as us," he said pointing to my ankle. "Same as everyone."

There was a long silence then, like I was laid out on the couch for viewing and Double didn't know what to say now that I was dead. So much of what I wanted to say to him would cause one of us trouble. I kept my mouth shut and waited. I knew Charlotte would get tired of waiting and come to take me home.

Double offered me a drink. I asked for a Coke and he went to get it. When he came back I couldn't believe what I was seeing. There beside him, was my mother in a cotton dress that draped from her shoulders, bulged at her watermelon breasts, and spread even wider at a midsection that started at her thighs and defied any attempt to be stuffed into pants. She looked at me mockingly as if I was a big disappointment. The kid she'd threatened to kill at thirteen years old. The kid who had to run to the streets at fifteen because he was afraid to die at home. She looked at me as if I had failed to live up to her standard of apathetic underachievement.

She tilted side to side as she came over. The enormous weight on each trunk had to be balanced just so or she risked a catastrophic fall. She eyed the recliner where Double had been sitting, but her hips wouldn't fit between the armrests. She thumped on past the coffee table and settled onto the other half of the couch with a bounce that jostled me.

Emotions rampaged around in my head like little children set free in the midst of finger paints, amusement rides, and a truckload of candy. Ideas popped to life and like children without supervision, they whirled around with intense energy, but couldn't decide where to strike out first. Dangerous ideas yearned to be set free. I imagined screaming at her, pummeling her, choking her, shoving that same gun in her face and watching her turn pale with fear.

What held me back? Was it Wendell's lessons? Was it my fear of what Charlotte would do or that I'd be sent to the cat baggers if I fell out of line? Or was it because she was my mother and she still held some power over me, some control infused into my cells at birth? I didn't understand why, but I sat quietly while the angry thoughts rampaged.

She told me how much she missed me, but there wasn't an inkling of sadness in her eyes. She told me how long she'd looked for me, but I hadn't gone far. I'd never been more than ten miles from home for the last ten years. If she'd looked hard enough she would have found me. Truth was she kept on collecting like I was still at home and never went out of her way to bring me back. She didn't want the hassle. She wanted whatever she could get and that's why she was here in front of me now. Charlotte had offered her something. She looked me right in the eye without a hint of guilt for what she'd done.

She told me I should give the boy up. She hadn't even bothered to learn Jonathan's name. I wanted nothing more than to see she didn't get what Charlotte promised her.

"I'm going to take parenting advice from you? Charlotte should know whatever advice you give, I'm going to do the opposite."

CHAPTER FIFTY-THREE

Charlotte dropped me home at lunchtime, but I couldn't eat. The confrontation with my mother had been due for a long time. I was proud of myself for not screaming at her, but the little I'd said wasn't satisfying at all. She had driven me here. She'd pushed me out when I was too young to survive without turning to crime. She didn't apologize. She didn't even look guilty. Some family counselor Charlotte was. She never mentioned the gun. All she wanted was for me to sign those papers and give my son to a stranger.

For a long while I thought I was missing the lesson in all of this. I couldn't tell if I was succeeding by refusing to give up my son. Was taking responsibility keeping me safe from the cat baggers? Or would I be viewed more positively if I put the boy's interests first and gave him a father without a criminal past? I wanted to see him grow up. Right or wrong, I wanted to know him, to stay connected to him.

I picked up *Tom Sawyer* but saw only a jumble of disconnected words.

I kept wondering about Nathan Farnsworth and how he could be so sure the people he chose wouldn't get into trouble again. They looked different over there. There were no tattoos. Shorter hair. Neater clothes. Did those things really matter? Did choosing to be clean-cut really make a difference in life? I hoped not.

His relearners were wealthier. They were softer, but there was another thing Nathan used to pick the relearners he wanted. It was about history. He'd take someone if they were in for the first time. Otherwise he wouldn't be in business at all. But once they non-conformed, Nathan didn't want them anymore. He didn't want guys who'd been in and out of the system over and over. He wouldn't save them in court like Wendell would. Nathan Farnsworth didn't care about helping people. He'd set up his program to make money. His success came from selection.

It bothered me that Nathan didn't want me. I wondered if he was right. If I was hopeless. Was I destined to keep making the same mistakes over and over until they put me in the grave? Was I that broken? I wanted to change. I wondered if guys like Joel wanted to change as much as I did. Had we gotten such a bad start that we were beyond repair? Wendell was giving me his best. He paid for my apartment and all these people to track, watch, and in their own strange way, try to help me.

I stared at the southern boy on the cover of my book. Would Jonathan grow up to be like Tom? Would he take things from other people? That was my life. It was never really a choice for me. Maybe it was, but I'd made it too long ago to remember. No one had stood up and told me I was headed down the wrong path. They'd wrestled me and arrested me, but no one ever got through to me.

That was a job for parents. They had the first shot. The first chance to teach the right way to do things, to treat people. What could I offer Jonathan? Could I teach him what I didn't seem to know even now? Probably not. I still had to have something valuable to give him. I had enjoyed our time in the sand more than I thought possible. I still wanted to go back even with Nick guarding my every move. I wasn't fantasizing about getting back together with Kathleen anymore. That was impossible. But giving up on my son was giving up on myself.

I tried to read the book again and to listen to what Wendell was telling me. I was like Tom, a boy without guidance who learned to take what he needed. Was he telling me something about Jonathan? If there was something I needed to do, it wasn't clear. Nothing with Wendell was clear. I paced. I stood rigid at the window with my hands on the sill.

I was waiting for them to come for me, to finally realize I'd been in the control room and needed to be punished. But no one came that afternoon.

Charlotte didn't mention it. In fact, she'd said little at all. Dealing with me was distasteful for her. She wanted me to sign those papers so she could hand me off to Joanne. Thinking about Charlotte and my mother only made me angrier. I paced more. Finally I detoured to the kitchen for a change of scenery or maybe just a longer track. Then I saw it.

There on the kitchen table was a pen camera exactly like the one Wendell had given me. I rushed it to the television and played the contents, but there was nothing recorded inside. The original was gone. I didn't know if that interview had been erased or if someone had collected the camera and brought it to Wendell. What a hopelessly optimistic thought. When I really thought about it I knew Nathan Farnsworth had the camera. Somehow he could watch me in my apartment even though I wasn't in his program. I didn't know how he did it, but I knew it was him.

The blank camera was a new start, another chance. I'd be smarter this time. I'd get the evidence to Wendell even if I had to stand at his gate and scream for him to come out and get it. I was angry then, angrier than I'd been in a long time. I rededicated myself to proving Farnsworth wrong. I was going to come out of this. My success would reward Wendell for believing in me. It was small thanks, but it was all I could give. He needed all of his students to make it from now on, or he'd lose his business. I was risking my life, but from that moment on, I was taking control.

I'd spent so much time reading and pacing, it was too late for what I wanted to do next. So I sat down with my book and scoured for any clue Wendell meant for me.

CHAPTER FIFTY-FOUR

I'd never read so long in my life. All the ideas hit me like a sleeping pill and replaced my cat bagger nightmares with dreams of a backwoods southern boy. I slept soundly and woke energized. I felt accomplished for all I'd read and optimistic about my mission to relearner court. When I arrived and read the posted hours, I realized I could have come the night before, but that didn't bring me down. Non-conforming relearners streamed in ahead of me. A week earlier I would have felt bad for them, but that morning they were my opportunity to graduate back into the real world.

The visitor entrance was around back of the building by the parking lot. I guess they didn't expect relearners to be curious about this place when they weren't on trial, even though our apartments were clustered nearby. Honestly, I was only there because fighting crime was my way out.

The guard looked surprised to see me come in with an ankle bracelet but no escort. I placed my key, my book, and the pen camera in a plastic dish and it rode a conveyor through an X-ray machine. When the dish came out the other side, the guard kept my pen camera and waved me through the metal detector.

"Can't take this in there," he said. "I'll hold it for you."

I collected the book and the Budweiser key ring I'd swiped at a carnival. Most people carried car keys, house keys, post office box keys. They were a symbol of trust and power. My single apartment key identified my miniscule station in the world. I was glad when I turned the corner and found clusters of people talking. Counselors talked with troubled relearners heading in or out of hearings. Prosecutors and police officers whispered case details and prepared cases they were certain to win.

I followed the hall, uncertain where I was going, angling toward each little group I passed. Conversations stopped. Eyes glared. I moved on past the front entrance, around the hearing rooms until the hall dead ended. I hadn't really thought this through. I was looking for wrongdoing in a building with the word justice hanging above the front entrance. This would take more than a quick walk through the building.

Back at the front, I chose a bench that allowed a long view of the lobby where I could see relearners entering, meeting their counselors, and heading off to hearings. I picked up my book and opened it, but I focused my eyes well beyond the words to the knots of conversation spread in front of me. Several times I watched the police bring in a new offender, take off his cuffs, and hand him over to a counselor. It was odd to think relearners didn't need handcuffs, but they could never truly escape, not with tracking devices sewn into their heads. I wondered how many of them turned violent after losing their cases inside. These were the worst of the worst offenders, but things were different now. To law abiding citizens this system seemed like the proverbial slap on the wrist, but we knew different. Any relearner who lost control here earned a short drive to a locked room he could only leave by jumping.

That's why the relearners behaved. They were afraid.

I didn't have to ask myself *if* I was afraid, but *when* my fear began driving everything I did. I was afraid to go to prison the first time, before I was shot, before everything changed, but that was a different sort of fear. I wasn't afraid for my life, but the cuts and bruises I'd collect, not to mention the emotional scars from years of abuse. My new fears built slowly. I wasn't truly scared until the night in the car with Dr. Blake. I understood then how fragile my life was and how horrible it could be to wake up with my fingers sewn together or my eyes glued shut.

Wendell and Farnsworth had created the ideal system. On the outside it seemed almost childish in its kid-glove approach to reforming criminals—that's what we were, criminals not relearners. Those inside understood how insidious their captors could be. The two faces of the system protected it from righteous dogooders. They would never discover the truth. At least not in time to save me. Back in the old system I would have been short to the gate because I'd served most of my time while I was asleep. Instead of counting the days until I was free, I was stalking criminals, hoping to trap someone infinitely more powerful than me just to save my skin.

The man in the bloodied golf shirt snapped me from my self-pity. I'd seen him during a Wiffle ball game. His huge biceps and pecs made it hard for him to catch up with a fastball, but he was a master at hitting balls that darted and weaved toward the plate. When he walked through the lobby, he had a white bandage plastering his ear down to the side of his face. His shirt was torn open in three or four places and the white fabric was covered in blood. It looked like he'd been stabbed, but he walked steadily. It was someone else's blood. That's why he was surrounded by cops.

I got up and hurried to the corner so I could see where they took him.

As I got closer I saw that his jeans had been muddied and then rinsed. They stopped at the double doors. I thought they were going to take the cuffs off before bringing him inside, but they didn't. I'd never seen that before. He must have gone nuts and beaten someone to death. This guy was in serious trouble and I was positive Nathan Farnsworth would do his best to dump him off on Wendell.

I tried to be casual as I came down the hall, but there was no mistaking where I was headed. I paused outside the double doors, hoping to hear what I could from outside. The court officer stationed there pulled a door open and held it for me. I balked and he looked at me strangely for a second. I wasn't dressed like an attorney and he couldn't have missed the ankle bracelet. Everyone checked when they met someone new. Still, he held the door and waited. I moved inside and eased into the audience.

In the old system the majority of trials were public and the gallery had at least a few interested parties watching. Three wide rows of seats waited for an audience, but there wasn't a single soul in the wooden chairs, nor had there been when I'd been brought here for judgment. Up front the prosecutor and three officers were ready to present. The accused, a man I'd known, but could not recall his name, pointed at me and then urgently to the door. A second later Nathan Farnsworth came in through the door to the judge's chambers. His eyes locked on me and he faltered like he wanted to turn back the way he'd just come. He didn't. He started to his seat and the judge followed a few seconds behind.

The accused turned and faced me menacingly, like he wanted to jump up from his chair and attack me. Even cuffed he could pound me before the cops pulled him off. Behind him the judge said, "Motion denied," and banged his gavel.

The defendant scowled like it was my fault. Had he been promised the same deal as the Wiffle ball pitcher? Was Nathan bribing the judge to get his record erased so he could be admitted into Wendell's program? The judge and Nathan Farnsworth both looked flustered. The accused wanted to rip me apart.

The trial, like all relearner trials, didn't last long. There was a scuffle in a bar the night before and it was captured on tape. The man at the defense table had been insulted by a few guys playing pool and eventually he snapped. He grabbed a man, pool cue and all, and pummeled him bloody. Another three guys joined in to help their friend, but they were no match for the hulk at the defense table. They armed themselves with chairs and beer bottles. Still, they took the worst of it.

When the fight was over, the chase was on. I'd seen the computer tracking before, but by his reaction, the defendant didn't know they could trace his every move. Nathan Farnsworth's relearners didn't get a chance to see this room too many times. This would be the big guy's only chance to see how well the police could follow him.

He was pronounced guilty and Nathan Farnsworth did something I didn't expect. He walked forward and accepted his failure. Scanning his thumb cost him dearly. The defendant would pay an even higher price.

CHAPTER FIFTY-FIVE

The handcuffs came off right there in the courtroom. When they did, the hulking defendant turned in my direction and I got ready to run. He stopped short when Farnsworth stuck an angry finger in his face and growled something under his breath. Even the judge and the cops turned to hear. The threat was little more than a whisper, but everyone understood the message. One more mistake and Farnsworth would throw him out. The men who came to claim him wouldn't be kind. Had the big guy been for a drive in the woods to hear the screams? It didn't matter how big he was. He wouldn't stand up to the drugs and cats and scalpels. He'd wind up facedown on the asphalt like everyone else.

His demeanor changed immediately. His shoulders drooped. His eyes dipped for the floor and he shuffled out. I was convinced he was picturing the atrocities Blake had told me about. The images came back to me when I was caught in Wendell's house and hauled here. Anytime could be the last time in this room. The big guy was lucky. He had to be scolding himself for being sent here again. I hoped he wasn't blaming me for his trouble with the judge.

I fingered the pages of my book, let them fan over and over again while Nathan Farnsworth walked the big guy out. I wasn't sure exactly what to do then. I went and collected my pen camera from the security guard and walked the sidewalks, aimlessly I thought. Several blocks later I ended up facing the yard behind Stephan's apartment. I took up the bench overlooking the field and watched the teams organize for the next game.

The big guy was right there in the outfield. He'd changed into shorts and a T-shirt, but there was no denying the bulging muscles on his huge frame. The white bandage on his ear dispelled any doubt. I would have been cowering in my room that soon after court. I thought it was strange for him to play, but I was glad. The game gave me time to check his mood. I wanted to ask why he'd gotten so mad. I was sure he'd been offered the same deal as the pitcher who'd moved to my complex, but I wanted to hear it. I wanted to know the judge was the guy I should be following. Before any of that, I wanted to be sure I wasn't going to end up in a fist fight with a giant if I approached him.

I pretended to read my book and a few times I actually read three or four pages before looking back to the game. The big guy wasn't quick enough to run down liners, but he could get under a drifting fly ball well enough. He stared me down a few times to say he knew I was watching, but when his team was at bat, he stayed around home plate instead of chasing me off. I took it as a good sign, a little hope that I might trick him into telling me what I wanted to know without needing to see a dentist afterward.

I got my chance when the game was over. He wandered away casually, arcing over to where I was on the bench. I clicked on the recorder and aimed it in front of me even though he wasn't quite there yet.

"Quit following me," he said. "Or we're going to have a problem."

"I don't need any trouble and you don't either."

His eyes narrowed on me and his shoulders clenched, but my words were enough to hold him back. "What do you want?"

I asked him why he was so mad in the courtroom. I told him I was just trying to figure things out. That I didn't want trouble.

He told me that I'd screwed things up. He told me they had worked out a deal with the judge. For a second I thought he was going to tell me what he'd been offered. Then I'd have exactly what I needed to implicate Farnsworth, to put him out of business and make Wendell king of reeducation. I must have twitched with the camera because he spotted it and ripped it from my hands. In one violent jerk, my camera snapped in half. Tiny components dropped to the ground like tobacco from a broken cigarette. My second camera and my second opportunity to help myself lay in pieces.

"Don't let me see you again," he barked. Then he turned and stomped off across the grass behind the control room. He headed between the ball field and the building, turning for a back entrance I'd seen dozens of players use.

How stupid of me not to hide the camera. I looked back and forth from the pieces to the man who'd just admitted everything I needed to prove. I cursed myself as I watched the broad back rush away. Then the big guy straightened abruptly. No one was around him. To me it looked like a heart attack. Wendell's lessons must have kicked in because I dropped my book and ran across the yard in spite of what he might do when I got there. Two more tremors shook his massive body and he collapsed.

I was panting when I reached him. I started shaking when I saw the blood. I wheeled around and screamed, "Someone call nine-one-one!"

Four splotches painted his T-shirt red. His eyes were closed and he lay still on the grass. I reached for his wrist to check his pulse, but two strong hands pulled me back. "He's dead," I yelled as I was dragged away.

I didn't resist. I'd learned that at least. I let myself be pulled away from the body, and while my eyes searched everywhere to make sense of what had happened a second floor window pulled closed. I pointed for the police officer wresting me back, but he didn't even look in that direction. He patted me down for a weapon instead. Another officer retrieved my book and the pieces of my camera. They didn't bother to ask what I'd been doing. They took my name and made me wait while one of them went back to his car. Later I learned they had played the audio from my conversation with the big guy.

After forty minutes discussing my fate, they decided they didn't have a case they could win, so they let me go. As far as I know they never looked for the guy at the window.

CHAPTER FIFTY-SIX

My legs shook as I topped the stairs and opened my apartment door. I stepped hesitantly over the threshold and listened for movement before I went deeper inside. Who did I think was in there? Wendell? Farnsworth? Either of them could have had a key. Even without one it was easy to get into someone else's home. I'd made a profession of it. What would they do if I surprised them inside? I always hid when that happened, but they had nothing to fear from the law. They could slash me open and walk away. I trembled with the thought after what I'd just witnessed.

I checked the kitchen, bedroom, and bathroom. There was no place to hide in the living room. I was as alone as I could be in a room fitted with microphones and cameras. I still didn't know who was watching me or when. That was worse than knowing people came and went when I was gone. I could clear the apartment, but I could never relax there.

I kept seeing the big guy quiver and fall to the ground. He'd only been out of court two hours before he died. He blamed me for ruining his shady deal with Farnsworth and the judge. The big guy was my chance to learn about that deal, and Farnsworth had made sure he couldn't talk. Farnsworth also ensured that the big guy wouldn't non-conform again. He didn't care about relearners. All he cared about was his rating. His technology and power made him nearly impossible to catch. That's why Wendell was so generous. He probably couldn't catch Farnsworth either.

I settled on the couch and opened *Tom Sawyer*. I saw the Wiffle ball pitcher's face in the pages and realized I hadn't seen him in person since I recorded him across my kitchen table. Could Farnsworth get to him here? Of course he could. Fighting Farnsworth was futile, but it was my only way out. I tried to use the book to forget what I was up against, but I'd already read it three times. I tossed it aside and turned on the black box.

My fear of the black box wasn't gone, but without Blake threatening me and without the wrist strap and the gray pads, it was easier to concentrate. I was still five years away from finishing even with Wendell's help. Turning on that box meant I believed I could finish. I believed I could outsmart Farnsworth and learn what most American teenagers learn. I had hope after all I'd been through. I hope you'll understand that and believe in me, too.

Wendell had told me to read the book twice. I'd read it three times and then skipped around here and there to interesting parts. Unlike the impossible division problems Blake assigned, I knew the answers to these questions on sight. I had the book beside me on the couch, but I never even glanced at it. I didn't need to. The thing that slowed me down most was typing my answers. I'd never used a computer for more than checking the weather or mapping an address. Typing word after word took longer than it should, but as I was typing I noticed something I hadn't expected. I could spell. Not perfectly but a lot better. I remembered seeing the words in the book and they came out the same way on the screen. When the test was graded, I passed something I didn't realize I was even being tested for. I received an eighty-seven on comprehension and an eighty-four on spelling.

Fireworks lit up the screen and this time I felt a rise in my chest. I wasn't sure if an eighty-seven was an A- or a B+. Either one was an achievement to be proud of. I was more hopeful at that moment than when I'd just finished recording my conversation with the Wiffle ball pitcher. I could learn what I needed to learn. It just took patience.

I placed *Tom Sawyer* on the floor next to the television. I visualized a stack of completed books and projects there. Maybe I'd even buy a bookshelf to arrange them where I could see what I'd done. Maybe I'd even want to reread that book someday just for fun. I picked *Lord of the Flies* from the pile of books Wendell left, opened the cover, and started reading. I was surprised by how little I needed the dictionary even on the first time through. I understood what was happening. Reading wasn't labor anymore. I was excited about the second time I would read this book. If Wendell had told me when I woke up in the prison hospital that I'd be excited to read a book for the second time, I wouldn't have believed him.

I read for hours, word by word, and as the story progressed, I was amazed at how savage the boys were. I was proud to be following the story so easily. Right away I saw why Wendell had picked this book for me. It probably had special meaning for all relearners, but I felt like he'd singled me out for this. Order among the boys was broken down by fear, superstition, and disobedience. When Simon was killed I stopped reading and looked around the room, expecting to see sand and ocean on one side and jungle on the other.

Fear had driven me onto the streets. I'd become a thief, afraid to go home and afraid to find help. What if I had stayed at home and worked as hard in school as I was working now? Would my mother have killed me? Probably not. It took Charlotte's meddling to teach me that she just didn't understand how to raise children. She was a teenager when I started getting into trouble. She was only my age when I started stealing from convenience stores. Could I raise Jonathan any better? She surely hadn't taught me how.

I wondered what Wendell was trying to tell me with this book. Was he suggesting I needed to be brave? Did he think I'd be reading this book when I felt my struggle against Farnsworth was hopeless? Was he trying to tell me to use my head and keep my cool?

I paced around the apartment for a while, thinking about the boys and how much trouble their fear caused. I had to be cool and rational, to look at Farnsworth as a man with weaknesses just like me. I realized where I could compete with him on almost equal footing. He controlled the relearners, but that wasn't where his clients came from.

CHAPTER FIFTY-SEVEN

The new pen camera sat right in the middle of the kitchen table. I grabbed it and headed for the door. I didn't think about where it came from or when it had appeared. I was always being watched and things showed up when I needed them, but I accepted the meddling in my life a little too easily. My subconscious wanted to know if Wendell saw the big guy break my camera. It was a question I should have been asking, but I was feeling good about bringing down Nathan Farnsworth and I wanted to get going.

My eyes burned from reading so long, but I detoured over to the coffee table and picked up *Lord of the Flies*. I told myself I'd use the book as camouflage while I was busy, but I knew I'd spend time reading. As if to convince myself I wouldn't read for very long, I left the dictionary on the coffee table, but as soon as the driver pulled away to take me to the mall, I opened the book and picked up where I'd left off. The jostling made me carsick and I stopped. It wasn't a long ride.

The cab cruised through the expansive parking lot past two dozen rows of empty spaces. I worried that most people would be home getting ready for dinner, but as we got closer, I realized that housewives weren't likely criminals. There were plenty of cars clustered around the building. The people I was looking for would prefer tired salespeople and empty aisles. When we stopped at the curb I felt good about finding what I came for.

The exterior was imposing. Concrete walls rose straight up three floors. Tinted glass trimmed the entrances and roof, providing natural light inside. As I scanned my thumb to pay for my ride, I wondered how much a project like this cost and who decided to build a shopping center as big as my neighborhood. I humbly carried my book through the towering, forty-foot entrance and headed past a series of stores, all boasting something unique. Most offered ladies clothes, jewelry, or electronics.

I touched the pen camera in my breast pocket to reassure myself I was ready. I felt like a hunter prowling through the unshackled masses. The people I passed didn't check my ankle when they saw me. I was glad to be away from Nathan, Wendell, and anything to do with reeducation. I hoped I'd gone far enough to accomplish my mission. What would I steal here if I needed extra credits? What could I sell? The answer came inside a roomful of bright lights and clear glass.

I watched from a bench outside the store until three men started browsing the cases. Then I closed my book and headed in. I pretended to compare the ladies' rings in the first display case while I was evaluating the three men in the store. None had an ankle bracelet. One wore a tie and was a bit older. I assumed he could afford what he was looking for so I focused on the other two. I didn't notice the sensors by the door when I came in. There was no tone to indicate a relearner had entered and I felt comfortable looking at the case while I watched the younger men move around the displays. I should have known a jewelry store would be prepared to ward of relearners, but I was too focused on my mission.

Footsteps stopped behind me. A throat cleared. When I turned around, a large man with a blue uniform, but no gun, confronted me from two feet away. The smaller man beside him asked, "Can we help you find something in particular?"

"No thanks," I said dismissively. "I'm just browsing."

The two men parted and offered me a clear path to the door. The man in the suit, probably the store manager, said, "We don't want any trouble." He nodded toward my ankle. "It would be better for all concerned if you left."

I heard my breath rush in. I felt myself stiffen. They were throwing me out because I was a relearner. I couldn't believe such a thing could happen in America. I had rights. I'd never been discriminated against like this. I wanted to tell them what I was doing, but I couldn't give myself away. They wouldn't have believed I was fighting crime anyway.

All three of my potential jewel thieves turned to watch. There was no way I was going to catch them taking something now, not with the security guard threatening me. So I walked between the two men and out the door. How many times had this store been robbed when the prison doors first opened? How much had they spent to hide their scanner? And what would have happened if they posted a sign prohibiting relearners? Did people care? Or were they so fed up they'd be glad to shop where they were safe?

I'd never been so frustrated as when I sat back on the bench to rethink my strategy. Nathan and Wendell had a stranglehold on me if I stayed where I belonged. Out here with the unsuspecting public I had a chance until they realized I was a relearner. It didn't matter if I was trying to do the right thing or not. Honest citizens didn't want me near them. I thought about taking my ankle bracelet off, but I remembered the chip in my head and the chemicals dispersed through my body. I couldn't be sure either story was true, but I knew that when I took my ankle bracelet off, trouble came looking for me.

If someone was going to steal from another store in the mall, I guessed it would be electronics, movies, or video games. I slipped in with the flow of shoppers moving along the wall of display windows. The scanner at the entertainment store was low inside the door, so rather than walk in and become a target, I stayed outside with my camera and watched the shoppers browse.

A group of kids, all about fourteen years old, flocked up and down the counters lined with CDs. They stayed in the pop section and if I was going to catch someone taking a CD, I guessed it would be one of them. After several minutes watching them joke, text message each other from four feet away, and slap and poke each other for no reason, I realized that I couldn't capture a good enough image from outside the store. Even if I did, these kids would go to some sort of juvenile counseling. They wouldn't be relearners assigned to Nathan, and that wouldn't help me at all.

Further down, I stopped in front of two young women who looked suspicious in a lingerie shop. I couldn't tell if they were nervous about wearing the skimpy underwear they were about to buy, or if they were considering slipping it into a pocket. It was small enough to hide, but women didn't come to our complex, so I passed them up, too.

Several doors later, I spotted the guy I'd been looking for since I arrived. He was young, probably in his twenties, and he wore ratty clothes that were dirty in the butt and at the ankles like he'd been sitting in mud. He didn't look like he could afford new clothes, but he needed them.

He went into three clothing stores, but came out empty handed—empty pocketed, too. He stopped for an ice cream and sat on a bench, watching people walk by for a good fifteen minutes. After that he turned back the way we had come. Lucky I was reading my book or he might have noticed I'd been behind him for nearly an hour.

Near the center of the mall, he turned and followed a short corridor wide enough to build a house inside. There were a few stores here, but he didn't seem interested in what they had to offer. When he walked out to the parking lot, I absently followed. I wasn't going to catch anyone here at the mall. Maybe it was the wrong place. Maybe the surveillance was too good and people knew it. Maybe people outside the reeducation system didn't make a habit of stealing. That bothered me as I pushed through the glass doors. It was my life that didn't fit. These people were the norm.

When I reached for the second set of doors a hand grabbed my collar and yanked me back. I choked. My eyes watered so much I lost sight of the dark parking lot. Lights filled my watery eyes as I turned and all I could see was brilliant white streaks.

An angry face met mine when I blinked my eyes clear. I'd been grabbed because I was a relearner. It was wrong and my arm was cocked and ready to show him how wrong he was, but before I let loose I remembered seeing the big guy bloody and dying on the lawn.

Good thing I didn't turn around swinging. There were two more angry faces behind the first.

"I saw him," said the man dressed in jeans and a blue-striped dress shirt. "He's been following that guy for an hour. He was going to rob him in the parking lot."

"Why would I rob that guy?" I asked. "What could he possibly have that's worth taking?"

The guy said some nonsense about identity theft. That relearners cut off people's thumbs and preserved them so they could collect their government checks. The two mall security guards looked at me like I'd had a machete to the guy's hand.

"That's ridiculous."

The mall cops didn't think so. They brought me back to the security office, along with the guy who grabbed me. They took his version of events, then called the cops for a report on where I'd been for the last hour. My computer-generated trail lined up well with the vigilante's story. The mall cops called the police again. They listened to the audio from my anklet and found nothing suspicious.

The cops wanted cases they would win. Lucky for me, this wasn't one.

CHAPTER FIFTY-EIGHT

The traffic light had cars backed up all along the mall access road. I walked past them on the sidewalk and turned toward home. I wasn't going to walk the entire way. It was too far, but I wanted to get away from those mall cops before they invented a story good enough to get me back in front of the judge. The farther I walked, the darker the street became. The shadows would have bothered those shoppers who were freaked out by my ankle bracelet, but they didn't bother me. I'd used darkness to hide so close to people I could reach out and touch them. Most would run screaming if they discovered me in their home.

Regular people spent their lives afraid someone like me would take their stuff or hurt someone they cared about. Were we really that different? I was afraid, too. When I was younger, I worried my mother would kill me. Later, I worried about getting enough to eat. Still later, I was constantly dodging the police. The biggest difference was that I didn't have anything to protect. Once the cash and jewelry were taken from my safe deposit box, I didn't have anything to lose in this world. Those people in the mall spent their life on alert for danger all to save a bunch of stuff they really didn't need.

The road continued on for two miles without a bend or taxi stand. I walked through dozens of intersections and passed plenty of phones where I could have called for a ride, but I kept on walking and thinking about what happened in the mall. Then I wondered if all the pressure from Nick and Charlotte made sense. Jonathan shouldn't be subjected to this. Not for the sake of a few visits to the sandbox. I should have agreed to sign the papers. It sounded simple, but I couldn't give him up.

A while later I came to a series of three blocks where the streetlights were clustered close together and the sidewalks were so bright that the green grass shone along them. A red cart with a giant hot dog was angled at the corner to be visible to anyone leaving the five-story parking garage across the street. Beyond the cart was the entrance to an ice arena with an Italian name I couldn't pronounce. I sat on a bench just short of the cart, thinking if I was going to catch someone stealing something tonight, it would be when dozens of people rushed the cart for a cheap hot dog. The hot dog vendor couldn't afford surveillance cameras, or at least I didn't think he could. He did have a thumb scanner on his cart, which made me long for the good old days when you could whip out a five, get a hot dog and a Coke, and the government didn't need to know.

No one passed for the next ten minutes and I realized there must be a game going on inside. The vendor would make his sales when the flood of fans spilled out. I wasn't sure I wanted to sit on that bench for another hour for the slight chance someone might do something they shouldn't. Catching criminals was much harder than robbing houses. I could hit a house and get away clean on any given night. I'd spent a few days trying to catch a criminal without a hint of success. The problem was, you never knew where a criminal would be. Fancy houses didn't move.

A couple crossed the street, the man hurrying the woman along, clearly in more of a rush to see the game than she was. He waited at the corner for her to catch up and the hot dog man went to work shuffling things around his cart. It was an act to look busy, to make his product appear fresh even though those same hot dogs had been cooked and sitting on his cart for an hour or more. The woman slowed and took a step toward the vendor, but her companion urged her toward the arena. When they were past us and focused on the concrete building, the vendor shrugged and stood back from his cart. The work that had him focused seconds ago didn't matter until the next patron appeared.

"Slow night?" I asked.

"No, no," he said. "Business good. Game ends, customers come."

I wondered if he made more with his cart than the government was paying me to learn what I should have learned in school. If he did, it wasn't much more, and I didn't have to stand out in the dark and serve hot dogs and drinks. Judging by his clipped sentences and his accent, he could have benefited from the books Wendell forced me to read.

I gave him a thumbs up and felt weird about it.

He edged over toward my bench. "What you hide from?"

He was better off not knowing. I smiled and shrugged. "Just resting."

He pointed to my ankle bracelet and grimaced as if he'd worn one once and knew what I was going through. He saw *Lord of the Flies* in my hand and said, "Good book." Then he held his hand up over his shoulder like he was pumping a spear up and down and dancing in a circle.

"I haven't gotten to that part yet." It would take me another day of reading to get that far, but as the hot dog man sat down next to me in his dark blue jeans, white shirt, and long apron, I realized he'd been a relearner. Could he have graduated? I couldn't believe my luck.

"Wendell good guy," he said.

There next to me on the bench was a guy who could barely speak English but had graduated from Wendell's program. For a second I felt like I had it all wrong, like reading the book was a waste of time, but this guy knew the book. He'd read it and he still remembered it. I was in awe. I never really thought I'd graduate until that moment. If he could do it, I could. I wasn't even breathing on that bench. I was ready to grab onto anything he offered me.

He tapped the camera in my pocket. He knew exactly what it was, and I assumed a similar device had helped him to move from the brick complex to his own place, where he could walk here to sell hot dogs. He told me I could find what I was looking for if I waited for the game to end, then followed the tail end of the crowd.

I couldn't thank him enough.

Chapter Fifty-nine

The game lasted another hour. The night grew darker, the traffic lighter. I hadn't intended to stay that long, but I couldn't leave that bench after the hot dog vendor told me how to get what I came for. We sat together for a while. I asked him what it was like working the cart and he told me he'd always done it. He liked seeing the same fans at each game. He liked working for himself and he made a good living with the cart.

What would I do if I made it out? Would I end up behind the counter of some store? Would they trust me with the merchandise? Probably not. It was too early to know. David Jones, my employment counselor, hadn't even called me yet. He probably didn't want to waste his time with relearners who weren't going to make it. I was annoyed he hadn't spent two minutes to give me some hope. If I could follow the hot dog man's advice and get the video I needed, I'd call David Jones and give myself something to shoot for.

Doors clanked open. Heels clicked. Voices shouted.

The home team had won and the crowd jostled and cheered, rousing everyone for blocks. The hot dog man stepped up to attention and even though the first wave of fans rushed right by him, he soon had a line of hungry customers ready for a late snack. I shifted the camera to my palm even though I didn't expect to catch anything so easily. The line was well behaved and I realized that even if I had seen something, I wouldn't be able to catch the person in the act. To do that I would have to be recording the whole time. I didn't have, or at least I didn't believe the tiny camera had, that much capacity. So I sat and watched, waiting for the rush to slow.

When the crowd leaving the arena slowed to a trickle, I got up from the bench with my eyes locked on a group of older men in suits. The hot dog vendor waved me back to my seat with a flick of his wrist. I obeyed. I tried not to stare at him while I waited and wondered what he had in mind. Is this how he got himself out of Wendell's program? His success was enough for me to follow his every command, but my excitement dimmed as he kept me waiting another fifteen minutes. Maybe lots of relearners ended up here and this was his way of taunting us.

I was sure no one was left in the arena when I saw the fingers motion me to my feet. They came slowly, which accounted for the delay. They stumbled up the sidewalk, blathering and laughing. They came even and turned away from us. I followed with a wide smile of thanks to the hot dog man.

The pen was deep in the book, marking my page and recording the wobbly men as they stumbled along. I kept the camera running and aimed as well as I could with the book by my side. This moment was what I'd spent days looking for. The three drunk men were younger than the group I had intended to follow. I trusted the hot dog man's advice enough to use every bit of camera time so I didn't miss anything they did. Their ties and dress pants suggested they were here on business, but weren't senior enough to require suits to mingle. It was hard walking slow enough to stay behind, but they were so wasted they didn't notice me following them.

They stopped at an opening in a long brick building. I caught up to them quickly and had nowhere to turn. The three faced the building, where an office entrance allowed them to step into the shadows. Zippers lowered. Liquid splashed on concrete.

One man said, "I was dying."

"Oh, that feels better."

One of the men asked me to step up and block them in case anyone came along. I stepped closer, my arms crossed, the book carefully aimed from the crook of my elbow. Urine sprayed the sidewalk, pooled, and ran down. The men adjusted their stances to keep their shoes out of the streams that ran across the sidewalk for the storm drain. I kept the book aimed squarely at their midsections and the splashing urine now hitting the sidewalk and door equally. The people who worked inside were in for a nasty surprise in the morning. Maybe this was a regular occurrence.

Was this what the hot dog vendor had meant for me to capture? I didn't know the law. If I was going to catch criminals, knowing the law would have been helpful. I'd seen people arrested for being drunk in public. These guys certainly were. Was this public nudity or something like that? I didn't know if either offense would get someone sent into the programs, but I hoped it would.

The men finished and walked up the block. I thought about following them, but I was pretty sure this was the scene I was supposed to capture. I wondered if I'd caught anything I shouldn't have. If I'd filmed a penis, would that be viewed as pornography? Would I get myself locked up for turning in this video?

I turned and ran back to the corner, but the cart was gone.

I listened for wheels rolling in the distance. One minute was all I needed from him. In one minute he could tell me what I needed to have on that tape and what might get me in trouble, but he was gone. Like the guy in the donut shop he'd been very helpful and then he'd vanished. I wished there was a way to know when someone had graduated from reeducation. The ankle bracelets were helpful, but the people who could really help me blended in with everyone else.

CHAPTER SIXTY

The brick building stood alone with a wide drive on each side and six cruisers parked out front. The white sign with bold blue lettering told me I was in the right place. The camera hadn't left my hand since I stopped recording. The three clean-cut guys I filmed were the kind of relearners Nathan Farnsworth would surely gobble up. One of them could have priors and end up with Wendell, but I was betting that once the judge saw this recording, they'd all be carted off to Farnsworth's. A twinge of doubt flickered in my mind and kept me from climbing the stairs and going in. Was I missing something? Could I be incriminating myself?

I'd thought it over backward and forward a dozen times. If I went home to check the video I was just giving Farnsworth an opportunity to steal it. I shouldn't have hesitated so long to grab onto that handle and walk in. When I did the reaction was swift and surprising. The detector inside the door beeped and every visible officer lowered a hand to a holster. There were probably men in other rooms grabbing shotguns. I remembered the motto *to protect and to serve* from a cop show on television. Unfortunately, I was the one people needed protection from.

I froze with the pen camera clutched in my right hand and the book in my left. They didn't draw down and shoot me, and when I didn't come rushing in the mood in the lobby relaxed. Two suspects sat cuffed to heavy chairs at my left. Both were clean-cut kids in their twenties, not who I expected to see. Two officers leaned against a high counter in front of me. I eased up to the nearest officer, careful to keep my hands in sight.

I didn't know quite what to say. He gave a nod to my ankle bracelet and said, "Can we help you?" He'd checked both of my hands and it felt like he was eying my clothes, looking for a gun or a bomb. I guess they didn't have many relearners walk in and try to prove themselves by selling someone else out. In my neighborhood we were taught to hate cops in the kindergarten schoolyard. Snitching would get you beaten to death if you picked the wrong guy, but I wasn't in the neighborhood anymore and the guys I'd filmed were as harmless as criminals come.

"I've got something for you."

"For me?" the officer asked, poking hard against his sternum.

"All of you." That wasn't quite right. Guns and uniforms made me nervous. Cops had been chasing me since I was ten. They probably knew I'd be trouble even sooner.

I held out the camera and he instantly knew what it was. He looked at the counter and back at me. The official procedure was probably to wait my turn and talk to someone behind the counter and then wait for someone to come out and help me, but the officer held up the camera to the man behind the desk and pointed to himself, as if to say he'd take care of me. He led me to the corner of the room, through a narrow doorway, and down a long hall deep into the station.

The cops all looked the same in uniform. Faces shaved. Everything else covered except their hands. Most of them were fit. This guy I was following seemed like he was ten years older than me. He walked easily and I bet he'd be tough in a fight. He led me into a small room with a table and left me there. I'd been in rooms like this before. Nothing on the walls. Three heavy wooden chairs. No windows. My heart started thumping and I tried to keep calm by reminding myself that I hadn't done anything wrong.

In a minute he returned with a television on a rolling cart. I saw the camera on top of the cart and at that moment I felt like an undercover news reporter. I'd lived in some rough places. Maybe that was a job I could do when Wendell was finished with me.

He took the camera, pressed a few buttons and some random bits of conversation played on the screen. I must have mistakenly pressed the

216

record button a few times. We quickly moved on to the three drunk men walking down the dark sidewalk. The officer focused, realizing without me saying anything that this was what I wanted him to see. He measured their wobbling strides, and I felt like he was trying to judge whether the court would find them guilty of being drunk in public.

All three faces appeared on camera at one point or another. I wasn't sure I'd captured them, but each had turned to see what I was doing and their faces were clear enough for the officer to identify. Everything was fine until they stepped over to the entryway and started peeing. Then the officer pushed back.

"Is that it?"

"Yes."

He looked at me squarely and asked in carefully measured tones, "What do you want me to do with this?"

Wasn't that obvious? These men had broken the law. I caught them and there was no way to refute what they'd done. Why was he balking? This was a case he couldn't lose. When I was caught without my ankle bracelet, I was rushed to court and tried in minutes. When I broke into Wendell's house, I was arrested over his protests. Why were these men any different?

I didn't know what to say. Was I a loser for catching these guys breaking the law? Did this cop really want me to take my evidence and go away? He wasn't upset by what the tape showed. When I sat down I had visions of being rewarded for helping the police. How foolish.

"I want you to do your job," I said.

"You realize these men will be charged as sex offenders?" He paused to give me chance to relent. "We'll need you to come to court and testify."

I nodded. I didn't want to ruin anyone's life, but I desperately wanted to help Wendell, and more than anything I wanted to get rid of this ankle bracelet and be free.

CHAPTER SIXTY-ONE

Officer Roland Benson identified one of the suspects by showing the video around the precinct. Once word got out that the video was funny, the cops all came to see it. One of them had to know the other guys in the video, but no one would admit it. Strange that sixty cops would protect these guys, but that didn't matter. Once Roland had one name, he called him on the phone. I heard Roland lie about an accident the men might have witnessed somewhere near the arena. That lie quickly netted him the names and telephone numbers of the other two men. Soon after, I assured Benson that I would testify and he sent me home.

The taxi dropped me off at midnight. The new pen camera on the kitchen table didn't surprise me. At that point I would have been surprised not to find one. As I microwaved some chicken nuggets I imagined Wendell sneaking in and out. He was a busy guy, too busy to bother with me every day. He must have been sending someone. The control room downstairs had been empty the day I'd gone inside, so I wondered if the people delivering the cameras came from somewhere else. Were they watching me that very moment? Were they proud of my video?

It was a long day and a half wait for the arraignment of the urinating renegades. I wondered if they deserved to be hauled in. They'd broken the law and had been caught just like me. They didn't deserve special treatment, but I felt queasy about testifying. Everyone in the courtroom would know I was a snitch. It looked bad even to me, ruining these people to help myself, but there was no turning back.

The next morning I stopped for coffee and a donut, then hopped a cab for the address Roland gave me. When I stepped out in front of the courthouse, I was stunned by the massive columns that rose up to support the roof. The wide granite steps covered enough ground for a small yard in front of the building. I'd been here before, but the contrast to the modest brick relearner courthouse was unreal. What did that say about the people who were tried here? And there? The date 1902 was chiseled into a corner stone. The law had been applied here for over a century before the relearner laws were written. I felt unworthy climbing the steps to testify.

The security guard took my pen camera and held it aside.

The lobby rose two floors above. My steps echoed off the granite walls. Unlike relearner court, there seemed to be nothing happening here. Office doors were open. Clerks stood around counters inside the offices, but no one was in the lobby or the long hall that led to the back of the building. Fifteen minutes passed before the next person arrived, a slick man with hair that clung to his head as if it had been glued in place. His suit was probably expensive, but I couldn't tell for sure.

He got right up close to me on the bench. "I don't know what you think you're pulling here, but you're not going to get away with it."

I couldn't remember the faces from the video very well, but I was pretty sure this guy was older than the guys on the street that night. I pegged him for a defense attorney. "Are you threatening me?"

"You're not going to get away with this. I'll get my guys off."

If I didn't feel so guilty about pressing charges for urinating in public, I would have tried to incriminate the lawyer, too. It might have helped Wendell, but my heart wasn't in it, so I pointed to my ankle bracelet and told him he was being recorded. He looked at me like I was insane, then stormed off. Apparently he only represented first timers in criminal court. If he'd been to relearner court, he would have heard the recordings play. Maybe he was mad because he was losing business to the new system. Clients must have become hard to find after relearner court was established and there weren't many billable hours in a fifteen-minute trial.

The three guys I'd recorded came in together and scowled at me from a safe distance. A few other people came and went and finally Officer Benson came to me on the bench and led me back to the courtroom. We walked through the double doors to find the crowd I'd been expecting to see, though there were a lot fewer than had been in attendance when I'd come here for my trial on the credit card case.

The attorneys had their own reserved area behind the litigants. When they were waiting to argue a case, they sat on the bench that divided the room. A high railing kept them safely away from the clients and spectators. I joined the sparse group of spectators and looked on as the prosecution and defense argued before the judge.

There was a jury box in this courtroom, something that was absent from relearner court. Something else that was odd, there was no video presented as we watched an argument continue on for thirty minutes. My entire trials hadn't lasted that long. My eyes explored the room as the discussion came to a close. Three court officers stood by. Pretty standard, one on each side and one up front close to the judge.

The parties exited and the judge called, "People versus Branson, Henderson, and Rodrigues." Four men popped up. The three men I'd seen two days earlier climbed down from the gallery and made their way to the defense table. Their lawyer was waiting for them when they arrived. Officer Benson moved behind the prosecutor's table and eyed me before he sat down.

I imagined myself on the stand explaining why I recorded these men peeing on the sidewalk. It seemed foolish. I was embarrassed and my emotions blocked out the action. I heard the judge say, "...plea agreement. Counselors please approach."

The prosecutor and the defense attorney, who had threatened me earlier, approached the judge. The prosecutor handed a paper to the judge and he read it carefully while the counselors waited. When he was finished, the three talked back and forth in voices too soft for me to hear. The men at the defense table strained their ears, but couldn't hear either.

The bailiff was sent on an errand and soon returned with a television on wheels much like the one Benson had used back at the station. The television was turned toward the judge and he watched it for about three minutes without saying anything. Then he shooed the counselors back to their respective tables and explained that the video wasn't shown to the rest of us because it was graphic in nature.

"This clearly shows the defendants," the judge said. "We're pleading this?"

"Yes, Your Honor," the prosecutor answered.

"We've got a pretty strong case, wouldn't you agree?"

"These men are no threat, Your Honor. A guilty verdict would label them sex offenders and the people don't find that appropriate. I don't think we'll be seeing them again after this plea."

The defense attorney never said a thing.

"I'll go along," the judge said. "One hundred dollars each for disturbing the peace."

The defendants sighed in relief.

They wouldn't be assigned to reeducation, which meant I couldn't follow them to Nathan Farnsworth. I was crushed. It had taken me days to find these guys and now I had to start all over again. I thought I heard my name, but I wasn't sure. I shrugged it off, but Officer Benson waved at me to stand up.

"Michael O'Connor, are you in my courtroom?" the judge barked.

I stood up. "Yes, Your Honor."

"I don't know what fantasy you're fulfilling here, but don't waste my time with trivia like this again. Understood?"

CHAPTER SIXTY-TWO

Wasn't the law the law? How could a judge just throw it aside like that?

The three men stood and hugged behind the defense table. Hands slapped backs. Palms clapped together for powerful handshakes. The men chattered on their way out of the courtroom, but there would be screams of jubilation on the courthouse steps. Their lawyer shook his head dismissively at me as he left, as if what I'd done was repulsive. Did he know what reeducation was like? If he didn't know my ankle bracelet could record his voice, I'd bet he didn't know about the cat baggers. Maybe he hadn't lost a case since the laws changed. Or maybe he abandoned his clients once they were committed to a program.

The next hearing began and I listened for a full ten minutes to be sure the men were gone before I skulked through the double doors. A few young guys scowled as I slinked past their knees, but an older woman patted my arm and smiled. The recognition gave me a boost, but I still wanted to take a cab home and shut myself in my apartment for a few days. Something kept me there in the courthouse. Maybe I was afraid to see those guys outside. Whatever the reason, I saw the empty bench, went back there, and opened my book. I read about the deserted island and the pack of increasingly wild boys fighting for dominance.

The story was so engrossing I didn't notice Officer Benson standing in front of me. He waved over the top of my book and I lowered it to my lap. Before he said anything, he offered my pen camera. I took it, surprised that I'd be allowed to have it in the courthouse.

"I should have warned you it could go like that," he said.

Benson had never wanted to prosecute this case, but I'd given him no choice. He'd tried to warn me that night at the station, but those men had broken the law and I'd caught them doing it. Ok, so they didn't rob the district attorney's house and steal his Mercedes. They still deserved to be punished. Did they know the judge? Is that why they got off? They didn't act like big shots. Honestly, I didn't think they knew the judge was going to approve their deal. They were scared when they came in and they didn't even know how vicious the cat baggers could be. Was it right for me to send them to reeducation to get myself out?

Benson saw my struggle and sat down next to me. "We can't get in the middle of everything," he said, meaning the cops. "That's not what we're here for."

They sure got involved when I took that credit card.

"Our job is to keep society running smoothly. Those men didn't really hurt anyone. It doesn't make sense to punish them. Do you get that? I understand what you are going through is pretty tough, but those guys that just left here aren't dangerous."

I wanted to stand up and scream that I'd never hurt anyone. Sure I'd taken things from people, hundreds of people, but so what? They lived in huge houses and drove fancy cars. They replaced the stuff I took and life went on like nothing ever happened.

"I don't know what you did and you don't need to tell me, but right or wrong, someone decided that the good citizens of this state would be better off if you weren't around. That's what we made *prisons* for." He hesitated on the word as if the idea of reeducation sickened him and he wanted to spit. "Prisons were made to keep honest people safe. I don't know about this new age crap. We were a lot safer when dangerous people got locked up and didn't come out for a very long time."

I pushed away. Benson was getting angry and I hadn't done anything to him. He thought I was the problem. The judge probably did, too. They wanted me behind bars and they wouldn't accept me until the bracelet came off. They'd only accept me then because they couldn't tell me from anyone else.

"So what?" I asked. "You wish I was still locked up?"

"I don't know what you did," he said. "But my job would be a lot easier if the people I caught stayed caught. Emptying the prisons turned this city into a war zone. It took us years to get control."

I never learned what happened after the bus accident. The release of all those prisoners must have been mayhem, but that wasn't my fault. I was doing my best and this guy didn't want to give me a chance.

"I never hurt anyone," I said.

"But you must have done something."

I told him I'd taken a credit card and some cash and that the guy I'd taken it from could easily afford it.

Before I could move, Benson swiped *Lord of the Flies* from my hands. I could feel my face turning red. My first impulse was to jump him and get it back. I wanted to slug him right there, but cameras covered every inch of a building like this. A video of me hitting a police officer would send me to the cat baggers and it might put Wendell out of business.

"Funny," I said and I put my hand out.

"You have other books, don't you?"

I did, but I needed that one. I'd spent hours reading it and without finishing it I couldn't answer Wendell's questions. I stood up. "I believe that's mine," I said loud enough for anyone around us to hear.

No one moved in our direction.

"I'm not hurting you," he said.

"You made your point."

"Not yet."

I couldn't believe what happened next. He pulled a cigarette lighter from his pocket, hung the pages of the paperback wide open, and lit them on fire. The flames whooshed to life and I couldn't help myself. I jumped at him and grabbed the book. The flames were climbing eight inches off the pages when I slammed it closed.

Benson dropped the lighter on the floor and yelled, "You can't start a fire in here!"

Four uniformed men ran in my direction. They tackled me as I stomped out the flames. I scrambled for the book and was rewarded with a fist to my left cheekbone. My head snapped sideways, bounced off the marble, and I flattened on the floor. Smoke rose up from my book. The flames were out, but the book was ruined. The men on top of me compressed my chest so hard I could barely breathe. They didn't relax until I stopped struggling. Then they cuffed me with my face pressed against the floor.

When they finally let me up, Benson was gone.

"I didn't light it. It was that cop. Officer Benson is his name."

"Right." A pudgy man in uniform hauled me to my feet. He and his three partners led me out of the lobby to a back room of the courthouse. They sat me down and one of them saw the camera in my pocket. In spite of the commotion, it seemed to be in good working order.

"How'd you get that in here?"

"It was evidence. Officer Benson gave it to me there on the bench."

"Sure," the pudgy man said.

"Are there security cameras in this building?"

Pudgy nodded.

"Go play back what happened. Then you can let me go and I won't sue."

All four men laughed. In the old days convicts made a living suing the state for mistreatment. This would have been worth fifty grand at least. Why they laughed it off I didn't know, but at least they sent someone out to check the video. Sure enough, when he came back, he unlocked my cuffs and apologized for the mistake.

I was glad to be out of there even if I couldn't sue.

CHAPTER SIXTY-THREE

I burst into the marble hall, headed for the lobby and the quickest route to a cab when a white-shirted young man gripped my elbow reassuringly and asked if he could help. I told him I was fine and tried to pull away, but he didn't let go. He said I needed his help then he moved around in front of me so I couldn't get to the exit without knocking him over. I stopped, not because I was afraid of him or because I needed help, but somehow I knew he had something important to tell me. It wasn't in his words. It was his eyes. They were both grave and supportive, like he knew exactly the kind of trouble I was in.

He led me to a bench, and a minute later I had a towel filled with ice pressed to my cheek. I watched him through my unobstructed eye. He apologized for Officer Benson. He told me that Benson was a law-and-order guy. Benson didn't like relearners and he'd do anything to see them fail. He didn't know me, so it wasn't personal. It was the system that had let him down. He'd spent an entire career chasing bad guys. He'd seen partners shot, stabbed, and killed. Then with the swipe of a pen, some crazy judge swept away everything he'd worked his whole life for.

I thought about what Benson had said. How criminals needed to be kept away from decent people forever. Benson lumped me in with the rest and I worried he was right. Did I deserve to be free?

The court officer, Mandla, told me he could see I was a good guy. He reassured me that I could make it out.

I checked him for an ankle bracelet, but of course he didn't have one. They wouldn't let a relearner work here. Relearners didn't work. Even after graduation I doubted I could work in the courthouse.

"I know what you were trying to do," he said.

"Didn't work very well, did it?"

"Seems like you're on the right track," he said. "I'm proof. You can make it out."

The ice dropped from my face. I'd lost the hot dog vendor and that guy in the donut shop, but here was someone who'd actually graduated from the system. I wanted to grab onto him so he couldn't get away. I imagined another court officer would call him back to work any second and I wanted to learn everything I could before that happened. "You got out? How?"

Mandla told me he'd been one of the smallest kids in a rough neighborhood. His father was gone by the time he was two years old, so his mother enrolled him in self-defense lessons. He loved karate and became an excellent student. The problems started when larger kids began picking on him at school. Mandla sent them home with broken limbs, fractured ribs, and countless other injuries. Success brought opportunities to help his friends when they had a dispute. Finally, when he was eighteen, he was arrested and sent to prison for the first time. Years later, he was one of the first relearners.

"But here you are," I said.

At first he was enthralled by the black box. He spent weeks working through the playground stories. Back then they were full of bugs and the black boxes stopped working three or four times an hour. He asked if they were better now and I told him they were. He chuckled and said it didn't really matter anyway. The black box and all that stuff was just a distraction. The real test was what happened outside the black box—in the real world.

He told me he was a good student and had already finished high school. It only took him two weeks to finish the videos Wendell assigned. He expected to graduate then, but he didn't.

"Wendell came to me," he said, "and asked if I thought I'd made up for what I'd done. We both knew I hadn't. I was arrested for beating up three guys in a bar, but that was only my latest trouble. I had sent dozens of people to the hospital. Fact is, I enjoyed it."

He told me Wendell had challenged him to save three people from violent situations. It was something he was trained for. "I thought it would be easy, but every time I helped someone, Wendell disqualified it somehow. Finally, I found a domestic abuse shelter. I saved three women from abusive husbands. The first two men backed off when I told them I knew karate. The third one punched me in the face." He rubbed his jaw like it still hurt. "It was a good one, too. Didn't see it coming. I could have dropped him and broken him to pieces, but I just walked away."

"After that they let you go?"

They did. That was the lesson. Wendell wanted him to overcome the violence that led to his arrest. Standing up to the husband without hurting him was the proof Wendell needed.

I was fidgeting with my hands and he stopped me. "You don't need that book anymore. That cop, was probably working with them. They challenged you. Wendell challenged you to do something. You do that, and you'll make it out."

He wanted me to tell him what it was, but just then a flood of worry swept over me. What if Mandla was working for the cat baggers? What if he wanted me to stop studying so I'd be sent there? If I had to choose between Mandla and Benson, it'd be an easy choice. But I couldn't tell him what I'd been asked to do. Who knew how far Farnsworth's influence reached?

"I don't really know," I lied. "I thought if I caught someone doing something illegal and had them arrested, that would help me get out. But that didn't go well. I guess I need to understand the system better before I can do anything."

Mandla knew the system better than I ever would. He didn't disappear like the others. All he needed was a hint and he volunteered to help.

CHAPTER SIXTY-FOUR

Mandla led me downstairs through a hallway that ran directly under the courtroom and into a huge empty room with chairs and tables arranged wherever they would fit. Prospective jurors came in every morning and waited there in case they were needed. First time defendants had the right to a jury trial, but most of them opted for a judge. The people were angry, Mandla explained, and the accused got fairer treatment from judges than juries. The new rules also had a lot to do with the jury room being so quiet. In the old days, many convicts were given probation or some other short sentence, then they'd be right back in court, sometimes within months. Under the new rules, once you were convicted of a felony you went to reeducation. If you got in trouble again, you went to relearner court.

He led me through another large waiting room with magazines piled on long tables and blackened televisions mounted on the walls. A decades-old poster enumerated the rules for the new jurors who arrived each day. We were alone on the lower floor, but I wasn't worried Mandla would turn on me like Benson had. Mandla wanted to help. I could feel it in his stories.

We took a back stairway up to the main floor and when we came into the hall, Mandla looked around like we weren't supposed to be there. This hallway to the judges' chambers was off limits to the public. From there he took me back out to the lobby and showed me the district attorney's office. The clerks shuffled papers and looked at computer screens, pretending to be busy when we came in. He told me they were managing the prosecution of every case that came before the court. Things were hectic in the old days. Now they had so much free time they worried about layoffs.

Next door we visited the clerk and Mandla told me about all the scheduling and filings that happened in her office. I tried not to seem disinterested, but his tour of the workings of the court wasn't really helping. If someone here was helping Nathan Farnsworth, they'd be doing it with computers or calling him on the phone. I had no way of knowing who it was and even if I did, I had no way of intercepting their communication.

Mandla sensed my disappointment. He led me to a quiet corner of the lobby and said, "My tour's not that exciting, is it?"

I tried to reassure him, but wasn't convincing.

"If I knew what you were trying to do, maybe I could help."

I trusted Mandla after all the time he'd spent with me. He wanted to help, I could feel it in him, but I couldn't betray Wendell's trust. What I was doing was important, but I wasn't getting anywhere on my own. I decided to ask, "Who works with the reeducation programs?"

He turned and waved me to follow. The small office was at the back of the courthouse, tucked away from original offices that had managed the court's business for over one hundred years. The carpet was new, the walls freshly painted, and the desk was modern, not a built-in relic like the counters and connected desks in the district attorney's office. I wondered if the furnishings were bribes from Nathan Farnsworth, but realized that this program hadn't existed long. Everything about it was new, including the man behind the desk.

Marc introduced himself, pressed down on both arms of his chair as if he was going to get up and shake my hand, but it was a bluff. He settled back and waved instead. I didn't blame him. His bulk overfilled the chair. If he got up, he'd have to stuff himself between the bowed arms again. Standing across the desk, I couldn't help notice how he pulled the hair from one side over his head to cover up the bald patch on his crown.

Mandla told Marc I was curious about the workings of the court and that he was giving me a tour. He explained the important role Marc played assigning felons to reeducation programs.

"I thought it was a random thing. That you got assigned to whatever program was next and which one you got was the luck of the draw."

Marc gestured to the hanging bins on the wall, one for each of the five reeducation programs. The cat baggers had no official place on Marc's wall. "That's true in general," he said. "But it's important to make sure that the groups work well together. If two people have a history of assault or some other problem, I make sure they don't end up in the same program. It's not like prison. There's not a lot of supervision. So violence could be a real problem."

Not a lot of supervision? Who was he kidding? Obviously Marc hadn't looked over his desk and seen my ankle bracelet. I couldn't help feeling I was incredibly lucky. Marc was the one guy who controlled the fate of everyone coming from this court into reeducation. If Nathan Farnsworth was cheating the system, this is where he would start.

"What if people know each other? Do you put them together?"

"I try. But I need to be fair to all the programs. I can't send a bunch to one program because they're friends and send no one to the others. It takes some research." He pointed to the files on the wall and then to the computer system in front of him. "I've got to do what I can to make sure they're comfortable where they end up and that they have a fair chance."

Marc tried to show me his computer system, but there was no room to squeeze around his desk and I wasn't big on computers anyway. I didn't have to see it to know he had lots of leeway. I'd bet no one was watching who he assigned where. This fat guy was screwing Wendell and I was going to stop him.

Chapter Sixty-Five

Mandla didn't have to ask how glad I was for the last leg of our tour. When we got to the lobby, my mind was racing with ideas to catch Marc sliding marginal felons to Nathan Farnsworth and sending hardened criminals to Wendell. The locks on Marc's office were nothing special, but there were guards and cameras all around. Maybe if I waited for his lunch hour I could dig through his files without being seen. There was no one working in that area of the building, but if I got caught breaking into an office in the courthouse it would be the end for me. Ditto tapping his phone line from the basement.

The camera resting in my shirt pocket reminded me of my original plan. I pulled it out and tapped it against my palm. Mandla perked up. "You don't have to catch them yourself, you know. There are plenty coming through here. I'm not sure what you're trying to do, but why don't you just find your criminals in the lobby?"

What a fantastic idea. Rather than kick myself for not thinking of it on my own, I wondered if he could he read my mind. Maybe the camera was an obvious clue. Could the implant in the back of my skull be transmitting my thoughts? Even if it was, how would Mandla receive them? My paranoia was foolish, but something about Mandla was too good to be true.

He eyed me skeptically.

"Good idea," I said. "I'll park out front and get to work."

I thanked him for his help and he sauntered down the hall and disappeared into the courtroom. The proceedings inside must have been carrying on without him for an hour and a half. I wondered if he'd be in trouble when he got back or if, like so many government employees I'd heard about, no one was keeping track of how much he worked.

The lobby was mostly empty, the same bench waiting for me. Even without my book to disguise my surveillance, no one seemed to care that I was watching. They must have assumed I'd come early for trial and was nervously awaiting my appointment with justice.

The first man who came through the door wore a jean jacket with the sleeves cut off, circling his upper arms with frayed white threads. His hair looked scraggly, his beard unkempt. He was destined for Wendell's reeducation program. I didn't have to know what charges he faced. I'd never seen anyone like him at Nathan Farnsworth's. There was nothing to be proved by following this man. Marc had latitude to assign a single case where he wanted. I needed something bigger.

Two lawyers and a police officer came out of the courtroom a while later. Once they left, no one new came into the hall for the next two hours. A few of the ladies from the offices walked back and forth, but it was a long time before the next group streamed in through the metal detector and assembled in front of me. When I saw the third man come in, I knew this was the group I was looking for. Every one of them had a suit, not a borrowed suit, but one that fit them perfectly. The creases were sharp, the shoes shiny. Every one of them had his hair cut short. And the best thing about this group, aside from the fact that they were young, there were eleven of them. Marc had latitude, but he didn't have the latitude to assign eleven easy cases to Nathan. He wasn't supposed to, but I knew Nathan would pay him well if he did.

They talked with their lawyers. I assumed the three men with briefcases and a touch of gray hair to be lawyers and not defendants. The group huddled together for a while, nervously checking their watches every minute. Soon they marched down the hall to meet their fate. When I made it to the courtroom five minutes behind this group, I learned my assumption was correct. Another proceeding was in progress. All eyes were on the bench and no one paid any attention as I slipped up the stairs and sat in back.

When the case was decided several minutes later, the eleven young men filed up front. Their names were called, but without anything to write on, I couldn't commit eleven names to memory. I heard Murphy and Johnson, because I had dated girls with those names. The other nine escaped me.

The prosecution opened with a bold statement that the men had been caught on tape, confessed to a police officer, and when their lawyers were confronted with this evidence they advised their clients to plead guilty. The point of the day's hearing was to pass sentence. These days there were only two sentences for serious offenses. Either a defendant was innocent or he was headed to reeducation. The simplicity made the court amazingly efficient. Since no one went to prison anymore, defendants weren't afraid to plead guilty. If they knew what I knew, these guys would have fought harder.

The defense made a statement that convinced me these men were a prime opportunity for Nathan Farnsworth. The men had been at a house party for a friend who was going off to war. When the party wound down and the friends spilled outside, a car raced down the street, nearly hitting one of the men. Traffic stopped the car at the corner and the men ran and caught up. Someone recognized the driver as a suspect in a gang shooting a week earlier. The men pulled him from his car and held him for the police. The lawyer admitted his clients had been overzealous. They'd beaten the man and he had been taken to Massachusetts General Hospital with serious injuries, but the men had been trying to do the right thing.

The lawyer pleaded for leniency. The men went too far, but their intentions were honorable. For a few minutes I thought the judge was going to let them go and that I'd have to go back to the lobby and follow another case, but I didn't have to. The judge asked to see the footage from the traffic camera. When he did, he sentenced all eleven to reeducation.

I knew they'd all be headed to Nathan Farnsworth. Now all I had to do was follow them and prove that Farnsworth was paying Marc for the favor. I assumed the first part would be the easiest, but when the judge banged his gavel, the men were led to a doorway I hadn't noticed before. They disappeared into a part of the courthouse Mandla hadn't shown me.

I went out to the hall and circled around to where Marc sat, but saw no entrance along the left wall. It was as if the only entrance to the room they entered was through the courtroom. That door was guarded by the court officers and the bailiff. The only other possibility was the locked hall that led to the judge's chambers. I didn't remember a door that opened in the direction the men went, but we had only been in that hall for thirty seconds.

Retreating to the back corner of the courthouse, I camped on a bench that gave me a view of Marc's door and down the length of the building to the district attorney's office. I couldn't see inside Marc's office, but I knew he was in there. I couldn't quite see the front entrance, but there was no way to get to the front of the courthouse without following the hall. If those eleven guys went to see Marc, or went out the front door, I'd see them.

Court was open until five o'clock on weekdays. When that time came, Mandla told me they were locking up and that I'd have to leave. The men still hadn't come out. I wished I'd seen their cars to know if they were still there, but I was sure they were inside the building somewhere. As I reluctantly followed Mandla and picked up the pen camera at the checkpoint, I wondered if the eleven were getting their implants and ankle bracelets. They'd need to stay overnight for that. Once they were implanted, there was no escape for them. I waited outside the courthouse another two hours. No one came out. The seven cars remaining in the lot were proof enough that something was still going on in there. I couldn't risk breaking into the courthouse, so eventually I gave up and caught a cab home.

CHAPTER SIXTY-SIX

The cab dropped me at the curb and soon I was back in my apartment, trying to figure out how Nathan Farnsworth could bribe Marc in a world without paper money. He couldn't leave a trail at Govbank, so he couldn't pay him off that way. The drug dealers took electronics, but how many iPods and phones could one man use? Farnsworth could put Marc on the payroll in an unofficial way, but that trail would be too easy to follow. It had to be something valuable and untraceable. I'd spent most of my adult life shifting property around. In a world without cash it was almost impossible. Farnsworth knew more about this world than I did. I knew he'd found a way to make it work. The best way to find out how he was doing it was to follow Marc and see who he talked to and what he did.

On my way to bed, I picked up the next book off the stack, *Treasure Island*. Mandla said the program wasn't about the black box and its lessons. I believed him, but by that time, I'd been reading so much that I *wanted* to get inside the story. My English was improving every day. I could hear it when I talked to people on the street. Gone were the lazy words, *stuff* and *like* and *dude*. Instead of packing them into every third sentence, I used words with meaning and I was proud I did. I know that's hard for you to understand because you are only hearing me now, but if you had heard me when I first came here, you'd think I was a different person. You probably would have pressed the red button already.

When my eyelids were heavy from reading, I crashed and slept as long as I could. After my donut and coffee, I walked to the bench behind Nathan

Farnsworth's place. I worried that I'd see Stephan at the ballgame that morning or that he'd see me and come storming over. I felt bad about what happened with his camera and the subliminal messages we found, but I was trying to do the right thing that day. I had no idea then how overmatched I was. I hid my face in my book, but like most worries, the confrontation never happened. I read and watched the action on the field and never saw Stephan again.

The eleven men from the courthouse appeared around lunchtime. I couldn't recognize any one of them from where I was sitting, but they came out onto the field as a group, and as they introduced themselves around they moved in a pack. I recorded the group standing along the foul line. When they settled into playing, I had half of what I needed. These men shouldn't have all come to Farnsworth's program. They'd broken the law, but they had been trying to do the right thing. None of them was likely to wind up back here. Wendell needed his share of these guys to clean up his record, but Farnsworth stole them from him. All I needed to do was prove that Farnsworth paid to get them.

Instead of going straight to the courthouse, I went home and took a nap. It was hard falling asleep in the middle of the day, but I couldn't get close to Marc at work. I was planning to follow him around all night. My hope was that his payoff would come after hours and come soon.

I slept too long and worried that Marc could be gone for the day. The cab dropped me off at the courthouse around four o'clock. To be safe I walked in through the front door and followed the hall past Marc's door. He didn't look up from the file he was reading, but I felt like he knew it was me. I kept on going, waited five minutes like I had something to do at that end of the courthouse, and then walked back to the lobby without letting Marc see my face.

I went to the employee parking and took down the color and plate number of every car. I tried to act casual for the cameras on the light poles, but there were twenty cars back there and I couldn't write down so much information without paying attention to what I was doing. I hoped Marc didn't have access to the cameras, but why would he?

Settled on a bench at the sidewalk, I watched the employees filter out and scratched the cars off my list as I saw them. It took forty minutes before Marc's wide face came rolling toward me in a silver Camry. I turned for the street even as he waited to pull out into traffic. I found a cab quickly and a few blocks later we caught up to the Camry at a red light.

Marc stopped at The Last Call, a tiny brick building with neon signs advertising American beers and free nachos on Wednesdays. The days all ran together for me, but I was sure it was Wednesday when he rumbled inside. The cabbie parked half a block back. The fare was nine dollars and change.

"I need you to wait."

"Sure," he said.

I was convinced he'd be gone once I closed the door. I added a fifty-dollar tip and his eyes widened. "Listen, if you're not here when I get back, I'm going to tell your company you ripped me off. If you're here when I come back, it'll be clear what the tip was for. Deal?"

The cabbie gave me his word he'd be there and I rushed into the darkened bar after Marc. Pool balls clacked. Eight feet from the entrance I ran into a cluster of people circled around talking. The dress shirts and skirts suggested they'd come straight from a nearby office. I pushed my way through. They let me pass and immediately the men and women pulled their conversations back together. All the tables were filled. Every chair had a coat draped over it, so I worked my way over to the jukebox and stood against the wall where I could see Marc, or rather his back, at the bar.

I remembered the big guy I saw shot near the ball field. His problems started in a dive like this. I wasn't supposed to be here. I was glad there was no detector at the door to identify me, and when anyone sidled up to the jukebox or wanted to push by I was sure to make way. Mostly I hugged the wall and watched Marc through the sea of heads.

He shoveled in nachos for the next two hours and washed them down with three beers. He'd chosen his spot at the corner well. People kept pushing up beside him to order a drink. I couldn't hear what he was saying or see his facial expressions, but a few women walked away shaking their heads. I couldn't tell if he was hitting on them and failing miserably, or if it was the splattering of cheese and sauce on his face that turned them off.

I watched carefully, putting the camera on him every time someone stood beside him for more than a minute, but no one passed him anything and no one seemed interested in talking with him. He sat. He ate. He drank and finally he left with me right behind.

The cab was where I left it and the cabbie was pretty good at following the Camry without being noticed. Marc didn't strike me as someone particularly aware of his surroundings, but we stayed back half a block and followed him for twenty minutes to a neighborhood of high stone walls and wrought iron fences. Marc stopped at an entrance, spoke into a speaker, and a wide gate opened.

The place reminded me of Wendell's and I remembered how fast the cops swarmed me for jumping the wall. The cab stood out in this neighborhood of Beemers and chauffeurs, so I paid the fare and stepped out onto the naked curb. My book was useless as camouflage in the dark and people here parked behind high walls, so there were no cars to crouch behind. The only cover was the occasional tree and that was where I chose to hide.

The maple at the corner had low branches that made climbing into the canopy easy. Once I reached the height of the wall, I was enveloped by leaves that hid me from passing cars, but I could clearly see the circular drive up by the house. In the next hour, three cars arrived, each carrying a single man. I was positive this was Marc's payoff. I sat there on a thick branch, wondering what was going on inside. What could be so valuable to Marc that he'd be willing to risk his job?

After an hour of watching and worrying that Marc would leave and I'd have no way to follow, I crept out along the heavy branch until I could step over to the top of the wall. The flat surface had iron spikes on top, but once I stood astride them, I could walk along the wall comfortably, which I did until I drew even with the house.

Marc stumbled out to his car and drove away. I turned and *Treasure Island* slipped from my coat and fell eight feet to the grass. I suppressed a twinge of panic. I wanted to jump down and retrieve the book, but couldn't see an easy way out again. If there were dogs or sensors, I'd be hauled to relearner court for the last time. Marc had led me to what I needed. I let him go and followed the wall for a better look inside the lower windows.

Inside that monstrous house was a form of payment that made perfect sense for Marc. It was untraceable, yet incredibly valuable to someone like him. I wondered if the men I saw through the windows with lingerie-clad young women on their laps all worked in the court system or if there were some politicians thrown in. Once I proved Nathan Farnsworth was paying the bills, I'd have everything I needed. That would be no easy task, but I knew someone who could help me and I had something he desperately wanted.

CHAPTER SIXTY-SEVEN

My nap the day before messed up my schedule. When I got home and couldn't sleep, I spent most of the night reading another book I picked from Wendell's pile. I was angry I'd dropped *Treasure Island*, not because it could alert someone at the house that they were being watched and not because it could lead them to me, but because I was halfway through and I wanted to know how it ended.

I showered and shaved the next morning even though I could barely open my eyes that early. I skipped my donut shop ritual and jumped in a cab with my stomach gurgling and complaining that I was going the wrong way. The cabbie parked half a block from my destination. I paid him and walked through the neighborhood of tightly-packed houses as if I was out for a morning walk.

The car was locked but had no alarm and I was sitting in the passenger's seat within seconds. It was Thursday, surely a workday for anyone at the bank. I couldn't be sure what time he went to work, but both cars were parked at the house, his at the curb, hers in the driveway. I was dreaming when footsteps rounded the trunk. My subconscious screamed to try and wake me up, but my dreaming mind refused to alert me to what was happening outside the car.

The remote clicked and tried to push open the locks even though I'd already unlocked them to get in. The door swung open, the seat rocked, but my eyes didn't open until I heard the yelling beside me. I rubbed my eyes open and told Nick to relax and drive.

"Screw that. What the hell are you doing in my car?"

"It's your lucky day. I've got something you want. I need a little favor and if you can deliver, I'll sign the papers and you can forget I ever existed."

I thought I heard a door open and worried that Kathleen would come out and see us together. "Drive," I said. "Before your wife starts asking questions you can't answer."

Nick didn't hesitate. He started the car and sped off.

His arms were rigid on the wheel and I could tell he hated being that close to me. I hadn't done anything to him, but that didn't matter. I wondered if he was sterile or if Kathleen refused to have more kids. What did any of that matter to me? Nick hated me. I needed something from him and that was the extent of our relationship. I knew I'd miss Jonathan, but I needed someone inside Govbank and Nick was the only person I knew who had a chance of getting it.

A few blocks later we stopped at the edge of a park.

"What do you want?" he grumbled.

I handed him the slip of paper with Nathan Farnsworth's name, what I knew of Marc, and the address to what I suspected was a brothel.

"What am I supposed to do with this?"

"Nathan Farnsworth is bribing court employees by hooking them up with prostitutes. He's doing it in this house." I pointed to the address. "I want you to help me figure out how he's paying the girls and who is coming and going from this place. I'd also like to know who owns that house."

"I can't do that. They don't just let me wander around in people's financial records without a reason. I could be fired."

I didn't feel guilty about pulling Nick into this. He'd been nothing but an ass from the moment we met. Every time I saw him he wanted to come after me. Sharing Jonathan with him would have been a nightmare and it would have shown eventually in how my son treated me. I finally realized that I couldn't really be a part of Jonathan's life, but Nick didn't know that. All he saw was an opportunity to be rid of me.

"Get me what I need and I'll sign the papers."

Nick straightened.

I told him I needed to connect Marc to Nathan Farnsworth. It had to be a transaction within the last two days. I also needed to know who owned that house and who, if anyone, officially worked inside.

He told me I could find the owner by going to city hall. That information was public record.

"Are you not hearing me? I'm willing to sign over my son to you. I expect cooperation. I need Farnsworth wrapped up in a neat little package so I can go to the authorities and hand him over."

I never meant to prosecute Farnsworth, only to turn the information over to Wendell so the two of them could fight it out. If I went to the cops, they'd have me shipped off to the cat baggers before anyone knew I was gone. At least Wendell was someone important. Even Farnsworth couldn't make him disappear. That's why he was trying to run Wendell out of business.

Nick stared at the monument in front of us for a few minutes. His eyes shifted back and forth, not seeing the landscaping outside the car, but some task he'd stealthily do at work, some way of getting me what I needed without getting caught.

"All right," he said. "Meet me here at nine."

"Bring the papers."

"What happened to the last ones?"

"What do you think?" I said and stepped onto the curb.

243

CHAPTER SIXTY-EIGHT

It was a long day after I left Nick at seven-thirty A.M. I desperately needed sleep, but when my head hit the pillow all I could think about was Nick getting caught and implicating me. I rolled over again and again until the pillowcase irritated my skin. Then I got up and read about a family shipwrecked and deserted on a tropical island. They built amazing gadgets and created a life for themselves with nothing but what they salvaged from the ship and fashioned from things found on the island. They inspired me and I felt similarly creative in my pursuit of freedom.

Farnsworth kept coming to mind. He'd caught me with Stephan and paid someone to shoot at me outside the donut shop. When he saw me with the big guy at the Wiffle ball game, he had him killed right in front of me. Stephan had to be dead. But why wasn't anyone following me? Farnsworth had to know I was up to something. Did Wendell threaten him? Not likely. It was spooky waiting for Farnsworth's next move. I was glad to be inside for the day even if I was going stir crazy.

I pictured Marc's bulky image and put the book aside. Women at the bar had scoffed at his round torso and thinning hair. His eagerness for the nachos attested to his love of food, but he made enough at his job to feed himself. What he couldn't get was women. How perfect for Farnsworth to bribe him with something every man wanted, something Marc couldn't attain for himself. I knew I was right. All I needed was the proof.

I was exhausted, but I couldn't help thinking about what Nick would find. It might take him days to collect the evidence I needed. The police captured such things in minutes, but they had authority. Nick would be sneaking around when no one was watching and trying to cover himself with some legitimate reason for investigating Farnsworth. Nick was bold dealing with me, but at work he had to obey his boss and play by the rules. His tiny house was proof of his station at the bank.

I replayed everything I'd seen and heard over again. I was positive this would be one of my last days in reeducation. I saw myself handing the typewritten pages to Wendell and seeing him overjoyed at what I delivered. I would save his company and he would release me immediately. I tried to dampen my hope, but I couldn't. I knew I was at the end and I couldn't help feeling excited.

I tried to read. I compared lunch menus from local takeout places, anything to keep my mind off Nick and what he was doing. Finally after a whole day of waiting, I got in a cab to meet Nick and find out what happened at Govbank. When I got to the park, Nick's car was waiting right where we had parked that morning. I kicked myself for not coming sooner. When I finally opened the door and sat down beside him, I thought I saw a tight smile on his lips.

"How'd you do?" I asked.

"You're going to be happy." Nick shoved a few white pages into my hands. They were the custody papers.

"I can't sign these until I have what I need."

He had a thick folder on his lap and I knew they were the records on Farnsworth. Neither of us wanted to give the other anything and come away empty.

"I'm not here to screw you, Nick. If you've got what I need, I'll sign these. Jonathan is yours. Just let me see what you've got."

Nick started the engine. "You take off and I'll run your ass over. I risked my butt for this. I'm not giving it to you for nothing."

I promised him I was good to my word. We could have gone back and forth, but he decided he could trust me and pulled out a single printed page.

"The house. It's Farnsworth's. Belongs to his company."

I checked the address. The report had Town of Brookline printed across the top. Nick could have made it up, but I had come to him, not the other way around. Farnsworth Reeducation was listed as the owner.

Nick pulled out another four pages.

"These women are listed as employees of Farnsworth Reeducation. They earn double what most other employees make and there's something else interesting. When I researched their purchases, they were all made around that house. They go to lunch out there. Have their nails done. Those women live there. According to their financials, they don't go far. All his other employees spend time near his facilities. Breakfast, lunch, and dinner all have lots of hits."

"So the prostitutes are on the payroll?"

"That's what I'm saying."

"He doesn't call them that. That's the thing these days. You can't hide transactions completely. People like Farnsworth have to code transactions so they make sense. If you hadn't stumbled onto them, they never would have stood out on any report. They look like any other employee."

I took the whole folder and shuffled the custody papers to the top. My stomach felt empty, like I was defying some law of physics by not folding in half. The single line with my name below it mocked me as I signed and wrote the date. My claim to Jonathan was gone, but my life was about to restart.

Nick gunned the engine as soon as my door closed. Kathleen would hear the good news in minutes.

CHAPTER SIXTY-NINE

The car circled the park and disappeared toward Nick and Kathleen's house just a few blocks away. As I settled into the dark behind the monument to consider what to do next, Nick was almost home. He'd probably rush through the front door to show Kathleen that I'd signed. I wished I was there to see how happy she was. We'd had a great time together however short it was. If this made her happy, it was the right thing to do. I hadn't cared for Nick before that day, but he had opened the door for me to walk back into society. I was glad for what he'd done even if we'd never be friends.

In my hands I had proof Farnsworth was paying prostitutes. I'd seen them and I knew what they were doing, but if I brought this to Wendell and Farnsworth found out, the next time I saw those women they'd be in heels, suits, and they'd be carrying briefcases full of relearner files. The eleven men at the complex could be sent off to the cat baggers, but I had filmed them on Farnsworth's ball field. Their trial left a record even Farnsworth couldn't erase. That part of the scheme would be easy to expose. I needed proof the women were hookers. If I could show them with Marc, that would be the definitive end for Nathan Farnsworth.

Crossing the grass to the sidewalk, I looked for a cab but couldn't find one. Most of the park was dark. Anyone walking here was probably close to home. Not a good place to hail a cab, not this time of night. I started back toward the center of town, where there might be a cab cruising for a fare. I was thinking about the wall at the Brookline house and how I'd dropped *Treasure Island* when a thought came to me.

Mandla told me that the test was outside the black box, not inside. What if everything I was doing was a test? What if Nick was supposed to give me this stuff? Was it too easy?

I abandoned my search for a cab and turned down a side street. Four blocks later I was crouched between the base of a tree and the front tire of a Volkswagen. It was late, so the lights downstairs at Nick and Kathleen's house were out except one, their bedroom. I crouched there long after the tree bark began biting into my back. Finally the last light went out.

The neighbors were quiet, too. A few watched television, but most were asleep. I needed to get to Brookline, so I didn't wait as long as I normally would have. In the old days I wouldn't have gone into a house when I knew there were people inside, but this was different.

Nothing moved on the street as I crossed and eased along the foundation and around back. I could hear voices inside, but couldn't make out the words through the insulated walls. I waited a few seconds, hoping they'd get louder, but I learned nothing. Farther along, I found a rusty toolbox on the back porch, opened it, and found a screwdriver small enough for my purpose.

I'd worked my way inside hundred of doors. Even though I hadn't robbed a house in years, the old skills didn't fail me. The back door opened without alarming anyone and I slipped into the kitchen and crossed the linoleum.

There on the table were the papers I'd signed in Nick's car. I could have grabbed them and ran off with my rights to Jonathan restored, but that wasn't why I came. I stood in the middle of the room, a place where my silhouette would stand out even in the dark. Jonathan made no noise upstairs. I heard faint rumblings from the master bedroom and I inched over toward the wall to listen.

"Oh, baby, I can't believe you did it." It was Kathleen. She was in bed with him, praising him for getting me out of their life. She'd been so nice to me when I visited Jonathan and now she talked about me like I was a leper.

I didn't want to hear more, but I couldn't move. Kathleen moaned. "Oh, that's even better."

The dreamy voice reminded me of nights we spent together, when she whispered to me in the midst of lovemaking. I knew what was happening in the room and I wished it was me in there with her. Why I'd thought of Mandla at the park I don't know, but standing in that kitchen with my ear to the wall, I was convinced that Kathleen and Nick were truly husband and wife and that I'd just given them my son.

I left the house as quietly as I'd come in.

It was ridiculous of me to think Wendell could create a scenario so elaborate. Why would Nick and Kathleen go along with such a thing? And why would Wendell go to all the trouble? He didn't care that much about one relearner. He was watching me and I was helping him. I was about to help him more than any relearner ever had.

CHAPTER SEVENTY

On the cab ride over I thought of dozens of places to hide the paperwork Nick had given me, but with each one came a risk I wasn't willing to take. These papers proved Farnsworth was dirty. Once I delivered them to Wendell, everything would change. But first I had to make it through the night with them in my possession. Even my safe deposit box wasn't out of Farnsworth's reach. In the end, I stuffed the folder down my shirt and hoped it didn't catch on something and give me away. The cabbie thought it was strange for me to get out on the empty street, but I couldn't have him stop at the front gate and ask Farnsworth to buzz me in. I pressed my thumb to the scanner, climbed out, and waited for the red tail lights to disappear.

I went up the same maple, climbed to the top of the wall, and followed it to where *Treasure Island* lay in the grass. Seeing the book lying unmolested on the lawn convinced me there were no dogs inside the wall. I hadn't thought to bring meat and tranquilizers. Even if I had, I'm not sure I would have used them again after Wendell's tirade. Farnsworth was different, but right was right.

There were no trees against the inside of the wall. I lowered myself down until only my fingertips gripped the concrete edge. Then I let go and fell the remaining few feet to the ground. There was nowhere to hide out here on the lawn, but fortunately my instincts were right. No dogs responded to my landing. I trotted across the lawn and ducked into the shrubbery at the base of the house. Voices laughed inside. Dozens of voices.

Marc had only spoken a few sentences to me that day in his office. As I sat there in the bushes, I tried to pick his voice out of the crowd but soon realized it would be impossible. I didn't know how often he showed up here. Would he come two nights in a row? I was desperate to catch him. I should have waited in the bushes and watched the cars along the drive, but if I had, I would have missed my chance because Marc was already inside.

Eager to prove my case and desperate to get out of reeducation, I snuck along the edge of the bushes to the one sturdy tree that stood close to the house. The birch proved flimsy. Several branches cracked underfoot, but it was the only way up. I climbed to the roof without falling.

The roof was covered in slippery slate tiles and on my first step up to the gable window, my foot flew out from under me. I caught myself softly with my hands and made little noise even though I had to wedge my foot into the gutter to keep from slipping off the roof and back into the tree. Had the cameras been in my hands I would have lost them both and my adventure would have ended, but they were tucked into my shirt pocket and luckily they didn't fall.

I raised slowly into a crouch, pulled myself to the window, and worked it open. Nothing sounded inside. I stepped down to the floor and discovered a room arranged with couches and racks of clothing. I was lucky not to find a bed with a customer in it. I assumed this was where the girls came to get away from their customers. Farnsworth paid them well according to Nick, so they probably got breaks during the night. I needed to vacate the room quickly before one of them found me.

Outside was a hallway with a bunch of doors. The door directly across was narrower than the others, probably a closet, I thought. I listened outside the door and hearing nothing, I tried the knob. Locked. Voices rose from downstairs. A couple could come up any second. I slipped the folder from my shirt and used it to lever the latch open. The folder wasn't sturdy and by the time the knob turned, I was sweating.

I shut myself in and was plunged into complete darkness. I was glad for the time alone to collect my thoughts and listen to what was happening around me. The voices were completely muffled by the insulation. I listened, waited, and let my eyes adjust.

The room looked like a cleaning closet that had been emptied to make room for the ladder nailed to the wall. I climbed up. Still hearing nothing, I pushed my way through the hatch. I couldn't believe what I saw or how lucky I was that no one was up there when I stepped inside. Few people were ever meant to see this room. No one would be allowed up here while customers were being serviced, so this was the one place in the house I could be alone for the night. I closed the hatch and I was safe.

The carpeted walkway was ultra quiet; the entire space darkened to be sure no light found the one-way mirrors set into the floor. Six cameras looked down into bedrooms below.

I stalked along the walkway until I was looking down into the first room. A naked man, covered from the waist down in only a sheet, lay on top of a blonde who looked straight up at the camera. I focused my pen camera on the couple even though I knew it wasn't Marc down there. I waited for several minutes and when the man rolled over to rest, I was stunned to recognize the judge from the eleven-defendant trial the day before. I held in a squeal and stood silent until the judge turned his attention back to the blonde.

In the next room I found the prosecutor with a brunette. He was dressing to leave, but I took thirty seconds of video anyway. I'm sure his wife would want to know why he was getting dressed in a strange room while a naked woman looked on from the bed. I stopped and panned my camera around the attic room, taking in the cameras and the mirrors assembled to make their own recordings.

I passed over two empty rooms before I found Marc entangled with a girl too chunky for my taste. He was happier than I'd seen him before. He wouldn't have been if he'd known what I was doing. Even without me he was headed for trouble. If he crossed Farnsworth, the videos would surface and he'd lose his job. He might even end up in reeducation.

CHAPTER SEVENTY-ONE

Hours passed before all the men left and even after that, the women huddled in a few of the bedrooms beneath the one-way mirrors. I waited until I could see them sleeping before I climbed down into the closet. That's why I'm so exhausted standing here at the window. I had to make sure the lounge was empty or I never would have made it here alive.

When I went out the lounge window, I almost lost my balance because the slate tiles were slick with dew, but I got a toehold in the gutter and lay flat to catch my breath. It wasn't a smart decision to jump to the trunk of the birch tree, but I thought it was the safest way down. The flimsy branches folded underfoot and I slid down the first ten feet like a fireman's pole.

My feet caught two thick branches. I came to a hard stop and almost fell off, but I got my grip and climbed down one branch at a time, careful of the dew and thankful I didn't plunge all the way to the shrubs. I veered over and picked up *Treasure Island* and searched for a way over the wall. It was smooth on the inside and I finally settled for climbing the iron gate at the drive. There had to be cameras, but I wasn't worried about being seen going out. I scrambled up and over, then ran down the street with the pen cameras, my book, and the files Nick took from the bank.

It was seven blocks before I first saw the cab. I tried to flag him down, but he already had a fare. I walked another five blocks before that same cab came back and took me home. It was well after midnight when I walked into my apartment. I half fell onto the couch, but the moment I touched down the phone rang. Truthfully, I thought someone had seen me climb the gate at

Farnsworth's and that he was calling to make a deal. Who else could know what I'd been doing? I hauled myself up and answered.

"Hello, Michael," Wendell said.

I was stunned.

"Do you have something for me?"

He had been watching. He knew what I had and he was anxious to get it. A burst of pride filled me and I felt rejuvenated. When he saw what I'd accomplished, his life would be changed and he'd be so appreciative he'd set me free. Soon I'd be living in a little house like Nick and Kathleen. I'd find a wife and maybe have a couple kids. My path was so clear I could almost touch it.

"I do," I said. "You're going to be very happy. I think you can put Farnsworth away with what I've got."

"Excellent." He sounded excited on the other end of the line.

The black box watched me in silence. The two remaining books from Wendell's stack beckoned me. When Wendell asked me to meet him downstairs I almost took them with me. How foolish to think he'd set me free the moment I gave him the cameras and the files.

He told me to come around back of the building and not let anyone see me. I obliged, taking my book, the files, and the two cameras out into the hall, down two flights of stairs, and out the front door. As I skirted the edge of the building, I wondered why he wanted to meet so late. It was after two A.M. by that time, but you know that. You were here waiting for me. I don't know how he assembled you all, and of course he hadn't told me about you yet. All I knew as I walked over the grass was that I had proof that would put Nathan Farnsworth out of business. I'd accomplished my mission and I thought Wendell would be ecstatic.

When I reached the back corner of the building, I saw him standing with the control room door open. Light spilled outside, suggesting we were headed there. I didn't hurry across the grass. I kept thinking of Mandla and what he'd said about how my challenge was outside the black box. But I'd won. I was carrying a little piece of victory in each hand.

Wendell smiled when I finally reached him. He gestured inside and I stepped in. The door closed tightly, like a refrigerator sealing the air in, like nothing inside should ever be allowed out.

The monitors were all active, showing my apartment, the street, and a tracking map of where I had been that night. Wendell had followed my every move. He knew I'd completed my mission, but he didn't seem excited. Maybe he was as tired as I was.

I explained what I had for him. I handed him the printouts Nick traded me for my son, then I handed him the cameras with the video I shot from the attic of Nathan Farnsworth's brothel. He wasn't surprised in the least. He set them on the counter, then turned his back.

"Follow me."

We went around the corner to the place where I'd seen the glass partitions set into the floor. I sensed trouble and I rushed to keep up with him so he couldn't lock me into one space or another. I imagined gas spilling from the walls or gunmen emerging from around the corner, but he calmly led me to the darkened window where you're sitting now. When I was beside him, he pressed a button in his pocket and the two glass panels shot up from the floor and locked us in a narrow section of hallway. I'd just been standing over one-way mirrors in Nathan's attic, so it was easy for me to understand that I'd been locked into a space in front of one. Of course I told you a while ago that I've seen the inside of that room. I know there are thirteen chairs in there. The glass partitions have kept both of us in front of the window so you could see me the whole time I've been talking.

I tried to remain calm. I wanted to break through the glass and escape, but I knew that acquittal was the only way out. Honestly, I never thought of attacking Wendell for the remote. He trusted me. He came inside with me. I always felt I owed him something and even now I believe he wants to set me free. This is where you see me now. This is the final court. Where I came to beg for my life.

CHAPTER SEVENTY-TWO

I don't know when you started listening to Wendell and me here in the hall, but when I first got here, before I started telling you my story, this is what Wendell said to me.

"Try and relax, Michael.

"What Mandla told you was true. It seems you understood the message he gave you. What you did with the black box was good. You tried hard to learn what you neglected when you were a child in school. These things are important and if you do well here today, you'll have a chance to go back to school and earn your diploma. That will be the first step to living a successful life. But as Mandla said, the real test is what you do in your life when you think you're not being watched. That is what we are here to judge today."

I couldn't believe he was judging me then. It was almost three in the morning and I was exhausted from chasing evidence against Nathan Farnsworth.

"The court you have been going to, relearner court, is only for your benefit. Nothing that happens there has any meaning whatsoever. It is how you react to judgment that is important. The cat baggers don't really exist either. We convinced you they did, but the American people would never abide the torture of inmates."

I heard what he said, but I couldn't believe they hired all those people to conduct pretend trials. No wonder they were over so fast.

Wendell gestured to the window.

"Behind this glass, there are twelve jurors. They each have two buttons. If they press the green button, they are voting to let you free. If enough of them do so, you will be given an apartment, you'll be enrolled in a real school for adult learners, and when you complete your diploma, we'll help you find a job, provided you don't get into trouble again. The hot dog vendor you met was telling the truth. He is a graduate."

He paused then.

"And if they don't press the green button?" I asked.

"Each of them has a red button. If three or more jurors press the red button you'll be taken away for termination."

He didn't say prison, because prison didn't exist anymore. He didn't say how long I'd wait to be executed, but I was convinced one of the doors at the end of the hall served that purpose.

"Why now?" I asked.

Wendell quivered. I wondered for a moment if he'd ever had that question before. Everything seemed so well planned. It seemed he'd done this hundreds of times, but why did he bring me here at three A.M.?

"You've completed your quest. What we need to determine now is whether you can move back into society without being a danger to those you meet there."

Mandla had told me exactly what I needed to know. I just didn't think broadly enough. I knew Wendell was going to rehash every mistake I'd made since I'd been in reeducation. I almost couldn't listen, but he was talking to you, prosecuting my case, as much as he was talking to me.

"You took the lessons to heart, Michael. You trusted me and there is something to be applauded in that. Even after you found the subliminal messages in the videos with Stephan, you didn't think to check your own. There were thousands of them in yours. Stephan showed you how to find them, but you didn't look. I'm glad you trusted me, Michael. Trust is an important quality in this world, one that is particularly difficult for you since you felt betrayed by your own mother."

"Felt?"

He gave me a stern look, like sarcasm wasn't a good idea, and I guessed that you were already watching. I folded my hands and listened.

"When Dr. Blake accosted you in the car, you stood up for yourself without resorting to violence. I applaud you for that also, Michael. That was your most shining moment in the program. Many men attack Dr. Blake at that moment and have to be restrained. You succeeded at both protecting yourself and managing your relationship with Dr. Blake. You also worked incredibly hard to comply with his demands on the gray pads, even though you knew they were unreasonable. That is also to be commended."

I remembered how sore my arms were from the push-ups.

"From there things turned worse. I assigned you a difficult task. I asked you to enforce the law and you resorted to your old ways, Michael. You poisoned my dogs. You broke into my home. You sold stolen property. You took off your ankle bracelet after being ordered not to. You illegally entered this courtroom. In fact you illegally entered a number of buildings, including two within the last several hours.

"Michael, the end doesn't always justify the means. To enforce the law you can't run around breaking it. I understand you were trying to help me, and I appreciate your trust and your commitment, but we must determine whether you are a threat or an asset. There is no in-between."

CHAPTER SEVENTY-THREE

I told you how my mother pressed the .22 to my head. I believed she was going to kill me. And right now, I wish I knew what you are planning to do with me. It must be light outside now. I don't know how I even have the strength to stand anymore. You've heard my story. I'm sure that Wendell has played recordings of my voice and videos from cameras around my apartment. I want you to know that since I've been here, I've been doing my best to do the right thing.

I haven't hurt anyone since I've been in this program, actually I've never really hurt anyone in my life. Yes, I took things from people when I was young. I was just doing what I could to survive. I was on my own at fifteen years old. You can't know what that was like because Wendell didn't start recording me until we met in the hospital. I want each of you to imagine what you'd do if you were sent out into the street at fifteen. How would you eat? How would you stay warm in the winter? I ran out of choices fast. I didn't have friends to take me in. I didn't have money or a job to pay for the things I needed. Even when I lived with my mother I had to take what I needed or I wouldn't have had enough to eat.

I'm not sure you can understand what that's like.

I can't see you in there and I don't know what your life was like. I can only guess that you are sitting there because your life went a lot smoother than mine. Yes, I did some things wrong while you were watching me. But every time I slipped into someone's house or someone's car, my only goal was to help Wendell. Farnsworth is cheating the system and I wanted to help stop him. There isn't much difference between me and those kids I saw in court last week.

Huh.

I guess that was a message to me, too. I remember thinking they were trying to do the right thing, but they'd just gone too far. I felt for those guys. They didn't deserve to get reeducation. They should have been released. Maybe I still don't get it, but given where I came from, I'm doing my best. I hope when you look at me, you feel the way I did for them.

I know I've been talking for a long time, but I also know I've missed things. It's been months since I woke up in that hospital and I've only had a few hours to tell you my story. I've done my best with what I knew and what I'd been told. I wanted to help Wendell and I did the things I did because I thought they were the right thing to do, just like those guys I saw in court a few days ago.

So please remember that I worked hard to help Wendell. That I didn't hurt anyone. Even listening to me, you can hear what I've learned from those books. I talk like a new person. I can't believe it when I listen to myself. I hope you'll give me a chance to keep learning.

Please, if you haven't already, please press that green button.

CHAPTER SEVENTY-FOUR

When I turned toward Wendell, he had removed a remote control from his pocket. He stood just four feet from me. I could have pounced and wrestled it away, but I still didn't know the outcome of the vote and I didn't know what the buttons did either. I might press one trying to lower the partition and end up gassing both of us. I stood against the glass partition and watched as he pressed the first button.

The window I had been talking to for the last few hours brightened. Something had been blocking my view and now as if by magic, I could see the room beyond. I'd been in that room not long ago and what I saw this time startled me. I remembered two rows of chairs. When Wendell told me I was talking to twelve people who were going to decide my fate, I believed him, partly because I'd seen thirteen chairs in that room. He knew that. From the beginning he'd been showing me what he wanted me to believe and convincing me it was true. I don't know how he tricked me into breaking in here so I would see the thirteen chairs, but he did.

Through the window, the room was twice as big as I remember. The walls had been moved back somehow and several rows of chairs had been added. Wendell stood back as I took in the faces arranged to greet me.

My counselors lined much of the front row. Charlotte, Dr. Blake, and Morris Farnsworth sat together. I recognized Joanne Torrance and David Jones even though I'd only seen them once. Next to them sat Nathan Farnsworth, Joel, Tyrone, and Deone. In the row behind them I recognized Stephan, the big guy who'd been shot on the lawn, the hot dog vendor,

Mandla, and Marc. The prosecutors and judges I had faced were all aligned in the next row along with Officer Benson. Even the flat-nosed Wiffle ball pitcher was there.

"What are they all doing here?"

It was a stupid question, but the answer was too shocking for me to believe. How had he arranged for all of them to interact with me while I was walking around in public? I approached many of them myself. Several of them worked together to deceive me, but there were hundreds of people on the street I could have turned to. The woman I saw every morning at the donut shop wasn't there, but the relearner who helped me that one morning was sitting near the back.

"Wondering how we did it?" Wendell asked. "Your program. Those videos you watched when you first arrived. Every one of these people was in those videos. We told you to like them or hate them and for the most part, you followed our programming. We gave you friends and we gave you adversaries."

I'd never seen these people in my lessons. They'd been cut in, just like the images of Stephan being stabbed had been inserted into his videos. Too bad I hadn't used Stephan's camera to check my own. But what would have happened then? Wendell couldn't have let me go if I figured out the game before he taught me anything.

I noticed the three guys I'd caught peeing against the building and I chuckled without thinking. "Why go through all this trouble?"

"We have to know if you're a danger or not."

"I mean tonight. Why did you make me tell my whole story? I've been talking so long I can barely stand up."

"They were hanging on every word. What you say about them tells us how well we did our job. We have to know if you believed what you were supposed to believe. Otherwise, we'd never know how we were affecting people."

"What about me? What are you going to do with me?"

"This is a difficult decision for me," Wendell said, almost choking on his words.

Was it really his decision all along?

"From the beginning I was worried you wouldn't make it. The problem we are trying to combat is recidivism. You, Michael, have been stealing from people since you were a little boy. From the very start I knew you were going to be a hard case. We pulled out every trick we had, but you seemed determined to keep breaking the law. You don't understand that other people have the right to be safe. You wander into their houses because you know how to jimmy locks. You never stop to think whether it's right or not. You just surge ahead."

"You've known what you're going to do for a long time?"

"It wasn't that easy."

"It's been a hell of a lot harder for me."

Wendell pressed a button and the glass clouded over again. I assumed the actors could still hear us, but I didn't know for sure.

"Are you sure? Do you remember the test Charlotte ran for you when you first arrived? A DNA test to find your father?"

I remembered it was a failure.

He pulled a sheet of paper from his pocket and handed it to me. My name was printed across the top. My mother's name, address, and her parents' names were printed down the left hand column. On the right, the name Wendell Cummings appeared along with his address in Brookline and the names and birthplaces of his parents.

I crumpled it and threw it at his feet. "This is just more of your crap."

"No," he said. "I met your mother after I volunteered to help the poor in Boston. Your mother told me she wanted out of her mother's house. They were poor. She said her mother abused her. I learned later that was a sob story. Her mother and her grandmother had both done the same thing to escape their parents. They were packing in a generation every fifteen years. I was in my twenties at the time and should have known better, but I went right along and got her pregnant."

He looked like he was going to cry and I didn't want to watch. I didn't care if he wanted to be my father or not. He was threatening to kill me and I couldn't think about anything else. I was sure it was an act, another lie to confuse me. I couldn't figure out what he was trying to hide. It was a bit late for deception.

"I never thought of myself as a father, just like you never thought of yourself as Jonathan's father. But when we started working on your case and Charlotte dug up the DNA results, she connected me to you and to Jonathan."

Jonathan was his grandson.

"I did what I could, Michael. You kept breaking the law. I couldn't hide it. I had to keep going to my boss and telling him you were going to pan out. I was proud that no matter how Charlotte pressed, you wouldn't give Jonathan up. He's my grandson, Michael. I'd never done anything with you, but he was my opportunity to help raise a boy. I kept covering for you, but then last night you gave up your rights. You didn't know it, but you gave up my rights, too."

"And that's why I'm in here now."

"It's out of my hands."

He had the remote out in front of him. He held it loosely a foot beyond my reach. I made a show of looking toward the window and snatched at it. As my arm flew out, I heard the button click. Every muscle in my body refused to function all at once. I teetered and fell to the floor. The only place I had any feeling was the base of my skull where that implant burned me as it short-circuited my nerves. It wasn't a tracking device. It was an off switch. I was neutralized with the push of a button. Charlotte had that same button when I made her nervous in the car. Maybe all my counselors did.

I watched Wendell, unable to interfere with his plans.

He pulled out a small jar, carefully opened the lid and squeezed a single drop of liquid onto the exposed skin of my neck. My throat tightened, my chest pounded, and then the world faded to black.

CHAPTER SEVENTY-FIVE

Wendell clicked three buttons as he'd done many times before. The window cleared, the glass partitions lowered into the floor, and three gloved men came out of the conference room to haul away his only son. They dragged him to the end of the hallway and through the door where the hall dead ended. He couldn't stop watching even after the door closed and he knew the body was being dumped into a chemical bath to ensure no one came into contact with the poison.

A dark-suited man opened the only remaining door beyond the glass partitions. He held a thick folder in one hand, but extended the other to congratulate Wendell on a job well done. Michael O'Connor cost the state $765,000, far less than they'd spent executing a felon in the old days. This new system was a boon and it proved to anyone who watched the video that the convict deserved the ultimate punishment.

Wendell's boss handed him the thick folder that held his next assignment. "Problem?" he asked. "This never bothered you before?"

"I never killed my son before."

Wendell's boss grimaced.

"I gave him a chance to tell his story. I could have saved him or at least I could have tried. He told the truth there in front of the window. Why couldn't he understand it was wrong for him to take things from other people? He needed parents to teach him that. Yeah, he got gypped in the cosmic lottery and I have to take part of the blame for that. He never had a father or a grandfather, but I didn't know what I was doing back then. I thought I was helping a poor girl fix her life, but my meddling destroyed two lives, maybe more. I tried everything I know to help him see what he was doing wrong, but he was too far gone. Michael had been stealing since elementary school. His problems had been passed from generation to generation. Mother after mother had fewer and fewer parenting skills. Each one thought society owed them more. His mother taught him so little. I think he learned more on the street than he did at home. My son could not see his own criminality. In the end I was forced to do what his mother only threatened."

Author's Note

When any system has been in place long enough, the original intentions become obscured by the daily scuffles between participants. When the men who created a system are long dead and it has been tinkered with over the years by many hands with differing political and social agendas, we must ask ourselves if the system continues to serve its original purpose.

Our system of criminal justice is one such system and this book has explored an extreme case of change. Underlying all of this is the idea that the criminal justice system should be in the business of protecting citizens from those who cannot abide by society's rules and helping those who have lost their way to become productive and cooperative members of society. The current iteration of our penal system appears in many cases to have morphed from a punitive system to a society unto itself in which criminals battle their captors and are allowed to sue the government for the most trivial of oversights.

In my experience I have come to believe that many of those who end up in prison are there because they have not been taught the skills they need to be a productive member of our society. This is a combination of moral values, academics, and vocational skills. To retrain these individuals is a massive undertaking and should not be entered into lightly. Still, we are losing those who could turn their lives around by lumping them in with career criminals with no hope of reform. In the future, we may be more successful by separating the two and providing focused care to those willing and able to receive it and shorter, terminal sentences to those who cannot.

WE HOPE YOU ENJOY THE FOLLOWING PREVIEW

Addicted to Love

A Romantic Thriller
by CJ West
Coming in 2011

CHAPTER ONE

"Mmm. Your kisses are so addictive," Leah breathed.

Wes couldn't get enough. The taste of her soft lips easing over his, probing and retreating in rhythm kept him leaned over her on the couch despite the cramp in his triceps. His parents would call her common. His brother would say he could do better, but Wes's whole body surged for her, delighting in the touch of her lips, utterly satisfied by the supple connection.

Her hand patted the couch, found the remote. The television died.

He shifted to her neck. Breathed shampoo or conditioner or mousse as his lips pinched tiny tracks toward her earlobe. Strawberries maybe. The scent sparked memories of other nights, locked together kissing for hours like kids who hadn't been further. Every second with Leah was that special. A frontier crossed. A moment that commanded him to linger. He'd never imagined staying up until morning holding someone close, but that's what they'd done three nights running. Leah could barely work. Wes slept half the day while she was gone. He worried she'd crash her car. Worried about the Red Bull she drank to stay awake. But mostly he paced and waited for the moment she came back.

What would Lynne think? Six weeks after they'd split he found unimaginable passion with a woman he'd just met. In ten years together he'd never felt anything like this for Lynne. He couldn't even remember how it started with Leah. He hadn't come here for this. He wanted to get away. To find himself. To break free. Instead he found another anchor. One his heart would never let him untie.

His arm started to shake and still he couldn't deny himself another kiss.

She kneaded the strong muscles of his back, simultaneously worshiping his power and begging him not to break contact.

He stood, scooped her legs, and tilted her down on the couch, never letting their lips part for more than an instant. They lay face to face, pressed together. He teased her hair until his quivering arm refused to hold its own weight, then it flopped down on the pillow. They kissed with tender little touches, their lips coming apart to absorb the feeling of being completely consumed by the other. Breathing never felt so good. Dreamy looks never communicated so much.

How had this happened?

Slow, soft kisses. Ecstasy. Not drugs, but it might as well have been.

A haircut three weeks ago had turned into drinks and a kiss. A sweet kiss, but nothing special. A week later they'd had two more dates and he walked around all day remembering how he felt when their lips met. Kissing her was different now—an insatiable craving that demanded to be fed.

Was she so perfect for him that his body took control? Was love about chemical compatibility on a level he wasn't conscious of? Was that why things with Lynne fell apart?

"Upstairs?" she whispered.

"Mmm," was all he could reply between kisses. Neither of them could break away even though their passion would reach a new high in the bedroom.

Branches cracked and something fell hard in the leaves outside.

Wes snapped to the open window but couldn't see anything beyond the candle-lit living room. Leah tugged him down and kissed his neck until he turned back and gave her his lips.

More branches snapped. This time a woman moaned in pain. They both stopped and turned to the window. Footsteps rustled the leaves. He crawled over and cupped his hands to the screen. Still too dark to see, but the footsteps crunched up the mountain away from the road. His boots were at the foot of the couch. He pulled them on, laces flapping behind.

"You're not going out there."

"Someone needs help."

"What if it's a bear?"

His parents didn't keep a gun. It wasn't a bear he was worried about. He could handle any guy in town, any unarmed guy, but if the woman was running upslope in the dark, she had good reason. He grabbed the fire poker and rushed for the back door.

"Keep the doors locked and the lights off until I get back."

"Should I call the sheriff?"

"Not yet."

He raced across the dark lawn to the stonewall he'd been building for the last week. Everything under the pines was black and he had to stop to let his eyes adjust. A heavy crash sounded a hundred yards ahead toward the ski lodge.

"Wait," he yelled into the darkness. "I can help."

No response.

He hustled into the dark, dodging branches and getting whipped sharply three times. The last stung his upper lip and made his eyes water so much he couldn't see. He slowed, walking with his hands protecting his face.

"Hold on," he yelled louder this time.

He listened but the woods went quiet. Rather than turn back to him for help, the footfalls vanished deep in the forest. He should have gone back to the couch. He went back inside not for Leah, but for a light. He couldn't track anyone in the dark, but he didn't expect to catch the intruder. He just wanted to know if it was a human or a maimed animal crashing through the woods.

Leah was perched on the edge of the couch, mashing a throw pillow when he came in. She popped up and met him in the center of the living room. She gladly threw her arms around him, but when he pulled away and started rummaging around the kitchen for a flashlight, her face turned sullen.

"It's gone. Whatever it was," he said before he disappeared into the backyard.

"So why are you going back out?" she called through the screen.

"I need a better look."

The grass shone brilliant green under the light. He crossed through the opening in his unfinished wall. His eyes fell on the gaps he'd fill the next time he came out to work. He scanned the far side, his eyes drawn to the fit of the rocks under the light. He followed the wall west, guessing his visitor had followed the outside of the waist-high wall rather than climb over. He'd built his dry wall that high to discourage climbers from tumbling rocks out of place.

The forest floor looked undisturbed until he came to a flattened pile of small rocks he used to fit the larger stones together. Mostly picked over, it was a tripping hazard even to him. This was where his visitor had stumbled and fallen. No wonder. He'd fumbled around in the rocks plenty in the daytime.

Metal glinted as he passed the light back and forth. He couldn't believe what he saw. Beside the seven-inch Chef's knife, a softball-sized rock captured a bloody handprint. Someone had lost a lot of blood. Had the person running through the yard been in a knife fight? Did that sort of thing happen in Highland Falls?

Wes left the knife in the rock pile, hurdled the stone wall, and sprinted across the lawn for help.

Breinigsville, PA USA
09 May 2010
237621BV00003B/3/P